MURDER ME TOMORROW

A novel from the Inspector Stark series

Keith Wright

©Copyright Keith Wright 2020

All rights reserved ©Keith Wright 2020

For Jackie

All characters included in this book are fictitious and are not intended to bear any resemblance to any Individuals, alive or dead.

Contains realistic and graphic descriptions of death and sexual assault. Includes issues which some readers may find upsetting.

Reactions and conversations are of the period.

Some language, terminology and behaviours are a social commentary of the period and are offensive.

It is intended for adults only.

If you are affected by an issue in the book contact:
ChildLine, Parentline, The Samaritans, or check local charities.

1

'Whatever you want to do, do it now.

There are only so many tomorrows.'

Michael Landon.

I do not know what second it will be, what minute it will be, what hour, or even day, but it will come. You may see it coming. You may not. Regardless, I can guarantee you; there will be a moment like no other when you will draw your last breath. Like it or lump it. And at that moment you will see your final view of the world. However, what I do *not* know, is whether your last glimpse will be the sympathetic countenance of a loved one or the grotesque, contorted, teeth-clenched face of a deviant killer. Nor do you. That is yet to be determined. Other options are available.

Thankfully, for the late Gordon Masters, it was the former rather than the latter. In death, as in life, family and friends huddled around him in a wall of love, as they lowered his coffin into the ground. The finality of this manoeuvre always triggered an outburst of emotion. Gordon's daughter Ella was the first to break down. Sunglasses masked the family's grief, and their tears could be confused with sweat, on this, the hottest day of the summer.

Gordon chose the name of his daughter, Ella, after the soul singer, Ella Fitzgerald; she was his favourite, indeed both his and Brenda's. He and his beloved had been married for fifty-three years until she died some seven years ago.

Gordon was thrilled that his daughter too, seemed to have chosen well, with her life partner, Paul. He was a bit of a drip, but a good man at heart. The two of them had been together for twenty years now, so they should be fine.

There were over fifty mourners, 'a good …. …., *turn out, send off, last drink,*' choose your own phrase; all were said during this bleak afternoon; these being the default phrases of the awkwardly bereaved at a funeral.

1987 had been a good year for Paul and Ella Masters, it started well, with Paul's promotion, and a growing light at the end of a shortening financial tunnel. There was a mild Spring leading into a scorching Summer, but then, suddenly, out of the blue, Ella's dad decided to depart. In truth, he had wanted to go a few years earlier, but it's not easy to die by merely wishing it. Your body won't let you take your last breath until it has thrown the kitchen sink at pulling one more out of your lungs.

Not that Gordon wasn't comfortable living at his daughter's house; they were very kind and considerate. He had just had enough, that is all. Gordon found it harder to make conversation as he got into old age; everyone spoke so quickly, he didn't have time to formulate the words to join in, before they'd moved on to something else. He became the ornament in the corner. 'Are you alright, Dad?' was the constant chant. Often, Ella didn't wait for an answer. He became more and more invisible in between bouts of kind concerted efforts when it occasionally occurred to the rest of them, that he was still around. Once, they even locked up and turned the lights off, and he was still sitting in the bloody chair. No. It was time to go. He'd had a good life, marred only by the bits of tragedy all must endure, but, on balance, it was time to get his hat. He was ready to rock n roll again with Brenda in the hereafter.

At the graveside, Ella was clinging onto Paul, she was shaking, and he could feel the tremble as he stroked her hand. Ella could smell the soil and clay coming from the grave, and some loose mud was sticking to the souls of her shoes, seemingly reluctant to go back in the hole from whence it came. Naturally, she was upset, which in turn made Paul emotional, and then her daughter, Jemma, had to get her hanky out. It was a Mexican wave of grief without the rousing cheer.

After the grim ceremony had finished, Ella declined to throw soil on top of the coffin. She closed her eyes and grimaced as she heard the gravelly soil and pebbles hit the wood, thrown by others. No one knew entirely why this was done, but they joined in none-the-less. Paul led her away, and the mourners began to meander back towards their cars. The Braithwaites first, then the Smiths, followed by Ken and Audrey from number 78. Paul was glad to be moving again, as he had felt a bit giddy in the blazing sun, and sweat was trickling down his back. He loosened his tie and patted his brow with his handkerchief as he let out a sigh.

Young Jemma had hung back a little. She was intrigued by the man in the distance, leaning on a spade, waiting to fill the hole in. The heat was distorting the ether, and he seemed fluid in the haze. At 17, Jemma was feeling her feet and becoming more curious about the adult world. The dawning realisation that she would one day have to make her way in life ignited the interest. Just behind the gravedigger was another man. A guy in a hoody, on a bike. He seemed a little out of place; a curious bystander, presumably. Jemma glanced back at the hole, sighed, and shook her head. 'Bye, Grandad. Hug Nana for me.'

Jemma took a slow walk towards her parents, not relishing the impending interaction with semi-strangers, each slow step allowing others to peel away before she got there. She then felt something touch her feet. She stopped and looking down saw it was a tennis ball of all things. The man in the hoody had his hand up and seemed to be beckoning her to return it. She could see her Mum and Dad still saying their goodbyes, so Jemma picked the ball up, and after ignoring her initial instinct to try and throw it back, she awkwardly traipsed across the uneven grass towards the man. He was smiling.

*

Detective Inspector David Stark was pacing around his bathroom with the door locked. He was sweating and muttering to himself. 'Come on, man, pull yourself together.' 'Stop it.' 'Take some deep breaths.' He was agitated, his mind was racing and his breathing shallow.

His wife Carol was outside the door, nibbling at her nails. She had never bitten her nails, but this felt like a crisis. Was he having a breakdown? She tapped on the door. 'David?'

He tried to put on a normal voice, to disguise the tremor. 'Be out in a minute, love.'

She did likewise. 'Okay. See you downstairs.' She walked over to the bedroom door and shut it but stayed in the room. She tip-toed a couple of steps and sat on the bed quietly. After a minute or so, the bathroom door opened, and she saw a glimpse of David. She rushed over and put her foot in the door as he tried to close it again.

'David, come on, we need to talk. What the hell is going on?'

Stark came out of the bathroom. He was in the same underpants and T-shirt in which he had slept. His shoulders were hunched, and his face had a grey pallor to it. His handsome 'silver fox' features were now drawn and tormented as if he was in a permanent state of smelling mouldy cheese. He looked awful.

Carol sat on the bed and patted the quilt at the side of her. 'Come on, let's talk. Something is wrong. I can see that. We're supposed to be husband and wife, aren't we?'

'I'm fine; it's probably a cold or something.'

'David, it's me you're talking to, you look terrible, just tell me what's troubling you. You've been in there half an hour or more.'

Dave sat down next to her and stared at the carpet. He wiped his brow;

the sweat was trickling from his scalp.

'I don't know what it is.' He looked close to tears. She had never seen him like this, and it was frightening her.

'How long have you felt like this?'

'About a year, maybe eighteen months.'

'A year! Eighteen months! Why didn't you tell me about it, for God's sake?' Her stomach churned.

'Because it has been fine, it only happens now, and then, it seems to be when I have to speak in public, everything else is fine.'

'Is it when you have to address a crowd?'

'It seems to be. It is the only time I get these episodes. I've tried everything; I don't get it. I'm not even bothered about talking to groups of people, Christ. I've been doing it long enough.'

She held his hand and smiled at him. She had never seen him like this; vulnerable. It triggered her butterflies in her stomach; it was unsettling. It called into question everything she thought she knew about him and their life. It was quite a shock, but she was determined to remain resolute, for his sake, if nothing else.

'You're giving that talk at the training school today, aren't you?' She asked.

'That's probably why this has happened. It's ridiculous.'

'You know what it sounds like to me?' Carol said.

'It sounds like I've lost the fucking plot, I know.'

'Don't be daft. You're the best detective on the damned force; they always have you for the difficult murders. It's nothing to do with that. I think it is something called "social anxiety."'

'Social what? It sounds a load of bullshit to me.'

'David, I read about it in a magazine. There are all different types of anxiety.'

He held his head in his hands. 'Magazine. Jeez. Anxiety? What have I got to be anxious about? I'm invincible. I'm scared of nothing, didn't you know?' He tried a smile, but it didn't come off. 'I've tackled the hardest bastards, killers, maniacs, that exist on the planet, you think talking to a crowd bothers me?'

Carol shrugged out a laugh. 'Men.'

'What?'

'David, you can be the bloody King of England and have things like this come on. It is nothing to do with how tough you are or how macho. That's the "bullshit", right there.'

'I know you're trying to help, Carol. I'm grateful, love. I have tried breathing slower, and that can help sometimes. I think I'll be alright in a minute. I've got plenty of time to get there.'

'David, you aren't going in to work.'

'I am.'

'You're not.'

He stood up. 'I am Carol. I've got shit-loads to do.'

'You aren't I've already rung in sick for you.'

'You've done what?' He folded his arms. He was not happy.

'I've rung in sick for you, don't worry, I told them you have a bad case of food poisoning.'

'Carol, you should have spoken to me first.'

'I have spoken to you and look at the response I got.'

Stark was too exhausted to waste his energy on arguing about it. He sat back down next to Carol. 'I suppose, but what difference is a few days off going to make? I'm stuck with it.'

'For now. It will pass, all things pass, in time.'

'No, they don't.'

'They do. Look, I know a girl who I used to work with at the office, and she is a counsellor now, I want you to see her. She's nice.'

'A bloody shrink! No way. So, you do think I'm crazy, then. I knew it.' He stood again and started pacing around, rubbing his fingers through his sodden hair.

'David, stop it. You aren't crazy; you are just going through something that can be helped. Relax. We are going to get you through this.' She went over to him and put her arms around him as he stared out of the window. She kissed his cheek. 'Argh, your hair's wet.'

'Yes, sorry about that. This is what happens.'

'Don't be daft.' She rested her face against his back and squeezed him again. He took hold of her hand. 'She isn't a psychiatrist anyway; she just lets people talk through their problems. It is incredibly helpful.'

David went quiet again. He sighed. 'I'm not going. It's the beginning of the end, once you start that game.'

'No, it's the start of the beginning.'

'Hang on a minute, I don't know where the beginning starts, and the bloody end finishes.' They both laughed.

'She will help you get yourself sorted out.' Carol said pleadingly.

'She won't, because I'm not seeing her. I know you mean well, Carol, and I'm grateful, honestly, I am, but it's not an option. If it came out that I was seeing some voodoo bloody head doctor, it just doesn't bear thinking about what the consequences would be. I would be finished at work. I'm not going. That's the final word.'

Carol stood with that immoveable expression on her face that he had seen rarely over the years. Her arms were folded across her chest. 'You're seeing her at eleven o'clock. I've already booked you in.'

*

Nobby Clarke was Stark's right-hand man, his Detective Sergeant. An ex Regimental Sergeant Major in the parachute regiment. Old school. His style was "forthright", shall we say. He barked 'Good morning reprobates,' as he walked into the CID office at Nottingham Police Station. His suit jacket seemed to be hanging off his broads shoulders, his tie swinging loosely with the collar undone, and he looked liked he needed a shave. Even his walk was untidy – ungainly as he held onto several large arch-lever files, that seemed in danger of collapse.

There were only a few of the team in, and the others were out doing a search warrant. He poured the files on to his desk and sat down at the group of tables with detectives, Stephanie Dawson, Charlie Carter, Jim McIntyre and Ashley Stevens. As usual, the desks were a mess; papers, some with coffee rings on them, newspapers, folders, mugs, screwed up notes, overfilled ashtrays, videotapes and brown evidence bags.

'Stark's gone sick.' Nobby said.

'You're joking? That's a first.' Young Ashley seemed surprised.

Nobby explained. 'He had a bad Chinese last night, his Mrs….'

'Carol.' Steph corrected him.

'Yes, that's her, "Carol", said it'd given him the shits, well, she said food poisoning, but it's the same thing.'

Jim's broad Glaswegian accent boomed. 'No, it's not, Nobby, it can be quite serious; if it's food poisoning, people end up in the hospital with it. Is that what she said, food poisoning?'

'That's what it said on the note on my desk, Jim. It's what you get from eating foreign muck.'

'Nobby, you love a Chinese.' Steph said incredulously.

'I know I do, but, I also know it's a risky business.'

The group smiled and laughed as they glanced at each other. Steph shook her head.

Steph loved Nobby Clarke dearly, and it was now no longer a secret that she and her Detective Sergeant were an item. The team were still coming to terms with the change of dynamic this had created. Steph carried on as usual; used her beauty to charm admissions from criminals, swore like a trooper on occasion, and was relaxed about the set-up. Nobby, however, seemed to follow her around like a lapdog at times. It wasn't doing his street credibility much good with the detectives in his care.

'You'll never change him.' She said.

'Change what?' Nobby grunted taking a paper bag out of his pocket. He tore it opened to reveal two slices of toast which he began to demolish.

'Nothing. Do we know how long the boss will be off sick?' Steph asked.

'No idea.' Nobby sprayed out his crumbs. 'The note didn't say. As long as it takes, I guess. It shouldn't be too long I wouldn't have thought, a couple of days maybe, if that.'

Charlie lit up a cigar and immediately started coughing smoke around the room. His lungs hadn't warmed up properly yet. 'I think we can manage that long. Are you acting up as DI then, Nobby?' Charlie asked.

'Not officially, but I will be running things, as the senior detective sergeant in the city.'

There were some whoops and catcalls. 'Senior Sergeant? Senior citizen, more like.' Charlie said he knew it safe to do so, he and Nobby went back twenty years.

'Eh, you will be drawing your pension before me, Charlie Carter.'

'True, I think I've been there, and come back again, to be honest.'

'If a big job comes in, one of the DI's from the other section will take it, and we will take our orders from whoever it is.' Nobby told the gang.

'Please, God, it's not Lee Mole.' Ashley offered.

'I could'nae work with the guy.' Jim said.

'Apart from the fact he's an obnoxious, scheming little prick, I think he's great.' Steph laughed.

'Anyway, Stark will be back soon, so just keep your fingers crossed we don't get anything too big come in for a couple of days.'

'That means we will you watch.' Steph said.

Post toast, Nobby reached for his cigarettes. 'Who's prepared the briefing for this morning?'

'I have Sarge.' Ashley said.

'Off you go, then. Brief us on events. Is the world still a meadow full of love and butterflies?'

*

Dave Stark felt like a schoolboy being taken for his first dental appointment as Carol drove him to her friend's house. At one stage he thought she was going to wet a handkerchief and rub a bloody mark off his face. She had agreed not to go in the consultation with him, and that was the condition Stark insisted upon when reluctantly agreeing to give it a go. He felt much better after his shower, and now that the prospect of his lecture at training school had gone away, he was back to his usual self. Confidence had returned to his stride, as he and Carol walked up the long drive to the rather large house.

'I think I'm in the wrong job.' Dave said. 'Look at the size of the place. Talking bullshit clearly pays well.'

Carol didn't reply.

'Haven't you ever thought of taking up counselling, Carol?'

On they walked.

'How much is this costing, by the way?'

Carol stopped. 'David, I'm glad you're feeling better, but can you please take this seriously?'

'I am taking it seriously. I wouldn't be here otherwise, would I?'

'Good.'

'What's her name again?'

'Linda.'

'Lovely Linda, meter maid.'

'That's the Beatles, and it's "lovely Rita – meter maid", not Linda.'

'Oh, yes.'

After the initial screams and exaggerated greetings of the two old work colleagues had subsided, they got down to business. Stark settled into the chair, with Linda sitting opposite. Carol was reading magazines in the other room and would soon be lost to the latest Hollywood gossip.

"Not the best position to interview". Stark thought to himself as he smiled at the red-haired woman in the tweed suit. She looked a bit 'jolly-hockey sticks' for his liking. "This is going to be a complete waste of time." He thought.

'It's lovely to meet you, David. Can I call you, David?'

'Yes, of course.'

Stark was shifting about in his chair, crossing and uncrossing his legs, and feeling somewhat ill-at-ease. He was clearly out of his comfort zone. 'Shall I call you Rita, sorry, not Rita, Linda.' He chuckled to himself.

'Linda is fine. Rita, not so much.' She smiled. Linda spoke slowly and seemed to be studying him. In truth, they were both studying each other and positioning themselves mentally; like a bull and a matador armed only with feather pillows. It was a mental dance they were imbued in; a neurological Paso Doble. No-one was quite sure who was the bull and who was the matador.

There were a few minutes of general 'getting to know you,' pleasantries while Stark waited for phase two.

'So, what is it that is troubling you, David?'

There it was.

'Carol seems to think it is something called "social anxiety", but I've never heard of it, so, I'm not sure.'

'Never mind what Carol thinks, what do you think it is?'

He was warming to her. He was glad it was a woman; he could always relate better with women; he wouldn't be as comfortable with a man. He wasn't sure why.

'I think she's probably right. But I must confess I'm a bit old-school, I like to deal in facts; this all seems a bit wishy-washy to me, and I don't mean that disrespectfully, I realise it is me probably out of sync with others.'

'That's okay. I tend to prefer an objective approach. A lot of people who come in here don't acknowledge the *fact* that it is happening to them.'

Stark smiled. 'I get it. Fair do's.'

'Let me see, some facts for you, David. George Beard first described neurasthenia in 1869. You would have still been in short pants then, wouldn't you.'

Stark laughed. 'Just started secondary school.'

'Okay, well neurasthenia had many symptoms ranging from general malaise, body pains hysteria, leading to anxiety and then chronic depression.'

'Hysteria? I don't think I'm that far gone yet.'

'That's good to hear.' She grinned and took a sip of her drink. 'In truth, anxiety as such is fairly new to the world of psychoanalysis, and it was only seven years ago in 1980 in the Diagnostic and Statistical Manual of Mental Disorders that anxiety neurosis was dissected into General Anxiety Disorder and what was called panic disorder.'

'Interesting, you seem to know your stuff.'

'I hope I do, or we are both in trouble.' They laughed. 'To be honest, anxiety can manifest itself in many ways, both physically and mentally. There is a general anxiety disorder where a person feels bad on most days worrying about many different things, and there is social anxiety, specific phobias, panic disorder and obsessive-compulsive disorder.'

'And then there is me.'

'And then there is you.' She smiled warmly. 'That's a fair comment actually as we are all unique, let's face it.'

'We sure are.'

'What is your unique issue, David? Just describe what it is you feel and when it comes on, in your own words.'

In his own words? Whose words would he use? Stark pondered.

'It is when I have to do a major briefing or talk to large audiences or the press; the closer I get to do it, I start sweating, my heart starts to quicken, I'm agitated. Any other time, I am fine. I don't have any of this; I would sooner fight an armed maniac than stand at a podium. It is weird.'

'Okay, I get to see a lot of people like this, you would be surprised who suffers from anxiety of differing themes: Judges, CEO's, many strong, intelligent people. It's as random as anything it's a bit like catching a cold, it kind of just happens.'

'That's a relief. That's good to know, thank you.' Stark was beginning to relax.

'Thank *you* for taking the first steps to resolve it by coming to see me. We will sort you out, David, don't worry.' Her smile was comforting.

'I hope so because it seems to be getting worse.'

'It will get worse if it's left unchecked. Now, however, it will only get better.'

Stark was feeling energised; this woman was good.

Linda continued. 'This is likely to take a bit of time and a few visits, but in the first instance, we need to give you some tools to work with. Get you back to work, build your confidence up a bit, just in case you have to face these audience scenarios again.' She sipped at a glass of water. 'Now, the first thing we need to do is to give you a technique to combat the feeling when it first comes on. There are many, but let's start with tapping and association, along with some meditational breathing and imagery.'

'Great.' Stark said unconvincingly. 'As long as I don't have to sit cross-legged, say "Ohm" and ring a bell.'

She smiled. 'No, no tinkling is required.'

Stark smiled. They were going to get along just fine.

*

Paul Masters was dozing as he lay sprawled on the settee. It had been a long day yesterday, and they hadn't slept well once they got home. His tiredness had caught up with him. Funerals sap your strength and wear you down. It is a slap in the face with a wet fish that reminds you of *your* mortality, not just the poor soul they lower into the ground or slide into the pizza oven. Ella could see Paul's head lolling. He then awoke with a start, look over at her, bleary-eyed, with a silly smile on his face, but she had removed her gaze by then. Sometimes he would begin to snore and wheeze for a few breaths before jolting awake. Regardless of the funeral, in truth, this habit of evening snoozing was becoming a regular occurrence. They had been married for just over twenty years, and in the last year or so, he had put on more weight, and was getting more and more tired in the evenings. Paul had recently been promoted, and Ella was beginning to think that perhaps it wasn't worth the extra four grand a year. It had changed him. She felt that maybe it was a step too far, and their previously idyllic lifestyle had diminished since he took the role on. He snorted for the umpteenth time. She could stand it no longer.

'Paul!'

No response. Ella pushed her husband's shoulder, jarring him.

'Paul! Wake up!'

'What?'

'You were dropping to sleep.'

'I was just resting my eyes.'

She gave him one of her looks. 'I'm going to bed, Paul, I'm tired. Why don't you come up as well, you keep nodding off?'

'I'm fine. I might come up in a bit. I need to do Jemma's sandwiches for college, like the wonderful father that I am.'

She leaned over and kissed him. 'You *are* a wonderful father and a magnificent husband as well. Thanks again for all your support.'

'I'm sorry your Dad's gone. I'll miss the old fellow.'

'We all will, but he went with a happy heart. Anyway, don't set me off again.'

'I won't. I promise. Get some rest, yes?'

'I will be asleep before my head hits the pillow, but, please, tidy up after you've made the sandwiches. Goodnight.'

'I will. Goodnight. What time is Jemma at College in the morning?'

'Nine o'clock, I think. She hasn't said any different.'

'OK, I'll do her sandwiches now. It will save time in the morning. Goodnight, love.'

Ella smiled as she left the living room.

Paul heaved himself off the settee and walked to the kitchen. His head was thumping.

Paul put the kettle on; he would make just a small cup of tea; otherwise, he would be up three times in the night. He busied himself and made chicken and tomato sandwiches for Jemma, which he put in a Tupperware tub and placed in the fridge. Paul had got it off to fine art, the perfect amount of water in the kettle so that it boiled as he finished. Remembering Ella's request, he dutifully wiped the unit, the chopping board and the carving knife. Wiping the blade only, he put the knife on the sill above the sink.

After making his cuppa, he opened the window wide. He walked quietly towards the kitchen door and closed it making just a tiny click. He then went to his secret stash, hidden behind the plumbing of the sink in the utility room. He got a cigarette out and lit it, before placing his booty back, securely out of the way. Paul sighed with pleasure as he exhaled the smoke. Ella would kill him if she knew, but with the stress of this new nightmare promotion, he had succumbed again. Still, it was his only vice. He used to put the fancy new oven extractor hood on, to suck the smoke away, but Ella came down on one occasion because she heard the noise it made. 'Like a bloody Harrier Jump-jet.' She remembered from The Falklands War. Paul thought on his feet and came up with a cock-and-bull story, about burning some toast. He wasn't sure she believed him, but she never mentioned it again. Anyway, because of that little scare, he had to stand next to the open window now, come sun, rain, or frosty wind. The back door was too damned stiff and noisy.

After his nicotine addiction had been satisfied, he checked the doors were locked. He wanted to watch Blackadder, a comedy he had video-recorded, and then he would retire to bed. It was only on for half an hour. Eleven o'clock was too early to go to bed, and if he went up now, he would end up lying there with his eyes open for at least an hour.

As he got into the living room, he closed the door quietly behind him so that he wouldn't disturb the girls. Paul spread himself out on the settee, covering himself with the fleece blanket that he and Ella usually shared, and pressed *play* on his remote.

After what seemed like only two seconds, he awoke with a jump. He looked at the clock on the mantlepiece. 3:23 am. Oh, dear. He turned the

TV off and went back into the kitchen for another cig. It was ridiculous at this time of the bloody morning, but he was thirsty, and he wanted a cup of tea, and with a cuppa comes a ciggy.

He stopped in his tracks as he entered the kitchen. 'Shit!' He had left the window wide open. 'No harm done,' he muttered to himself. Paul chuffed on his cigarette and had his tea in the small china cup. This time he was resolute, and he pulled the window securely back into the frame. He looked around to make sure all was secure, inexplicably patting at his pockets as he did so.

The climb up the flight of stairs, late at night, always bore the risk of a creaky stair, and he was conscious that the two loves of his life, Ella and Jemma, were happily snoozing. He was practised at manoeuvring around the dark bedroom using just the landing light through the tiny crack in the door which he left slightly ajar. Once he got into the en-suite, he closed the door and switched on the light. He brushed his teeth and took his newly prescribed blood-pressure tablets. Paul turned the bathroom light off and fumbled his way through the darkness to his side of the bed, closing the bedroom door as he did. It was now pitch black. He threw off his cotton sweatpants and T-shirt; he always slept naked. He got into bed with Ella, and as ever she was facing away from him. She never stirred. He was tempted to have a feel of her backside, but she had complained that he woke her up when he did that so, no, he would be a good boy. It probably wasn't the time to try anything, and she might call his bluff. He wriggled around and finally got into his set sleep position, and within a minute, he was gone again—fast asleep.

*

The music from the radio alarm tapped into Paul's brain, with increasing loudness, as the layers of tiredness fell away with each line of the song. 'Someone saved my life tonight,' by Elton John. It was 07:15.

He lay there for a few seconds. Something wasn't right. He sat up and felt the wetness in between his legs. 'Oh, Christ, don't tell me that last cup of tea...' He hopped out of bed and was confused that his legs were covered in a red fluid. *'Ella!'* he shouted to his wife, who was still sleeping.

'Ella! I'm bleeding. Christ. What the hell? Ella, w*ake up!'*

He leaned across the bed and pulled at her shoulder. Her head lolled back, her eyes wide and unseeing. A slit spread across her throat exposed the cartilage and bone.

'Ah! My God! *Ella!'* Paul shook at her shoulders as if this would somehow wake her from death. It didn't. She was stiff.

He suddenly thought of his daughter. *'Jemma!'*

In a crazed panic, he ran naked across the landing and burst into the bedroom. Jemma too was naked; on her back on the floor; her mouth stretched open with a green tennis ball stuck into it. Her lips were stretched back, exposing her teeth as they clenched into the lime green ball in death. Her legs were open, bent at the knees. Jemma's throat had also been slit, but closer to the chin than her mother; the cut was deeper, and her tongue had been sucked down through the hole with the tip protruding through it. It was grotesque in its ugliness.

Paul gagged at the sight, collapsing to the floor, in front of her, sobbing. 'No! God – no!' He was dizzy, confused, horrified. His leg brushed hers as he wept; she was rigid. He started to crawl into the landing; his strength was gone from his legs. He managed to claw his way up the bannister and stagger downstairs to the hall telephone.

'Emergency. Which service do you require?' The female voice answered.

'What?'

'Fire, Police, Ambulance or Coastguard?' She clarified.

'Ambulance. No. Police.'

'Hello, police emergency.'

'Quick, help, my wife and daughter have been killed. Please, can you get here, straight away? We need help.'

'Is there an intruder on the premises?'

'No, there's only me in the house.'

The operator began tapping away at the keyboard.

'A unit is travelling sir; there is one close by - stay on the line, please.'

'Stay on the line? Okay, but hurry, please.'

He was sobbing, as she again tapped away on her keyboard. It was one of these new computer things, which were supposed to save time, yet everything seemed to take a damned sight longer in the name of progress. Paul was now whimpering and making strange, desperate noises and squeaks. He thought of the open kitchen window; the window *he* had left open before he fell asleep on the settee. 'What have I done? I must be losing it. This is my fault.'

'Sorry, sir?'

'Please, hurry.'

'Are you certain both parties are deceased? Do you require an ambulance?'

'No. Yes, they've gone. I mean, I don't need an ambulance. I've lost them both.' He sobbed with horror, confusion and sheer panic.

'Are you injured at all, sir?'

'No, I'm fine, but I do have blood all over me.'

'You have blood all over you?'

'It must have trickled out overnight.' He was whimpering and crying.

'Sir, how can that be?'

'I slept with my wife, and she must have been dead.'

'I'm sorry, sir, this is not making much sense. Stay on the line, and the unit will be with you shortly.' The line went quiet, briefly, as the operator broke off and radioed an update to the patrol officers.

Within a couple of minutes, Paul could hear a siren wailing and quickly put some underpants on from the drawer in his bedroom, not daring to glance toward the bed. He had forgotten he was naked. The strobing blue light was now intruding through the drawn curtains, and he started back down the stairs. His shoulders were heaving with his distress, his arms loose and by his side. The phone was still unhooked and on the table near the door.

The officers did not knock. One boot put the door in, and they ran up the stairs, taking hold of Paul as they did.

'Where are they?'

'In...in here.' He stammered.

The officers ushered him into the main bedroom and saw his dead wife.

'Has someone broken in?' The officer asked.

'No. Yes. I don't know. I can't process it. I can't get my head around it. My wife...'

'Where did they break in?' The cop asked.

'There is no break-in.'

Even the officers were shocked when they entered his daughter's bedroom. The officer pressed the button on his radio to speak: 'Papa Tango Four Five, there are two, repeat *two*, one oblique one's, here. Suspicious circumstances. Notify CID please, urgently.'

One of the police officers took hold of Paul's arm. They took him downstairs, as he continued to sob and wail in confusion and despair. He felt he was going insane; his brain could not take it all in. It was just too much. They entered the kitchen. The officers immediately homed in on the carving knife, on the draining board next to the sink.

'What's the knife doing there?'

'Oh, I thought I'd left it on the sill, that's weird. It's mine. I left it there.' Paul said.

The officer leaned in close to the knife. 'It's been wiped, but there is a tiny strand of blood, just near the handle.'

Paul was honest. 'I've wiped it. Could it be that? It's not blood. There was no…'

'*You've* wiped it? So, your fingerprints are going to be on it.'

'Of, course, yes. To get the erm, Christ I can't think straight, red stuff off.'

'Blood.'

'Tomato.' Paul said softly.

The officers exchanged glances.

The older one took out his handcuffs. 'I am arresting you on suspicion of the murder of your wife, and daughter. You do not have to say anything unless you wish to do so, but anything you do say will be given in evidence.'

'What? Why? Just because I wiped the knife down. Ella told me to. I don't understand. What's happening? I called you for Christ's sake.'

Paul was shocked as the cold metal cuffs wrapped around his wrists, and the ratchets clicked into place. The cops walked him towards the door; the phone still live in the hallway.

'It's my fault, I know, but I didn't mean it to happen.' Paul tried to explain, but his mind was addled, and his comments were not helping his cause.

He was bundled out of the house, and into the police car, as other police vehicles turned up at the suburban cul-de-sac. Some of the neighbours were standing in doorways, and others had ventured out on to the pavement. Lights in windows around the street were flickering on, and distant dogs were barking. Several neighbours were out, commentating and muttering to each other, including a man in his thirties, who looked a bit too old to be wearing a grey hoody. He was not known to the locals, but he was smiling as he watched the gabbling, confused, blood-stained man, in his underpants, being manhandled into the police car.

2

'Be the best at whatever you do, but first, make sure that what you are doing, is for the best.'

Shon Mehta.

The detective, in his early forties, had a skinny build and wore a beige summer suit that was too big for him. Detective Inspector Lee Mole looked like a little boy in his big brothers hand-me-down jacket. There was a small cigarette burn at the end of the left sleeve which he covered up subliminally by holding it with his fingers which only served to highlight the oversized nature of the garment. The CID office smelt of smoke and had three clusters of desks all facing in toward themselves where the different shifts of detectives plied their trade. A cigarette-smoke cloud hovered above Starks team in layers, like the striation marks of a cliff face, but shifting and rolling gently. The walls were adorned with ageing intelligence notices, ignored as much now as they were when first pinned to the walls. They were more an obligatory intermittent wallpaper than a source of information. Many were yellowing and dog-eared, interspersed with a calendar of naked ladies and ripped out topless models from Page 3 of The Sun newspaper.

The hideous DI Mole was addressing the assembled detectives. 'It's him. The father, Paul Masters; he's done it, he's a hundred per cent guilty, and that's the end of the matter. I don't want to hear any crazy theories or distractions claiming otherwise.' He paused to summon up the words to express his excitement. 'Two detected murders in the bag, sorted. No need to complicate matters. No need to go all Sherlock Holmes over this one. We are going to keep it nice and straightforward. No heroics. It is him. Okay?'

A new day had dawned, and Detective Inspector Lee Mole could not believe his luck. Superintendent Wagstaff had asked him to cover for DI Stark for 'a day or so,' on a 'red inker' of a murder. In other words, a crime that was already, self-evidently detected. Some 'looney-toon' had killed and raped his wife and daughter and was locked up in the cells. The fact that the Machiavellian Lee Mole and his sinister Detective Sergeant, Carl Davidson hated Stark's guts merely added to the thrill for them. It was a chance to get one over on Stark and rub his nose in it when he came back to work.

Mole paced around at the far end of the CID office and was addressing Stark's team of detectives as if he owned them. It had already got a little awkward, because DI Mole was at the far end of the room, along with his Detective Sergeant, Carl Davidson, while Nobby and Stark's crew stayed sitting at the other end at their cluster of desks. Neither moved toward the other, and empty desks filled the chasm, but Mole ploughed on regardless. The disdain between the two groups was palpable, and the misery that Stark's men were enduring seeped into the atmosphere like an unwanted fart at a wedding.

'You don't look a gift horse in the mouth, sir.' Mole's Detective Sergeant, Carl Davidson, said, before turning around to look at the others, pleased with himself, but they couldn't be less impressed, and he received a sea of expressionless faces.

'What's the motive?' Nobby Clarke asked sceptically.

'We are working on that. I would say that it is an infatuation with his daughter, which has all come to a head. His Mrs has found out, and there has been a massive argument.'

'Is there evidence of that yet, sir?' Young Ashley asked.

'No, it's more of a …, what's the word? More of a hypothesis, that's it, hypothesis.' Mole took his jacket off, displaying thick white braces over his dark blue shirt. He called them 'power' braces; he was truly a git of the highest order.

'Made up, yae mean.' Jim McIntyre smirked, causing a ripple of scornful laughter.

'Why were they both asleep when he killed them if it's come to a head? It's not a crime of passion. I don't get it?' Ashley asked, fiddling with his gold bracelet. His wealthy father had offered Ashley a place in his business many times, but he was too happy being a dashing detective while wearing Saville Row suits and having a stream of 'CID groupies' on the end of his arm. Then, later, on the end of his dick.

Mole raised a finger. 'It is a crime of passion, because' he paused, waiting for inspiration. Then it came to him, 'he has waited for the right moment, hasn't he?'

'Has he?' Ashley asked.

'Yes, he has waited, until the time was right; until they were both asleep and then pounced.' Mole repeated, more confidently this time as he developed his theories in the moment, by the seat of his pants, which, incidentally, were shiny.

'How do we know all of this, sir, if he hasn't been interviewed?' Steve Aston asked.

'We dinnae.' Jim answered in gruff Glaswegian slang.

'What's with the tennis ball in her mouth?' Charlie asked without looking at Mole; it was more to the group than to the DI.

Mole answered anyway. 'It must have been in her bedroom. She's a kid, so he's put it in her gob to shut her up. Simple. There you go.'

'She's seventeen, boss, hardly a kid. I mean, does she play tennis?' Ashley asked.

'I don't bleeding know, but there's no fucker else in the house, everywhere is locked up. Jesus Christ, you call yourselves detectives.' Mole was getting exasperated at the lack of support for his assumptions about the case.

Nobby lit a cigarette and sat back in his chair. 'You're running it, boss, but it just seems a bit odd, who knows, you could be right. I just think we need to be careful and just do it as normal and not merely investigate our assumptions.'

The point seemed lost on Mole. 'Do you? Anyway, thankfully I've already had my top man, Carl, speak with this shithead in the cell. All above board, obviously, and the guy has completely lost his marbles. He's a gibbering wreck.'

Davidson turned around again, smirking. 'Top man,' he mouthed to Stark's team and pointed at himself. He was like a small, sneaky child; a teacher's pet.

Steph couldn't bite her tongue anymore. 'Could he be a gibbering wreck because he found his wife and daughter with their throats slit wide open, perhaps?'

Mole had started twanging on his braces. 'It could be, yes, or is it because he knows he is guilty? Have you thought of that?'

'Sir, come off it...' Steph was losing it.

Nobby interrupted her. 'Hang on Steph. Boss, are we sure on this one? I think we need to be a bit careful we don't just jump in.'

'Can I refer you to my opening comments. "He's fucking done it." Alright?'

The detectives shook their heads and glanced around at each other uncomfortably.

'Don't worry. I'll speak to Stark, once he replaces Mole, we can sort it. Hopefully, the gaffer will be back tomorrow, if the case hasn't been totally fucked up between then and now.' Nobby whispered to the detectives with concerned faces. He said it quietly enough that Mole and

Davidson missed the detail of what was said.

Steve Aston muttered, this time a little too loudly, 'I don't want to get too involved in this, Sarge, I've not long got on CID, I don't want to get thrown off straight away.' He was chewing on a carrot. He was a vegetarian, it was a thing he started when the lads had left one on his desk as a joke, but Steve discovered he quite liked crunching on a carrot after all.

'That can soon be arranged, Bugsy.' DS Davidson sneered threateningly.

'Bugsy?' Steve looked quizzical.

'Yes, Bugs fucking bunny.'

Mole, his only ally, cackled uproariously at the lame joke and gave him a high-five.

'Seriously?' Ash said as he watched the dubious performance by the embarrassing detectives.

Mole took a few steps down towards them and raised his voice slightly. He thought it might give him some authority. It didn't.

'I can hear you all muttering and mumbling, but look at the evidence. This shithead has been found at the scene. He admits on the three nines call that it's his fault, and he has wiped the murder weapon clean, which had blood traces on it. Do I need to go on?'

Nobby sighed. 'I get that we can make it fit, very easily, but I wonder what drove him to do it, that's all—motive, method, means and opportunity. You would think he might have mentioned what drove him to do it. What did he say in the cell, Carl?'

'Not a lot. Just that he hasn't done it, we're going to interview him in a minute, me and the Kingpin.'

'Kingpin?' Steph asked.

'The boss.'

'Christ.' She stifled a laugh.

Mole spoke. 'While we interview him, Nobby, can you get the basics done? Your gaffer is going to love it when he comes back, and I've detected two murders on his patch, in his absence. Happy days.'

'That's what this is all about.' Charlie Carter said to the group.

'Come on Carl, let's get a bacon butty before we get into this guy's ribs.' Mole said.

'Good call, Kingpin.'

'See you losers later.' Mole said as they walked out. The stunned silence lay heavily in the room. Mole came back in, a second later, red-faced and grabbed his jacket.

'What are we going to do, Nobby?' Steph asked her Detective Sergeant.

'We are going to do what we are told, by DI Mole.' Jim said. On Nobby's behalf.

Nobby had little choice but to agree. 'He hasn't even got any actions arranged or anything. He just thinks he is going to con a cough out of the prisoner. We will do the normal, as Jim says. I'll write some actions out, but we deal with it flat, no assumptions of guilt, okay. Tomorrow will be a different day, and we will have a real detective in charge, instead of these pair of jokers.'

'That's if Stark is back tomorrow.' Ashley said.

'He will be if I have to drag his bed here myself.'

There was a chorus of 'Okay Sarge.' And 'Nice one, Nobby.'

Stark's DS continued. 'We need to get the gaffer back as soon as possible. I might ring him, but word is he is back tomorrow, or at least the day after anyway, and then all this madness can stop.'

'What about speaking to old Waggy?' Charlie asked. 'It's going to be a dodgy one with this pair of clowns, Nobby. Surely the Detective Superintendent wants it done properly?'

'Let me see if I can find out when Stark is back at work, first. He will do a proper job. In the meantime, avoid Mole and Davidson like the bloody plague. They are a liability.'

*

Paul Masters sat on the floor of the cell, it was cold concrete, and his back rested against the hard wood of the 'bed.' He remembered a man in a suit coming into the cell earlier, but couldn't recall what he wanted or what was said. He knew he hadn't been formally interviewed yet. He also knew it was a bad situation in which he had found himself. Even as he spoke to the officers back at the house, it sounded terrible, as the words came out of his mouth to the officers arresting him. He was disorientated, lost in shock and grief. How can you defend yourself when you have witnessed such trauma?

His eyes were closed, and his arms folded as he rocked backwards and forwards. He had no-one. He was confused. He'd had a breakdown of sorts, and was not capable of thinking properly. He was haunted by the images of his loved ones in the vilest of circumstances. The officer said that he had killed them. Had he? Had he gone berserk and then blanked his memory of the carnage? He began thrashing his head to one side and screaming at the top of his voice. 'No!'

He heard the faraway yell of the custody sergeant. 'Cell 7. Shut the hell up!'

Paul began sobbing again, and more tears and mucus fell out of his nose, onto his white waxed paper overall that they had given him when they took his underpants off him for forensics. He was shivering now and tired. So tired. His brain wanted to close down. Was this a dream? How had this happened in a matter of a few hours? He had gone from well-revered business-man. The wealthiest on the cul-de-sac, let it be known, to a half-crazed, animalistic figure, snarling in a prison cell. And now he was about to be interviewed about the murder of his lovely wife and daughter. Not only that; horror upon horror, the *rape* of his precious daughter. His shoulders heaved as he began sobbing again, this time it grew into a sort of wail.

'Cell 7. I've told you; stop screaming and bloody wailing!'

Paul could hear footsteps. Was he in trouble for shouting? The key was for his door, and he clumsily got to his feet.

'Come on. You've got an interview. Get walking. I will follow you.' The sergeant steered him into interview room 2 and sat him on a chair. Paul did not look directly at the two men seated at the table but was aware of them.

Detective Inspector Mole and Carl Davidson were sitting opposite Paul Masters who was sniffling. They were pleased to see how dishevelled he looked. These rooms were always quite bleak, windowless, with sticky carpets and dirty walls. It was made even grimmer by the heartache ripping the prisoner apart as he sat squirming on the chair, gasping for air in between intermittent episodes of sobbing. Carl had got Paul Masters to sign away his rights to have a solicitor when he spoke with him earlier in the cell. The poor sod had no idea what he was signing.

Davidson was still eating his bacon sandwich and making a mess of it. Mole was staring at the pitiful wreck in front of him with a misplaced look of superiority spanning his Weasley face.

Mole wanted to secure the deal first. 'We are trialling new tape machines for interviews. They are rolling them out next year, but you don't want to do that, do you? You prefer handwritten notes surely?'

'I don't get it. What?'

'Do you want us to record everything you say? What if you say the wrong thing? If we take notes, you can read them afterwards before signing them.' Mole kicked Carl under the desk.

Davidson spoke. 'It's better for us, boss if we tape him.'

'I know, but we have to be fair, Carl. Shall we take notes instead of using the tape recorder. Yes?'

'Yes, whatever.' Paul had his head down, not acknowledging the officers. Occasionally a tear would drop down on to the carpet. He wasn't in a fit state of mind to be interviewed.

Mole looked at Davidson and winked. 'Just notes then, Carl, yes?'

'If that's what Paul wants to do, fine.' He grinned.

Silence fell on the room as Carl sorted his paperwork out. Mole allowed the silence to perpetuate; he wanted a big full stop to separate the interview proper. Eventually, he spoke.

'You've done this. You've killed them.' Mole said, matter-of-factly.

'I haven't. I wouldn't.' Paul said, shaking his head. 'I don't even know why I'm here.' He was fighting a constant battle to shake off the hideous images of his dead wife and daughter tattooed onto his brain and haunting his every waking moment.

'You're not listening. You've done this, you have.'

'But I haven't. Why would I?' Paul spoke through his tears.

'You have done this, Paul Masters, and you are going to prison for life, kid.' Mole said, not entirely carrying it off.

'That's not fair. It's not right. I don't know what is going on? I can't think straight. You need to catch this bloke, he's out there, on the loose.' Paul put his arms on the desk and rested his head on them. It was as if the storm in his brain was making it too heavy to support. He couldn't cope with the situation of which he had no escape. He wasn't resting; he was trying to find a way of not being there.

Mole shoved Pauls arms off the desk. 'He's not on the loose, Paul; he is sat opposite us. It's you. Sit up. Who do you think you are?'

'I'm tired. I've lost everything, can't you see that? I'm confused, I've never been in trouble in my life. I'm sorry if I have done something wrong.'

'I'll give you some advice to help you.' Mole said before leaning forward and staring into Paul's eyes. 'You just need to say three words.

"I. Did. It". Does that help?'

DS Davidson chimed in. 'That's when the good times start for you, Paul.' He was spitting crumbs on to the table as he spoke. Davidson was still chewing his sandwich, and he sipped his tea. He was used to this style of interviewing by his D.I.

'I can't say that. It's not true. Is it?'

'Only it is true, Paul, that's your problem. Your life is in a total mess, and you need to take responsibility for that. But, trust me, we can help you.'

'My life is over, anyway. Who cares?' Paul said more to himself than the officers.

'Your life will be over when you get to prison, and Mr Big drops the soap in the showers and asks you to pick it up, my friend.' Mole said with a snigger.

'I don't want to go to prison. Why am I going to prison?'

'You *are* going to prison. Of that, there is no doubt, my friend. You just need to think about how you are going to get to an *open* prison, with weekends home, and all the trimmings.'

'I can't do that. What do you mean? How can I influence that?'

'How, Paul? Through me, that's how. It's your lucky day because all you have to do is exactly what I say and you will be fine. Yes?'

'Yes, but…'

'Do what your Uncle Lee tells you, and you can get a cushy number. If you are going to fuck about, its Mr Big for you, all day long. Maybe he should share a cell with you. What do you think, Carl?'

'Definitely boss. Do you want me to ring them now? The prison, I mean, to arrange for Mr Big to double up with Paul?'

'No, wait.' Paul said, struggling to catch his breath through his tears. 'What about the bloke that did it?'

'We're talking to him right now. I'm looking right at him. It's up to you, Paul, what's it going to be?' Davidson said as he wiped tomato sauce off his fingers with a napkin. The sauce stunk and added a momentary release from the smell of body odour that permeated the interview room; the funk now a permanent feature, etched into the walls by a thousand sweaty prisoners.

'Maybe I had a dream or something? I don't remember doing anything.' Paul said, trying to grasp a solution to an impossible situation.

'Maybe. Let's put it this way, Paul, if you haven't done it who has?' Mole sat back.

'I don't know. How can I know that? Surely you will find him, though, won't you?'

'Exactly.'

'What do you mean, "exactly"? I just don't remember, maybe I blacked out or something. Is that what you mean?'

DS Davidson started scribbling on his notes for the first time.

'There you go. We are making progress. You tell me. So you blacked out? Yes?'

Paul fell quiet again. He had a fuzziness in his head. As if the air in the room had turned to treacle, with every movement being slow and difficult.

Mole continued. 'If we get to the other side of the interview and you've been wasting our time, DS Davidson here is going to make that call to the prison. Is that clear?'

Paul's shoulders shrugged, and tears rolled down his face. His nose was snotty, and he couldn't rationalise what was happening. He was spaced out like it was someone else, not him going through this hell.

'I can see you're very upset, Mr Masters. I understand, just take your time.'

Paul couldn't see the face of the Custody Officer peering through the small perspex window of the interview room, but Mole could, hence his change of tone.

'I don't know, I'm worried, I don't want that man to get me, that big bloke in jail.'

The custody sergeant's visage disappeared from the murky, smeared hole.

'We can't help you with that until you help us, can we? Listen. Just tell us what happened. What can you remember?'

Davidson's pen halted whenever anything too contentious was said. He had started to write generalised questions cutting out the veiled threats.

'I don't remember anything. I went to bed, and when I woke up, they were dead. That's all I know.'

'That could happen, Paul, if it were natural causes or something like that, but there is a slight problem when both have had their throats cut, and they are pissing blood. I think it is asking a lot to expect any of us to believe that, don't you?'

Paul gasped. 'I don't want to talk about it.'

'You did this, didn't you, Paul? You killed them.'

'No. I can't have. I loved them both very much. I don't know.'

Lee spoke to Carl. 'Do you need to make that telephone call, Carl?'

Paul panicked. 'Hang on. Okay, it must be me, but I don't remember. I just don't remember.'

'You accept that you did it?'

'Who else can it be? I must have blacked out, or something. I honestly don't remember what happened. I don't.' He wiped the tears from his cheeks. It was the calmest he had been.

'I will ask again, Paul. Did you kill your wife and daughter?'

'I must have.'

'Did you kill your wife and daughter?'

'I don't know.'

'You've just said you did. Who else could have?'

'No-one.'

'Did you?

'Yes. I don't know. I don't remember.'

'So, you did it.'

'I must have.'

'No, "must-have", Paul. You did it didn't you?'

'Yes. Can I go back to the cell now?'

'How did you do it?'

'It must have been with the knife.'

'What knife is this? The one you wiped the blood off?'

'Yes, I wiped it, but it was tomato juice, wasn't it?'

'Why wipe it?'

'I don't know I've told you, I can't remember. That was before, I think, when I did the sandwiches, not after.' Paul put his hands on the desk again and then remembered the detective had pushed his arms off, so he sat back and rubbed at his face.

'There's only one reason to wipe that knife. The knife that slit the throats of your wife and daughter; to hide evidence. That's right, isn't it?'

'I suppose so. I don't care anymore. Whatever. You've made your minds up anyway.'

'No. We need to get to the truth, Paul. Why did you do it?'

His body crumpled, and his shoulders fell with a huge sigh. 'I've no idea.'

'Let us just recap then. You accept you killed your wife and daughter and wiped the knife afterwards, but you don't know why you did it.'

'I don't remember.'

'Hang on, Paul, that's what you've told us so far. These are your words, not mine.'

'Fine.'

'So, you did kill them?'

Paul muttered something under his breath.

'I didn't hear that. Did you kill them, Paul? It's a simple question.'

'Yes. Can I go back to my cell now?'

'We need you to sign the notes first.' Davidson said. He threw them across the table for Paul.

Paul didn't bother reading them. 'Do I just sign at the end?'

'At the bottom of every page, please, Paul, there's a good chap.' Davidson had left a large blank at the end of the last page, enough for a final paragraph to be inserted.

*

DI Lee Mole and his hand-wringing cohort, Carl Davidson, were drinking pints like it was going out of fashion in the Police Station bar. Detective Superintendent Wagstaff, with a handlebar moustache and military bearing, was in their company; he looked like a bemused RAF wing commander as he listened to Lee and Carl regale him with stories of how wonderful they were.

Stark's men were huddled at the end of the bar, looking somewhat dour and threw the occasional glare towards the excuses of detectives.

'He's charged with two counts of murder and the rape of the daughter, sir. All done and dusted, on to the next one.'

'It's a job well done, Lee. I know the Chief is very pleased. It will be a feather in your cap, this one.'

'Good to hear, sir, good to hear. The elite are awaiting instructions for the next big job, aren't we, Carl?'

'We are, sir.' Carl raised his glass, and Lee clinked it with his own.

'What has the offender said?' Superintendent Wagstaff asked.

'He's said he'd done it, that's all we need.' Mole said.

Wagstaff laughed. 'We need a bit more than that, Lee. What made him do such a thing, for Heaven's sake?'

'He wouldn't say. He realised we were a bit too street-wise to be conned, so after his admission, he packed up saying too much, didn't he, Carl?'

'Yes, boss. You wrapped him up in bloody knots. It was brilliant.'

'Very nice of you to say, Sergeant.'

'Mon pleasure, sil vous plait.'

DC Cynthia Walker shuddered. 'Have you heard that pair?' She said to Steph. Cynthia was of mixed race, a beautifully elegant young lady, new to the department.

Steph took a cigarette out. 'Don't start me off, Cynthia, what a pair of prize pricks they are.'

'Mr Stark isn't going to be too impressed.' Cynthia caressed her gin and tonic, as she mentioned her boss's name; her long painted nails immaculate.

'I just hope to God he is back in time to sort this shit-show out.' Steph puffed at her cigarette.

'He should be back soon, Steph. If it's a bit of food poisoning.'

'Hopefully, depends how bad he's got it, I suppose.'

There was more exaggerated, over-loud, laughter from Mole and Davison, which cut through the group, mocking them.

Nobby suddenly burst out of the group, heading towards Lee Mole. Steph put her hand on his chest, blocking his path. She had been keeping an eye on him for a while, waiting for him to blow. 'Where do you think you are going, Sergeant Clarke?'

'To tell that pair some bloody home truths.'

'No, you're not. You are going to get another drink, and I'll tell you why.' She nodded to Steve Aston. 'Get the Sarge a pint, Steve, please, will you?'

Nobby was Stoney-faced. 'I can't stand this bullshit any more.' He raised his voice. 'They're a pair of incompetent, bent, fucking idiots!'

Wagstaff and the brace of clowns looked over towards the disturbance to discover that it was DS Nobby Clarke causing it. Was he drunk? Wagstaff appeared confused; he hadn't quite heard what had been shouted but could tell something was awry.

Steph continued. 'Let me tell you why you are not going over there to tell them what a pair of incompetent, bent fucking idiots they are.'

'Go on then, let's hear it, Confucius.' Nobby said with steam coming out of his ears.

'Because, we all know this poor sod in the cells, hasn't done it, and do you know what else we know?'

'What?' Nobby grunted. Steph could wrap him around her little finger.

'The mad bastard that *did* kill the Masters, is still out there, and you know what that means don't you?'

Nobby frowned. 'The killer's going to do it again.' It was as if it had suddenly dawned on him.

'Bang on, Sergeant Clarke. He's going to do it again. And when he does, the Chuckle brothers over there, are going to have a shit-load of egg on their face.'

'One question.' Nobby said.

'Go on.'

'Who the hell are the Chuckle brothers?'

Steph laughed. 'They've got a new television show, have you not seen Chucklevison?'

'Funnily enough, I haven't.'

Steve handed Nobby his pint. 'Cheers, Steve.'

'You're welcome, Sarge. Remember me when it's assessment time.' Steve said.

'It'll need more than a pint to get you off the bloody hook, Mr Aston.'

Nobby was drawn back into the conversation with the lads.

Cynthia spoke quietly. 'Steph, it needs sorting. Other people could die because of this. We need to sort it before the next one if we can.'

Steph sighed. 'I know, Cynthia, I was just stopping old firey breeches from popping his cork. We need to find the real killer soon, we need Stark back, sharpish.' Her attention was diverted. 'Oh, hello, sir.'

Wagstaff, nearly thirty years on the job; 8th August 1958, to be precise, was older than old school seemed possible. 'Let me give my favourite detective policewoman a hug before I get going.'

Steph obliged. He was harmless enough, bless him. Nobby's radar went off, and he turned around and saw Wagstaff.

'What are you lot so glum about? I would have thought you would be celebrating a good result.' Mr Wagstaff said.

Nobby was never one to hold back. 'You're joking, sir. This one's a wrong 'un.'

'What do you mean exactly, sergeant?' There was a hint of ice in Wagstaff's question.

Nobby continued, 'I mean we aren't very comfortable that this bloke has done it, sir. That's why we ain't doing the bloody hokey-kokey with that pair.' Steph kicked him.

Wagstaff twiddled his moustache. 'That's rather a serious thing to say. Are you prepared to put your money where your mouth is?'

Nobby paused. 'Damned right I will.'

Steph intervened once more. 'Hang on Nobby. We need to prove it if we make a complaint. On the face of it, you can make a case for Paul Masters being guilty, and that is exactly what they have done.'

Wagstaff was getting a bit twitchy. 'This is the first I've heard of this. I wasn't aware of any dissent. Just be mindful that if you are going to cast aspersions, you need to have dotted the I's and crossed the T's. Is that clear? Idle gossip won't be entertained.'

'Yes, sir.'

Mr Wagstaff leaned into Steph. 'I'm going to bid you goodnight. Listen, those fellows over there don't have the monopoly on being right. Have a word with DI Stark. He's back tomorrow. I will ask him to keep me posted. Okay?' He winked.

Steph spoke. 'We will, sir, thank you. That's good news about Mr Stark. Thank God he's back. And thank you.'

'You're welcome. Relax, enjoy your drink. Goodnight.' He turned to leave.

The chorus of goodnights was far more energised than they had been before Mr Wagstaff's little chat with Steph.

'He ain't as daft as many people think.' Nobby said.

'He certainly is not.' Steph smiled. 'Happy now?'

'I'm always happy when I'm with you, Steph, you know that.'

3

'Heroes are not known by the loftiness of their carriage;

the greatest braggarts are generally the merest cowards.'

Jean-Jacques Rousseau.

Nobby threw the tennis ball to Ashley who quickly offloaded it to Steve Aston who dropped it, and as he tried to catch it at the second attempt it ended up under the desk amidst groans of "butter-fingers". He had to crawl underneath among the telephone wires to retrieve it. He didn't see the man enter the office.

'I see nothing has changed; it is still like a bloody kindergarten.'

It is nice to be appreciated. There were cheers as Stark's muscular frame appeared in the doorway of the CID office. He was smiling as the detectives clapped and whooped his return, it turned into being over the top and a semi-piss take. He had regained his twinkle; his Italian looking olive skin and thick dark hair accentuated his white toothy grin. He wore a grey suit, expensive shoes, and was holding a leather notebook as he gave a bow.

'Give us a twirl, give us a twirl.' Charlie Carter said. Stark duly obliged.

'I understand you've been having fun.' Stark said.

'The tennis ball? It's just a stress reliever, that's all.' Nobby said as he caught the ball from Steve's throw. He placed it back into his bottom desk drawer somewhat sheepishly.

'No, you plonker, I mean you've been having fun with a certain, Lee Mole.' Stark said.

'Boss it's no joke, it's been an absolute nightmare.' Ashley was serious.

'Come and have a seat, sir, and we can tell you all about it.' Nobby patted the chair in between him and Steph Dawson.

'Sure, let me get a cuppa, first.'

'Steve, get the boss a coffee.' Nobby barked, and Steve readily got up to do just that, but Cynthia stopped him. 'It's fine, let me do it.'

'Thanks, Cynthia.' Stark smiled and walked past her towards the desks. Cynthia moved with feline grace and an extra wiggle for her Detective Inspector. She was so pleased he was back. It was becoming more and more apparent that she had a bit of a crush on him, even if he was nearly twenty years her senior.

Stark stretched, just before he plonked his backside onto the chair next to Steph. He shook his head despairingly as he noticed Steph's three stationary trays labelled, 'In,' 'Out,' and 'Shake it all about.'

'How's your arse?' Nobby asked.

'Arse?'

'Your food poisoning, is it sorted?'

'Oh, that. Yes, thanks, I feel much better than I did on day one, let me just say that.'

Ashley sat next to Steve. 'Pleased to have you back boss, trust me, we will never slag you off again. Not that we ever have, of course. Ahem.'

'I believe you. How's your dad, Steph?'

'He's fine thanks, I've not had a chance to see him the last couple of days, but our Margaret has been to the hospital, and he was laughing and joking, so all is well. He'll stay at mine when we get him home.'

'It's the second time he's had a fall, isn't it?' Stark said. He was guessing.

'Three times now. We need to think about what the hell to do with him. Now he's broken his hip he can't afford to have another fall.'

'I'd start with keeping him off the bloody sherry.' Nobby contributed with a wink.

'He doesn't even drink, and you bloody well know it. It's you that needs to keep off the booze, if anybody.' Steph was quick to defend her father; her nerves had been a bit on edge with all the worry about him.

'Alright, I was only joking, bloody hell.'

'How come you know about all the aggro we've had with Mole?' Charlie Carter asked.

'Wagstaff rang me first thing and said he sensed a bit of concern amongst the troops. He asked if I could *tactfully* have a look at the evidence under the auspice that the murders are on my patch.'

'We mentioned it to him last night in the bar; it's good of him to talk to you about it.' Steph said.

'You can do what you want, boss, you don't need Moles' permission.' Steve commented, he was still under the misbelief that his DI was all-powerful when, in reality, he was just as much in the food chain as anyone else.

'I wish, Steve, and anyway it's *DI* Mole to you.'

'Sorry, sir.'

'We still have to be respectful to DI Mole or if not him, the rank at least. He was good enough to cover for me, even though we know he is a hideous creature, spawned from the bowels of hell.'

Murder Me Tomorrow

They laughed. 'Mole never showed *you* any respect, governor.' Jim McIntyre said in his Scottish drawl, tapping a cigarette on the table prior to lighting it.

'Nothing new, there Jim, but we mustn't stoop to their level.'

'It's every time, though sir. It's bang out of order.' Ashley said, leaning back, his expensive made-to-measure suit jacket flapping at the sides of the chair.

'Oh, well, we're better than that. Let's just worry about what we do. I know its not nice when you are being steamrollered. Leave all the politics to me, though.'

The team muttered a reluctant agreement. Stark didn't want their judgement about the murders being clouded by the desire to prove themselves right to Mole.

Charlie piped up. 'Just let Mole keep digging a big hole for himself, you mean.' Charlie laughed uproariously and slapped the desk. There were groans and a few giggles.

Cynthia brought Stark his coffee. Her long nails wrapped around the mug.

'Thanks, Cynth.'

'Made with love, sir.'

'I'm sure it was, thank you.' He smiled at her, and she returned it with an extra helping of jam.

Stark took a slurp and opened his writing pad before clicking his pen into action. 'Come on, then; I'm all ears.'

Stark had to shush them, as they all began talking at once. He decided to do it in order around the table. By the end, he had a lot of notes, but there were four sections of text which he had drawn a circle around:

'Tennis ball,'

'Pubic hair,'

'Access?'

'Motive.'

'Please tell me that tennis ball you've been throwing around is not the one from the scene.'

Nobby seemed put-out. 'Of course, not, give us some bloody credit, boss. It's just that you don't normally see us throwing it around. It's got more service on CID than Steve Aston has.'

Stark offered a view, with all the detectives waiting to see if he shared their doubts about the case. He was less committed to the cause than they thought he would be. It seemed a bit flat.

'Okay, I can see why you have reservations, but it wouldn't be the first time that a husband has lost it and wiped out his family. I think we can get more certainty on it, though, from what I've heard. Nobby, are you going to take me up to the scene; there are a few things I want to explore.'

'Absolutely, we've got the door key back off Scenes Of Crime. I'll get the CID car keys, and we can shoot.'

'Okay, just let me finish my coffee first. It was made with love, after all.' He winked at Cynthia.

*

Paul Masters home was a typical detached house, built 'out-of-the-box' in the 1970s, with a bit of a garden at the back and open plan at the front. It was a cul-de-sac with many similar, cloned houses surrounding each other. It had a small extension at the side.

As Stark surveyed the street, sunlight glinted from windows across the way. One or two curtains were twitching. The heat was unbearable, and they were in short-sleeved shirts and sunglasses.

One woman emerged with hedge cutters, another rolled her dustbin out, and the children bicycled and scooted towards the house. It was exciting to see some activity at the place where the husband and father had so savagely slain Ella and her daughter. They had known all along there was something dodgy about that Paul Masters. He scarcely spoke, just nodded or waved, and hardly ever smiled, clearly a man with something to hide. Flora at number 63 said she had predicted something like this would happen, but nobody listened, she was called judgemental, but now; now it was a different kettle of fish.

The key slid in easily, and both Nobby and Stark gasped as he pushed the front door open. It stunk to high heaven, and a dozen or so huge meat flies flew out. Many others were buzzing around in a circular pattern, inside the hallway. They stepped backwards. 'Jesus. Nobby, didn't Mole get the council to clean the place?'

'It doesn't look like it, boss. There was a lot of blood, so it will be that causing the stink.'

'This is ridiculous. This is going to be pleasant, isn't it?' Stark said sardonically.

'Let's go around the back and open up the back door to get some air in, at least.' His DS suggested. 'I will keep this front one open.'

Once they were at the back of the house, Stark let Nobby chase around inside, opening as many windows as possible while he had a mooch around the garden. He was just looking, observing whatever seemed right or wrong.

Stark looked up the building and then down to the floor. It was a well-kept garden with a lovely lawn and patio. Again, pretty standard, but cared for by the owners, none-the-less.

'Ready when you are, Dave.' Nobby shouted.

'Yes, hang on. I'm just having a gander out here a minute. Never rush a scene, Nobby.'

His DS came to the kitchen door and pulled some clean air into his lungs before replacing it with smoke from his Park Drive cigarette.

Murder scenes always made him reach for the cigs, he felt them odd, a bit spooky, which of course they were. Anything to do with the after-life or death, and Nobby got the jitters, 'You can't punch fucking ghosts,' he would say.

'What are you looking for, boss?'

'Nothing in particular, just whatever is here. If we take our time, anything abnormal will show itself. It always does.'

At the side of the house was a small gap between wall and fence, that just accommodated the width of a man, so long as you weren't as wide as Nobby Clarke. The ground had gravel down the length of it.

'Have the family got a bike?' Stark asked his Detective Sergeant.

'Not that I know of, there's no shed or anything, just that box thing, so I don't think they have. I mean, where is it if there's no shed?'

'I only ask because, come here, look.'

Nobby joined him. 'If you look down the side of the house, in the middle of the gravel is a groove, looks like a bike might have caused it. The indentation goes on for some way, look, and curves slightly, and it follows down onto the patio, do you see what I mean? That's not a garden implement that has caused that.'

'I see what you mean. It could be anything, though.'

'You're right, it could, but it's most likely a bike, I reckon.' Stark said with a shrug.

The DI squatted down and looked closely at the gravel which led to the patio slabs and on to a flower bed.

'A nice display of flowers, don't you think?'

'I suppose.' Nobby grunted. He wanted to get inside rather than messing around out here.

'That doesn't happen by accident, Nobby, you need to tend them and care for them. It takes time and effort and lots of fussing around to keep them so pristine.'

'I'm sure it does, but…' Nobby's voice trailed off.

Stark finished his question for him. 'What does it have to do with the murder?'

Nobby was scratching at his head again. 'Well, yeah.'

'Why is that end flower squashed? They look like they are pretty proud of their garden. I reckon it's a shoe that has caused that, look at the soil indentation.'

'It's not a footprint, though boss, not enough to make anything of, at least.'

'There is a ridge, don't you reckon?'

'Possibly.' Nobby scratched at his thinly shaved hair once more.

'I'm just thinking out loud, Nobby. We are trying to find anything that suggests an intruder, or a third party, aren't we? If you're saying Lee Mole has just taken the gift horse sitting in the cells, then Mole won't have thought about any of this. Come on then, let's go in. I can see you're champing at the bit.'

The kitchen was dark and much cooler than the sunny exterior. It was made chillier by the vibe that lingers in all death houses: the quiet, and the ambience of doom that shadows you around wherever you go. This was the feeling that gave Nobby the collywobbles.

Stark stood still and looked around the kitchen as his eyes adjusted from the bright sunlight.

'This is where the uniformed lads found the carving knife, is it?' He asked.

'Yes, on the windowsill, or sink.'

'Which was it? Windowsill or sink?' Stark stared at his Sergeant.

'Windowsill.'

Stark gave him a sideways look. 'You're not guessing, are you?'

'No.' Nobby looked at his shoes.

'Regardless, it is a little odd, don't you think?'

'What's that, boss?'

'Taking the knife downstairs, why not leave it at the scene with the body or take it away with you? That's the norm, isn't it?'

'Yes, it is thinking about it. That Paul Masters told the cops, he wiped it, don't forget.' Nobby said.

'No. I get that. I'm just running it through as if it is *not* Paul Masters but a third party, so let's do that. Why would the killer bring it down?'

'Not to wipe it, that is for sure.'

'No, he would have gloves on. Why bring it down unless he knew our friend Mr Masters, was in the living room and thought he might need it if challenged.'

'Could be.'

Stark peered at the draining board next to the sink. 'A little bit of pinking still there from blood residue mixed with water. Where's the rag or towel?'

'What rag is that, boss?'

'What has the knife been wiped on?'

'SOCO has the dishcloth, but it was tomato juice on it; no blood was evident.'

'You're missing my point Nobby. There is blood on the knife, and so it is the murder weapon, we know that. According to Sherlock Mole, Paul Masters has killed them and wiped the knife, so what has he wiped the blood-stained knife with? It has to be here, with Paul Masters or with SOCO, so where is it?'

'That's a point. I don't think it's on the list of property from SOCO. Can I just mention that I have not been to the scene, and I don't think Lee Mole did until SOCO had finished?'

'So, it's been overlooked. Is that what you are saying?'

'I guess it has.'

'Make a note to check the prisoner's property back at the nick, will you? Because whatever the knife was wiped on exists and has to be somewhere and let's face it, it is here, or it's with the prisoner or…another third party. It could be the killer used his clothing, I guess.'

'Masters was in his undies when he got nicked.' Nobby remembered.

'SOCO would have taken anything blood-stained; have a look in the dirty clothes basket when we see one, will you? And the bins. Anything blood-stained, clothing or rags.'

'Yep, no problem. I think Mole thought about getting the place searched, but then said there was no point because Masters had "kind of coughed it"; his words not mine, and so he asked what the point was?'

'Seriously?'

'Seriously.' Nobby shrugged. 'See what I mean? This is what we've had to put up with.'

Stark led the way at an amble into the hall and then the living room. He tapped on the wood of the door. 'Old style, reasonably thick doors, to say it is a new house, so in theory, if Masters was asleep in the living room, it is at least feasible that an intruder could go past unnoticed.'

'No doubt, boss. Particularly if he is fast asleep.'

'And that any noises were masked by the door and indeed by the telly, assuming it was on.'

Stark took hold of the TV remote and turned the box on. The channel that was being watched before it was turned off came on. 'BBC 1. Get a schedule for all the TV programmes that were shown on the night in question Nobby, will you?'

The Detective Sergeant sighed and reached into his pocket again for his scrap of paper, writing 'TV schedules,' on it.

Having discovered nothing further in the living room, they took to the stairs, the foul stench getting stronger with every step. They turned left into the master bedroom.

'Fuck me!' Nobby exclaimed.

'This is what happens when you don't get a scene cleaned in the hottest summer for ten years.' Stark said while holding his nose.

The bed was swarming with maggots and scores of flies buzzed around, causing the pair to gag and cough. The centre of the bed was blackened and putrid. A hole had formed in the mattress—the centre of which had a wriggling mass of hundreds of yellow pupae.

'Look at the quilt, what's left of it.' Stark said, his voice whiny because of the constriction to his nose, which he pinched with thumb and forefinger.

Nobby whined back, adopting a similar strategy. 'What?'

'Paul's side of the quilt is folded back as if he had got out of bed.'

'How do you know that's his side?' Nobby was swatting at the flies – they had chosen him.

'He's got a fucking problem if he sleeps on the other side. It's got five pints of blood all over it.'

'I know I was just about to say that.' Nobby said a little sheepishly.

'Stuff this. It's a bloody health hazard in here. I'll have to have a proper look at the SOCO photos and video. Let me just stick my head in the teenager's room.'

It was a similar sight with maggots this time infesting the carpet.

'Any other tennis balls or a racket or anything like that?'

'Not according to the search log. I can't see any, can you, boss?'

'No. I've got a feeling that ball might be the attacker's, you know.'

'That's was Ashley said yesterday.'

'Let's go back outside.' Stark said. 'We can't stay here; it's fucking humming. Christ, it stinks.'

Once in the garden, the two men lit up tobacco. Stark enjoyed an occasional small cigar and Nobby liked his ciggies. They were suitable for just this occasion, to get rid of the murder pong.

Stark sat on a small garden wall, and Nobby leaned against the fence.

'Tell me the highlights of the main bedroom, again, Nobby.' Stark asked.

'Sure, Ella Masters, that's the wife, she was lying on her back in the bed with her throat cut. Unmolested, no rape or sexual assault. The blood spattering suggested she was attacked while sleeping on her side. Maybe Paul pulled her onto her back.'

'And he is suggesting that he slept with her despite her throat having been cut.'

'On the three nines call, he said that apparently, to the officers attending as well I think.'

'I need to listen to the tape of that call.'

'Is it even possible to sleep with a dead person and not notice?' Nobby asked.

'It's not so much sleeping with a dead person, per se; it is sleeping with a woman who has had her throat cut. It's possible but seems a little remiss. You might have to question how attentive you are as a husband.' Stark grinned. 'If she was decomposing, it might be a bit more difficult to believe.'

Nobby smiled as he sucked on his cigarette; it was good to have the boss back.

*

'Murder room, DC Stevens.' As ever the damned telephone cord was wrapped around itself and Ashley stretched it as he took it to his ear. He had drawn his white shirt sleeves back a couple of folds, exposing his tan, gold bracelet and Rolex watch.

'Is DC Stephanie Dawson there, please?' It was a female, and she sounded upset, or she had a cold; one of the two.

Ashley swivelled on his chair and shouted across the room. 'Steph, call for you.'

'Thow it over then.'

'What's your extension, again?'

'Christ, Ash, you'd think you'd know it by now, 3639.'

'I'm no good with figures.' He grinned.

'That's not what I've heard.'

'Cheeky. I'll put her through, hang on.'

'Who is it?'

'I don't know.' He shrugged.

Steph tutted and shook her head. 'DC Dawson,' she answered.

'Steph, it's Margaret.'

'Oh, hi sis, what's up?'

'It's dad, we've lost him.' She began crying.

'Lost him? Hang on, what? You mean he's passed away?' Steph could feel her stomach churn and her breathing quicken. Ash swivelled around and looked on concerned. She was aware that he was watching her and this somehow enabled Steph to cling on to her emotions, by the thinnest of threads. Her heart was pounding, and she stood up.

'Sorry, Steph, according to the hospital, he just deteriorated in the night, and then this morning he let go. I've only just found out myself.' She sniffled. 'I can't believe it.'

'Why the hell didn't they ring us?' Steph asked, feeling her tears forming in her eyes. She grabbed for her cigarettes and hastily lit one.

'I don't know, I'm going over to the QMC now, he's on Ward E10, but they are only keeping him there for an hour, and they will move him somewhere, but I can't remember where they said.'

'The morgue, Margaret. I'll meet you at the QMC. Ward E10.'

Steph slammed the phone down and paused as the tears began to come.

Ash was shocked by the news. Steph had said he had been laughing and joking just the night before. 'I'm sorry, Steph,' He muttered, feeling he ought to say something but not being sure quite what.

Steph grabbed her bag and keys and headed out of the office. 'Tell, Nobby when he gets back, will you, Ash?' There were tears in her voice.

'Of course, do you need…'

She had gone.

*

Stark and Nobby continued with their garden discussion, basking in the heat. Sweat had re-formed on their foreheads.

'There was more evidence in the girl's room, you said?' Stark asked.

'Just a bit. She had a fucking great tennis ball rammed in her mouth, for a start.'

'Yes, I know that hence looking for a bloody tennis racket, Nobby. It was an improvised gag, I presume.' Stark said.

'Yes, but that begs the question if she kicked off, and started shouting and screaming and needed gagging, with your mystery third party, surely this would have alerted Daddy, downstairs?' Nobby moved his position slightly, as the wood of the fence he was leaning on was splintering slightly and digging into his shoulder.

Stark seemed unconvinced. 'Not necessarily, it depends if he was awake; he could have dozed off. Maybe he stuck the tennis ball in her mouth as a precaution before she made a noise. He raped her, don't forget. Mum was just one clean cut.'

'Two cuts, boss, I've seen the photos. No tentative cuts at the edges though, he was confident. I don't think this is his first time, somehow.'

'Interesting. What bothers me more is where the tennis ball came from?' Stark mused.

'I just thought it was from the room; I don't know why.' Nobby shrugged dismissively.

'Maybe, but does she play tennis? She's a bit old for toys, don't you think?'

'Yes, fair point. As I said, Ashley said the same yesterday; we need to find out, boss.'

'Get SOCO to test the ball for whatever they can, as if it is owned by the offender, rather than improvised by him at the moment of truth.'

'I can do, boss, but Lee Mole will go ballistic if he knows I'm sticking my nose in. SOCO is bound to tell him.' Nobby looked concerned.

'Leave that to me; I'm going to meet Mole, later, with Waggy.'

'Oh, to be a fly on the wall.'

Stark flicked some ash onto the soil. 'I think we've got enough flies, don't you? You'll have even more when you go back in and search that washbin and bins like I asked you to.'

'Oh, shit.'

'Yes, oh, shit. Add to your list, to check that SOCO has photographed the gravel for the tyre indentation if that's what it is, and the flower bed, with samples of the soil taken for future reference. I will be surprised if they haven't.'

'No problem.' Nobby's list was getting longer, and he scribbled notes on a scrap of paper he kept getting out of his trouser pocket and putting back in again, repeatedly. The writing was getting smaller to fit each new reminder on the finite space.

'What else was relevant in the girl's room?'

'Let me think. She'd been raped, of course.'

'Ejaculation?' Stark said hastily.

'Bless you.' The two laughed. Nobby continued, 'Yes, there was ejaculation, but they still won't do this new DNA thing, not for weeks or months, anyway.'

'It's fine, Nobby. It makes no odds anyway, not until we catch the guy, then it's great, but we've got to catch the bastard first.'

'So, do you have doubts as well?'

'I think there are big holes that need filling…'

'To coin a phrase.'

'To coin a phrase.' He laughed. 'Anything else?'

'Yes, they found a single pubic hair that did not match any of the people in the house.'

'Yes, you said. That's important Nobby. I mean unless she's had a boyfriend in.'

'No, it can't be that. It was stuck to Jemma's inner thigh.'

'If Paul Masters raped and killed her with no one else present, that pubic hair cannot exist. It cannot be true.' Stark said.

'I know, but it does exist.' Nobby said.

'So, there is a high likelihood that it was a third party. I would represent Paul Masters, as it stands?'

'You agree it's dodgy, boss?'

'It's quite dodgy.'

'I knew you would.' Nobby wiped at his forehead. 'Christ, it's a warm one.'

'It's too hot. We spend all year moaning about the cold, and when we get the heat, guess what?'

'I know, we whinge about that as well.' The two of them laughed.

'Anything else, Dave?'

'What has this, Paul Masters said in the interview?'

'I've no idea; Mole and Davidson implied they'd got a half cough, but they are guarding the interview notes like they're Princess Di.'

'Nobody is guarding Princess Di, mate; let's face it who would hurt her? She's too much of a sweetheart. The only people pointing anything dangerous at her is the paparazzi.'

'And Dodi, of course.' They both laughed.

'Yes, and Dodi, he must be pointing something really dangerous at her.' Stark laughed as he stood up. The wall he'd been balancing on was giving him a numb backside. 'Anyway, we digress, why are they so precious about the interview notes, do you think?'

'I don't know. Who can tell with that pair? To be honest, they've hardly told us anything that has been going on.'

'You don't think they've written him up, do you?' Stark asked. Aware that the practice of adding confessions or elaborating confessions on to notes was rare, but not unheard of.

Nobby shrugged. 'I wouldn't put anything past them; they're a pair of glory hunters. Anything is possible.'

Stark stubbed his cigar against the wall on which he had been sitting. He pinched it with his fingers to check it was out and put it in his pocket so that he could bin it later. Nobby threw his Park Drive on to the grass and trod on it. 'Are you ready to head back then, boss?'

'Yes, when you've checked the bloody wash basket, and bins, as I asked you to six fucking times.'

'Oh, yeah.'

'Are you alright, Nobby? You don't seem with it today. It's not like you. Are you and Steph all loved up again is that it? You need to screw your head on a bit tighter, mate.'

'No, it's not Steph. To be honest, I just don't feel like I've got a handle on this at all. I've never seen such a shower of shit in my life. We've been kept at arm's length. It knocks you bloody sideways.'

'Incompetence is contagious.'

'It's not just that they are incompetent, Dave, I think they're bent bastards, and because of them we are now a couple of days behind catching a killer who is going to kill again, while we are still scratching our arses and playing catch-up.'

4

'How lucky am I to have something that makes saying goodbye so hard.'

A.A.Milne – Winnie The Pooh.

The little boy had never worn a suit before, and it felt funny. Toby was hot, his cheeks were red, and Mummy had left his sun hat in the car. He kept blowing air out of his mouth, upwards to try to cool his face, and his breath wafted his blond fringe. Toby was fidgety, and he kept pulling at his collar, it was rubbing at his skin. His bowtie was askew; part of the elastic had wriggled from the shirt collar and was pinching the skin around his neck. It was digging in. He couldn't manipulate it back again, so he endured it. Toby wanted to put his hand up to ask to go to the toilet, but he knew he couldn't, because the man was talking. His Mummy was crying, and that made him feel sad, and a little afraid. He'd got 'tummy worms.'

The man was saying weird things that sounded like a foreign language; *'Into your hands, O Merciful God, we commend your servant...'*

Aunty Dot had her arm around Mummy, and she kept pulling Mummy into her shoulder and wiping her hand over her head. Then Mummy would blow her nose on her handkerchief. He had never seen anything like this before, and it wasn't nice; he didn't like it. Maybe she had hurt her leg or something. She used to hug him if he had a graze on his knee. Toby kept shuffling his feet and kicking at the grass on the ground, just out of boredom mixed with unease.

All of the grown-ups were standing around the big hole, which he sort of wanted to jump into, but he daren't go too near the edge, in case he got a telling off. Everyone was staring towards it as if it was important. It was just a hole in the ground.

There was a man in a large black dress and a scarf that kept flapping in the hot wind that occasionally gusted. He was the one saying weird words, and now and then someone would shout out in a cry or begin sobbing.

'...we humbly beseech you, a sheep of your own fold, a lamb of your own flock, a sinner of your own redeeming.'

Toby didn't feel very well, and he wanted to go. He kept pulling at his mother's skirt, but she was just ignoring him, which wasn't like her. She was usually lovely. He must have done something wrong. Toby fiddled with a zip that was on the side of his Mummy's dress, but she batted his hand away. He felt like he wanted to cry but didn't know why. He was uncomfortable and felt a little bit frightened.

Toby looked around at everyone, quickly averting his gaze if they met his. There were some people that he knew and others he did not. Toby was the only child there, which made it even more boring. He wondered why daddy wasn't there. His Daddy hadn't been home for ages and Mummy looked like she was missing him. Maybe he was on holiday somewhere. But he usually took them with him. Daddy wouldn't go to the seaside without them, surely? Daddy was always kind, not like Mummy, who would shout at him sometimes. The man with the flappy scarf kept saying his Daddy's name, every now and then, but he wasn't even there. So why say it?

'Receive Mark Stanley Teversall into the arms of your mercy, into the blessed rest of everlasting peace, and into the glorious company of the saints of light.'

Unless it was a surprise party and he had not come, for some reason. It didn't look like a party, though. Everyone seemed sad. They kept saying Amen, without warning, which made him jump, but nobody was praying, they were just standing there.

Somebody threw some soil in the hole which looked like fun, so he got some off the ground, and he could feel pebbles in amongst it too. He had got some of it under his nails. Toby threw it overarm towards the hole, but some went on an old man's shoes on the opposite side, and the man scowled at him. Could he throw some more? Nobody else was. You only had one go apparently. He had tried to peek inside, but he couldn't see all of the way to the bottom. They had lowered a huge box thing in there. Maybe it was treasure, or something?

This was awful. It was worse than school. No wonder everyone was crying. Toby had cried earlier in the church, but he wasn't sure why, probably because everyone else seemed upset, he just got overwhelmed by it all.

Finally, everyone started to move, and Toby ran a few yards at full pelt along the grass and stopped. He didn't know why; it was just a burst of energy. He had been fed up just standing there for no reason. He ran back to his Mummy and held her hand. He pulled at her dress yet again.

'Will, Daddy be home when we get back?'

This seemed to upset her, but he was only asking.

'Not now, darling.'

Mummy's face looked funny. Her eyes were red, and she had got black marks around them, smeared above and below her eyelids. A bit like black paint, but they hadn't been painting or doing any craftwork or anything like they did at Play Group. Mummy's face was a bit floppy as if it didn't fit her and her bottom lip kept trembling. She screwed her eyes up now and then forcing out the merest trickle of a tear. She was either mad or upset about something, and he had never seen her like this before. She rubbed at Toby's hair. 'Go and play with this, sweetheart, and mummy will be with you in a minute.' Her voice trailed off into a high pitch. What was the matter with her voice? It didn't even sound like

Mummy. It was crackly and squeaky. Weird. She reached into her pocket and pulled out a matchbox toy car. 'Brilliant!'

Toby grabbed it and ran towards the bench near the church, and skipped for the final twenty yards. He sat on the wooden seat, and the heat stored from the sun burned the back of his legs. Toby was focussed on his toy car and making driving noises, but he noticed that some of the people in the distance, talking to Mummy, kept looking over and shaking their heads at him, as if he'd been naughty. He couldn't wait to get home, but at least he had something to play with for now.

It wasn't long before a green tennis ball rolled down the grass to where his feet didn't meet the floor. The ball nestled just under the seat of the bench. He jumped down and picked up the ball, looking around for its owner.

'Hey, little dude.' It was a man near the car park.

The boy didn't reply but gave a half-smile. He was shy.

'Y'all wanna play catch?' This person had a funny voice as well. He sounded strange, but he was friendly, and he had got a bike, which looked really cool, it was bright orange, but it was too big for Toby to have a go. Toby looked around and could see Mummy still talking to her party friends.

'Hurl it over, champ.'

Toby threw it, but it wasn't a very good effort, and the man had to run a few yards to retrieve it. It was a little like his attempt with the soil earlier. The man with the ball walked over and seemed to be glancing at Mummy as well.

'Don't I know you?' He said.

'No.' The boy muttered and fiddled with his car, spinning the wheels.

'Your place is on Montague Road, ain't it?'

'I don't know what you mean.'

'Where do you live?'

'I can't say because you're a stranger.'

'Good boy. Here's some candy.' He gave him a fruit salad, chew. 'Great job. Anyways, strangers are people who don't talk to each other, but we are talking, so how can we even be strangers?'

Toby was thinking. 'I suppose.'

'I guess you are too small to know where you live. It's all good. You probably can't remember.'

'I am not too small. I *can* remember it.'

'Can't.'

'Can.'

'Can't.'

'Can.'

'It's Montague Road like I said.' The man was smiling. He seemed nice.

'No, it's not.' Toby said, seemingly affronted.

'Is.'

'Isn't.'

'Is.'

'Isn't.'

'What is it then?'

'64 Watnall Road, Hucknall, Nottingham, NG18 2JB.'

'Wow, you're smart.'

'Told you.'

He heard his mother calling. 'Toby?' When he turned, she was beckoning him.

'I've got to go.' Toby said.

'See ya later, champ.' The man in the grey hoody watched the boy run back to his mother. He bounced the tennis ball on the grass which gave off a dull thud. The boy turned and waved. The man waved back.

He muttered again. 'See ya later, kid. And Mummy too.'

*

The door to DI Stark's office was closed, but Nobby could hear muffled voices as he stood outside in the corridor. He couldn't make out all the words, just some of them. Inside, Stark sat at his desk, and Det Superintendent Wagstaff sat in an armchair. DI Mole sat opposite with a pissed off look on his face. No-one was talking, because Stark was playing back the recording of the 999 call by Paul Masters.

'Emergency. Which service do you require?'

'What?'

'Fire, Police, Ambulance or Coastguard?'

'Ambulance. No. Police.'

'Hello, police emergency.'

'Quick, help, my wife and daughter have been killed. Please, can you get here, straight away? We need help.'

'Is there an intruder on the premises?'

'No, there's only me in the house.'

'A unit is travelling sir; there is one close by - stay on the line, please.'

'What have I done? I must be losing it. This is my fault.'

'Sorry, sir?'

'Please, hurry.'

'Are you certain both parties are deceased? Do you require an ambulance?'

'No. Yes, they've gone. I mean, I don't need an ambulance. I've lost them both.'

'Are you injured at all, sir?'

'No, I'm fine, but I do have blood all over me.'

'You have blood all over you?'

'It must have trickled out overnight.'

'Sir, how can that be?'

'I slept with my wife, and she must have been dead.'

'I'm sorry, sir, this is not making much sense. Stay on the line, and the unit will be with you shortly.'

Stark pressed the white peg-button on the tape machine, and it snapped to a stop. 'It is somewhat confused; I think you will agree.'

Mole shrugged. 'No, it's not, he has admitted it pretty much, he said it was his fault for a start.'

'Come on, Lee, that's not an admission.' Stark grimaced.

'He says, "What have I done" and then "It's all my fault," for Christ's sake.'

'So what?'

'What is it then?'

'What do you mean?'

'Come on. Mr Big Shot, if it isn't an admission, what is it? A denial?' Mole was agitated.

'Lee...'

Wagstaff interjected. 'Alright, let's not bicker. What are your thoughts, having had a look at it, David?' Wagstaff was twiddling his waxed moustache.

'I've only had a brief look, but I must say, I do have some concerns.' He glanced at Mole.

'What are they?' Wagstaff asked. 'Don't be coy, David. Lee might be able to answer them for you. This is the whole point of the meeting to share information and expertise. I don't think anyone is suggesting that Lee has just polled up and decided it was this Paul Masters fellow without considering every option. He is open to all suggestions, aren't you, Lee?'

'Erm. Yes, I suppose so, sir. It depends on what they are.'

Stark glanced at Mole, who was sneering at him with disdain.

'It looks to me like a third party has been at the house.' Stark said.

'Here we go. What makes you say that, Sherlock?' Mole was immediately on the defensive. He was laying back in the chair, his top button undone and his tie bedraggled and twisted.

'Well there is a bike track in the gravel, a flower has been trodden on…' Stark said.

'Ha! A fucking flower, God, help us.' Mole appealed to Wagstaff. 'Come on, sir; this is bloody ridiculous.'

'Just hear him out, Lee.' Wagstaff sounded tetchy; he was hoping for something a little more tangible, in truth.

Stark continued. 'There are some question marks around Masters being the offender, for example, why take the knife downstairs and wipe it? You accept the knife was wiped after the murder, I assume, Lee?'

'Obviously, you can still see a tiny bit of blood smeared down it. It has been wiped alright, by Masters.' Mole tapped his fingers on the wooden arm of the chair, and he began to fiddle about with his suit jacket, trying to locate the pocket for his cigarettes.

'What was it wiped with?' Stark asked.

'Eh?'

'What was it wiped with? There is no cloth remaining, no rag with bloodstains.'

'We aren't sure about that yet.' Mole sat up a little in the chair; his confidence was waning. Having found the packet, Mole tipped a cigarette out and lit it with a match. He threw it onto the ashtray on Starks desk, it missed and smouldered on the wood until it died down.

'Okay. That is strange.' Wagstaff said as he scribbled some notes on his pad.

Stark picked the match end up and put it into the ashtray. 'If it is Masters there must be a rag, a piece of clothing or something. It cannot have just disappeared, and it is not at the scene and not in the prisoner's property.'

'What about the prisoner's clothes?' Mole said as if he had discovered electricity.

'He was in his bloody undercrackers when he was arrested, wasn't he? And they were clean, only the inside of them had blood on it because he had put them over his bloodstained legs.'

'Could he have wiped it on the inside of his undies?' Mole asked.

'Really? You think he's wiped the razor-sharp knife with his bollocks?' Stark looked at him incredulously.

'That is odd, granted.' Wagstaff said, glancing at Mole.

Mole scoffed as he took a puff on his cigarette, 'Nah, there are a thousand explanations for that.'

'Like what?' Stark asked.

'I don't know; I can't just come up with it like that, can I?'

'You said there were thousands.'

'For fuck's sake, when you compare it to the evidence pointing to him doing it, against these...these suppositions, it still looks a bit lame don't you think?'

Wagstaff noded. 'He's got a point, David.'

'I haven't finished yet. What about the tennis ball?'

'What about it?' Mole asked.

'Somebody has brought that into the house. It's not Jemma's, and it certainly doesn't belong to the parents.'

'You don't know that.' Mole said.

'Do you?'

'No, but it must be theirs.'

'So, you are guessing. That needs following up. What about the biggest concern of all?'

'What's that?' Wagstaff enquired, his brow furrowed into a frown.

'Jemma, the daughter, has got a pubic hair stuck to her inner thigh, believed by semen, which is a hair that does not belong to the three of them. The pubic hair cannot exist if there is no third party.'

'It could be anybody's.' Mole said without really thinking, flicking ash on to the carpet of Stark's office.

'I know, that's the point I'm making. But it ain't the bloke who stands accused of raping her, so it needs to be eliminated. Can you use the bloody ashtray, Lee?' He handed him the glass bowl.

'That is quite alarming, don't you think, Lee? I mean, where has that pubic hair come from, if it isn't any of the Masters?' Wagstaff said.

Mole felt like it was slipping away from him, so he reached into his briefcase and pulled the interview notes out and threw them on to Stark's desk. 'Read the bit where he says he's fucking done it. It's something of a clue.'

Stark took hold of the notes. 'Four pages. Is that it?'

Mole shrugged as he stubbed the cigarette out and put some chewing gum into his mouth. 'He didn't say a lot.'

Stark shook his head as he read down them.

'What?' Mole said.

'Nothing, it is just the coincidence of it all.'

'What coincidence? There ain't no coincidence.'

'What is it, David?' Wagstaff enquired.

'It's all up and down, and vague until you get to the final paragraph, which is in a different vein to the previous conversation, by the way, and miraculously stops at the foot of the final page where the scribbled signature is.'

'There is nothing miraculous about that.' Mole protested.

'Let me read the final paragraph to you.' Stark said to Wagstaff.

'"*I would like to add for clarity that I am gilty...*" No u in guilty would you believe. "*of the murder of my wife Ella and daughter Jemma. I cut both of there throats.*" I won't keep commenting on the spelling and grammar, but it looks like Carl Davidson needs to go back to school. And by that, I mean primary.'

'Get on with it, David.' Wagstaff said.

'"*I have grown more and more turned on by my daughter now she's grown up and we were close and I wanted to fuck her.*" Really?'

'He said it.' Mole started to bite his nails at the same time as he was chewing gum which is a good trick if you can pull it off.

'No, he fucking didn't, Lee. He didn't say it, and you know he didn't. If I go and see him, he won't even know about this last paragraph. We didn't just fall off a Christmas Tree. It fucking stinks.'

Mole folded his arms in defiance. 'I don't know what you mean. It is what it is.'

'Yes, a bloody setup. You've written him up on the last paragraph to try to get it over the line.'

Mole stood up. 'Say that to my fucking face.'

Stark stood up. 'I just fucking have done.'

'Let's take it outside, if you're calling me bent, That ain't on.' He pushed Stark's chest, which had little effect and Stark pushed Mole in retaliation and he staggered backwards.

'Fuck you!' Mole shouted through spittle which had formed around his mouth.

Wagstaff stood up and got between the two men. 'Now, listen here. I want no more. You should be setting an example. Keep your damned voices down for a start. Half the station can hear you.'

Wagstaff opened the office door. Nobby stood there firmly to attention, staring at them all. His eyeballs flicked left and right as he stood there frozen.

'Yes? What do you want?' Wagstaff asked.

'Anyone want a cuppa?'

Wagstaff slammed the door. 'See. This is what happens. You come across to the lower ranks as complete bloody arseholes. Now both of you sit down, and I will tell you my thoughts.'

The two Detective Inspectors complied, as did Wagstaff who explained his view. 'Okay. First of all. I want no talk of anybody being "written up" unless and until there is any hard, and I mean *hard* proof of that, which given Masters' mental state, is highly unlikely.'

'That's why he shouldn't have been interviewed.' Stark said.

'Shut up, David. I'm telling you my thoughts, not asking for opinions.'

Mole grinned at Stark like the child he was.

Wagstaff sighed. 'Let me make it simple. There are notes with an admission on it, so he cannot be freed, and the judicial process needs to run its course.'

'Thank you, sir.' Mole said.

'Hang on, Lee, I've not finished. David does make some good points, and there are too many pieces of the jigsaw missing. I want these pieces found, and they need to be pieces that fit the space properly, not hammered in with a fist. I want it reviewing. I want the gaps filled, which David will do.'

'Why him? It's my case.' Mole protested.

'Because you don't review your own case, Lee, it is not how it works. He's already familiar with it, and it is on his patch. And also, because I bloody well say so.'

Mole sighed. 'It's bullshit, but go ahead, fill your boots, Stark. If you need to know anything, don't bother giving me a call.' Mole stood to leave.

'Don't worry, I won't.' Stark said, immediately annoyed with himself for yet again being drawn into Lee Mole's childish world. It happened every time.

Mole walked out, and Stark noticed Wagstaff with his head in hands. 'There is nothing like a happy ship is there?' Wagstaff muttered.

Stark was fatalistic. He shrugged. 'And this is nothing like a happy ship.'

5

'Anyone for tennis?'

Variously attributed.

Sandra Teversal was an attractive lady in her mid-thirties. She had shoulder-length black hair, trim waist and full figure and her hair complimented the black dress she had worn at her husband, Mark's funeral. Sandra did not deserve to be made a widow at such a tender age; nobody does. Naturally, Mark's death was a huge shock. He was only 39 years old, and he had just dropped dead at work; an embolism. Sandra now had to contemplate what to do with her life. Should she spend the rest of it alone? She had a five-year-old son, Toby, so who was going to want her? She had just to take a day at a time. That's what Aunty Dot said to her, who was still fussing around in the kitchen, washing pots.

'He's there again.'

'Who is, Aunty Dot?' Sandra asked. She was tired, and her mind was getting fuzzy. Her eyes sore through all the crying.

'That bloke I told you about in the grey hoody, he keeps cycling up and down and looking in.'

'We often have kids come up and down the drive, Aunty Dot. It's a long drive, and there are no cars. It is fun for them. I don't mind if it keeps them safe.'

'He doesn't look like a kid to me, soft bogger, what's up with the idiot?' Aunty Dot was never backwards at coming forwards.

'Aunty Dot, please, leave the pots, let me get some time to process the day if you don't mind. You have been so helpful, and I will remember your kindness forever, I really will. I am so grateful. I just need some space, that's all.'

'Just let me dry them for you.'

'No. It's fine honestly, you've done enough.' Sandra held her hands together as if in prayer.

'I still think I should stay with you for a couple of nights.' Dot put her hands on her hips, seemingly to emphasise the point.

'And sleep on the sofa. No, there is no need, Aunty Dot, but thank you anyway. It is so kind of you to offer. I'm really grateful, honestly.'

'Are you sure you'll be okay? What about this bloke on his bike? Don't forget there was that murder the other day.'

Sandra's shrugged out a laugh, which turned into a sigh. 'He has been arrested, Aunty…'

'Whose to say he was alone? Shall I call the police? He could be a murderer. I've seen him twice now. I'm telling you he keeps looking in.'

'No, there is no need to bother the police, and if he's the murderer tell him he can murder me tomorrow, I'm too tired tonight.'

'Oh, Sandra, you are terrible, saying things like that.'

'Well, I am.'

Sandra took Aunty Dot into the living room with her arm around her shoulder. She shouted. 'Toby!'

There was no sound of movement.

'Hasn't he been a brave little soldier, bless him.' Aunty Dot said as she tilted her head.

'He has, he's too young to understand what is going on, which is probably a good thing.'

'Have you still not said anything to him?'

'Not yet. I will do, all in good time when he is used to his Dad not being around, and it is less of a hit for him. Toby!' Sandra shouted again.

She heard the scampering of tiny feet and her son ran into the living room.

'Yes, Mummy?'

'Aunty Dot is going now. Give her a big kiss and a hug.' Dot picked him up.

'Goodness me, you are getting big. I won't be able to pick you up soon. Give Aunty Dot a big smudger.' She kissed him, and he backed away, rubbing his sleeves across his lips and shuddering. She put him down to the floor and Sandra opened the front door. The warmth of the summer afternoon surprised her.

'Thanks again, Dotty, you're a star.'

'You're the star, you've been amazing, everyone has said so.'

'Thank you. It has been exhausting, but we got through it somehow. I won't need much rocking tonight, that's for sure. I will be asleep as soon as my head hits the pillow.'

'It'll do you good.' The two hugged and held hands as they parted. 'Are you sure you'll be alright?'

Sandra began to walk with Dot towards her car. 'I've got to be, haven't I? For Toby's sake, if nothing else.'

Toby watched from the open front door. He glanced to his right and saw the man from earlier on, with the bike and the tennis ball. The man waved at Toby and smiled, and Toby waved back excitedly at his new friend.

*

Detective Inspector Lee Mole warmed his hands on his mug of coffee. At 42 years old, with 20 years police service, this was not the first time he had sat around a table trying to determine someone's fate. The DI had brought the meeting with CPS forward, now that it was all getting a bit slippery. The meeting with Stark and Wagstaff had thrown Mole off-kilter a little, and he regretted acting so impulsively with Paul Masters. But the die was cast. He was no mastermind, but he had to try to figure some way out of the approaching menace, not for the sake of a potentially innocent man, but his own damned skin. Mole was chewing gum again. He hated these meetings, the shiny boys with their law degrees and their 'devil's advocate' bullshit. Half of them wouldn't know a criminal if he was being throttled by one. They were all 'wankers' in Lee Mole's mind, but then again, so were most people. 'Wankers' and 'Tossers' was how he described pretty much everyone but himself. He lacked self-awareness and the knowledge that if at every meeting you attend you think everyone is a wanker, the reality is that the wanker is undoubtedly you.

Others at the meeting were the young, clean-cut, career-minded Rupert Mandrake for the Crown Prosecution Service and Detective Superintendent Fox, who was retiring on Friday. Mole had chosen to bring Fox, knowing that he couldn't give a damn, now that he was all but out of the force.

They had been going at this for an hour or more in the bland office. DI Mole was getting a little frustrated, with conversations about the 'what-if's,' rather than the facts of the case. Mole had said nothing about the testy exchange with Stark and Wagstaff, nor the ongoing review of the case. That could wait. Telling CPS would start the hares running. If they thought there could be a miss-trial, or worse discover it to be an unsafe conviction, there would be no way it would get off the ground as a trial. They would stack their hand in right now.

'It's him, isn't it?' Mole said, 'It has to be the husband; there is no other rational explanation.'

They were sitting in the sterile environment of The Crown Prosecution offices at King Edward Court. The conference room differed slightly from the main office because it had two pictures on the walls. They were pictures of several swipes of different coloured paints across the canvas; it must have taken the artist six weeks of summoning up the motivation and 30 seconds of doing the damned thing. The subsequent wait for some sucker to buy it must indeed have been longer?

'I suppose it begs the question; what the motive is?' Rupert mused. He kept preening himself, fiddling with his gelled hair. Mole had noticed Rupert was doodling the picture of a face on his pad, presumably his own.

'Insanity, drugs, who the hell knows? But the facts speak for themselves; it couldn't be anyone else, it's a locked house mystery with only one suspect. It is not rocket science. If we cannot prosecute this, it's a bloody sorry tale.' Mole was looking at Rupert as though it was madness even to question the case. Mole seemed sold on it. 'Don't you agree, Superintendent Fox?'

Detective Superintendent Fox was fiddling with a rubber band. He didn't seem overly interested. His head was in the Maldives, and his heart was not in this murder. 'Sorry? Yes, absolutely.'

Mole always had the urge to press home a conviction. He counted the reasons on his fingers as he spoke. 'Look at the evidence we have: Paul Masters is alone in a locked house where two people are murdered. There is no forced entry. He says it is his fault, both on the phone when he rings 999, *and* to the officers at the scene. Masters admits to killing them in the damned interview. He is mentally unstable, and the police surgeon says he has had some sort of a breakdown.'

'I know, but wouldn't you if you had found your family butchered?' Rupert offered.

'That depends whether he had the break down before or after the murders. We don't know, do we, now?'

Rupert twiddled with his diamond-set cuff-link. 'Exactly we don't know…'

'And the knife used to kill them, by his admission is *his* knife, and he has wiped it clean, for Christ's sake!'

'I suppose you have a point.'

Mole shrugged out a laugh. 'Of course, I have a point. Come on.'

Rupert suddenly perked up; his mind had been racing when it suddenly landed on something of note. He pointed at DI Mole. 'Aha, but the cloth or clothing, I asked you about, or whatever was used to wipe it, was never found, now was it? Don't you think that is very odd? Where has that disappeared to, I wonder? That's impossible, isn't it? It can't just *not* be there. We can't just ignore it.'

'I do think it's odd, it is an imponderable, Rupert, but is it enough of a reasonable doubt for the jury that Masters hasn't done it? That is for the defence to pursue should they so wish. Anyway, I haven't finished yet. The evidence is overwhelming, as well as all of the evidence I've outlined, he is covered in his wife's blood. The same blood, his wife's, is then discovered on the inside of his dead daughter's thigh. Then there is the pubic hair.'

'No, we mustn't forget the pubic hair.' Rupert said with a smirk. He liked a good old verbal scrap.

Mole ignored the sarcasm. 'A pubic hair belonging to the accused is found on the carpet in front of the dead girl's vagina.'

Rupert played devil's advocate once again, but he was losing heart. 'Tricky, granted. But I've also read through the SOCO report and something you have neglected to mention; is that there is another pubic hair, yet to be identified, which was found on Jemma's body. Another miracle?'

Mole shook his head. 'Tricky? Christ. Tricky ain't the word. Can we, in all honestly and in all good conscience, *not* prosecute this man for the murders? Would it seem appropriate to let him walk for a case as serious as this, or do we put it to a jury? Be honest, Rupert.'

Rupert glanced at Superintendent Fox, who had moved on to fiddling with a paper clip, looking pretty disinterested. He merely shrugged and then shook his head.

Rupert sighed. 'I suppose when you put it like that it does look like a bit of a mountain for the defence. Let's take a vote. Do we withdraw the charges, or do we prosecute?'

The three men spoke in unison. 'Prosecute.'

*

Nobby and Steph sat in the lounge of the Little John pub in Ravenshead. It was a rustic setting, a typical country hostelry, with wooden tables, fireplace, brasses and obscure country pictures framing the walls. There were only a handful of other customers pitted around the room all talking in hushed tones. Steph hadn't said much; they just held hands across the table for most of the time. Occasionally Nobby would just smile at her, but she was lost in her thoughts and her grief.

Nobby could smell the food being cooked, and it was making him salivate. 'Do you want anything to eat, Steph?'

'No, I'm fine, thanks.'

'Okay, let me know if you do.'

'You have something if you want.'

'No, I'm fine. I'm not going to sit here tucking into pie and chips while you're breaking your heart, now am I?'

'I'm surprised. It's never bothered you before.' She managed a smile.

'I have had the steak and ale pie here before, and it is the dog's bollocks.'

'Aren't they a bit chewy?' She smiled again and then burst into tears. It drew attention from the other customers. She wiped her eyes with a handkerchief, which had been in her handbag for two years unused, until now. It smelt new and felt scratchy on her face.

'Sorry.' Steph said, looking around at the punters through tear-filled eyes.

'No need to apologise, don't be daft.' Nobby turned to look at those staring over, and they all averted their eyes.

'I'm embarrassing you.' She sniffed.

'Steph, seriously? Do you think I am bothered about anyone on the damned planet? Other than you?'

Tears continued to stream down her face, reddening her cheeks. She couldn't help it, they just came. Steph could feel the calloused hands of Nobby as she stroked at them.

'I don't know what to say, Steph. I'm just gutted for you.' Nobby said awkwardly. The smell of the food cooking was making his stomach grumble.

'It's fine. It had to happen one day. He was old, but you never think it's going to happen to your own.'

'I know.'

'But, of course, it does, and then it hits you like a bloody ten-ton truck.'

'He was one of the good guys, Steph. He wouldn't hurt a soul.' Nobby tried a sympathetic smile. Steph had never seen that expression on his face before; it seemed odd.

'He wouldn't, you're right, he wouldn't hurt a fly. It's the finality of it, Nobby. All the things unsaid, all of that stuff.'

'Hey, don't start that, Steph, you were a terrific daughter to him. He knew how much you loved him, and he loved you to bits. Everyone could see that. Come on, love.'

'I know, but aren't daughters supposed to be sugar and spice and all things nice?'

'You are.'

'Really? That armed robber didn't think so when I kicked him in the goolies last week.'

Nobby laughed. 'No, I don't suppose he did. But your Dad was so proud of you being a detective because he knew you were doing good and you had principles. Plus he knew you loved the damned job. He was proud as punch.'

'I know. My head's all over the place at the moment. You get funny ideas pop up.'

'No change there then.' Nobby smiled.

'Get stuffed.'

Another tear trickled down her face, and she quickly wiped it away. 'This is going to play havoc with my mascara. Just look at me; this is silly.'

'Of course, it's not silly; it's silly to say it's silly.'

She smacked his hand. 'Oh, Nobby, you daft bugger.'

He smiled. 'You're coming back with me tonight, yes? Stay at mine for a while until you feel a little bit better.'

'No, I want to be at mine, Nobby, if you don't mind. Thanks anyway, but I just want a little bit of space. I'll be back at work tomorrow.'

'Oh, no, you won't.'

'I will.'

'You won't.'

'Nobby, I am not moping around the house on my own, all bloody day. That will just make me worse.'

'You said you needed time alone.'

'No, I didn't, well, I did, but I didn't mean twenty-four-seven.'

Nobby seemed a little exasperated and rested his chin on his palm, his elbow on the table.

'Steph, you shouldn't be alone. Anyway, what about all the funeral arrangements? There's a lot to sort out. You are going to need time off to sort all of that out. And you need someone to bounce ideas off, someone to open up to; you know it makes sense.'

'All the arrangements are in hand, Nobby, typical Dad, everything is signed up and paid for, even down to the music he wants.'

'What's he gone for, "The Ace of Spades" by Motorhead?'

She smacked his hand again. 'No, he went for "Ballroom Blitz" by Sweet.'

'You're joking.'

Steph smiled. 'What do you think?'

'Bloody hell, Steph. I thought you were serious.'

'Two can play at that game, Sergeant Clarke.'

'Is there anything I can help with? Just say the word.'

'No, I'm fine. Don't fuss, Nobby, just let me get on with it.' She pulled her hand away and leaned back into the chair; it was one of those with a moveable cushion, tied onto the back, on a wooden spoked chair and it kept threatening to fall off. She hutched her backside up and slid it back underneath.

Nobby was frowning. 'I'm not happy with you coming back to work Steph. You're entitled to a week off, at least.'

'We'll see. Maybe I will take some time off after the funeral. It hasn't really sunk in, yet. I don't want the lads tip-toeing around me either, tell them to just treat me as normal.'

'But, you're not normal.'

'Haha, very funny, you know what I mean.'

'I will tell them, don't worry about that. If you insist on coming back.'

'I do. The last thing I want is to bring the whole place down.'

'I'll be guided by you, Steph, but if you need to go home at any time, or change your mind, just say the word, and I will sort it.'

'Thanks, Nobby.'

'Another drink?'

'G&T please, and make it a double.'

*

The killer had developed a fascination with attending funerals. It was a recent thing. A natural progression, probably emanating from when he was younger and scouring the newspapers for obituaries. The depths of the communal sadness and tragedy made him want to laugh out loud, and sometimes he couldn't contain himself. He had felt like that when he was around death for as long as he could remember. Maybe the urge to laugh started as a coping strategy, but bearing in mind the depths of his depravity, it seemed more likely he was just a sick bastard.

The emotions at funerals, or cremations, seemed to seep into him and overwhelm him. He thought it was fucking hilarious. He liked death.

Probably because he didn't value life; his own or anybody else's. There were a few things he liked about death; one was the finality of it, the irrevocability that was so powerful, nothing could reverse it, nothing in the universe.

The second thing was that you could poke, pull, cut, punch, or do anything you want to a dead body, and it was still. It looked like a human, but it wasn't, he loved that lie. He once popped an eye out for giggles, but that was back in the States. He didn't fuck about with bodies too much after he killed them, nowadays.

Another thing about death, which was terrific, was how much people would struggle to avoid it. It is the holy grail of possessions. You simply cannot drop the ball where death is concerned. It often takes a whole lot of effort to wrest it from their grasp, and then sometimes, right near the end, they often give it to you. It is a gift. You feel them stop the struggle. It is an acquiescence; it is quite beautiful. It is the ultimate submission.

He was quite aware that he was perverse in these views, a psychopath, but if he were bipolar, or suffered from anxiety, people would be falling over themselves to help him or at least to sympathise and understand. Not with his condition though, not with psycho's, they can't be helped, just avoided. The consequences of his illness outweighed any potential for sympathy or help. The only good criminal psychopath is a dead one.

Unsurprisingly he felt it was hypocritical of people to lack any compassion for his plight. It was so hurtful that just because he was born with a penchant for ripping people apart with a butcher's knife, that no-one could love him and help him.

He first started using death as a theme to his criminality back in the States. His dad had left when he was born, never to be seen again, and his mother well, she did try to support him, even if it was a bit half-hearted. She was an addict, and so children come down the priority list. His Mama was missing a lot, but she was thoughtful enough to leave whatever food scraps she had on the table for him, as soon as he was old enough to clamber on the bench and grab it. She would replenish the stocks later that day by shoplifting on her way home. If she got arrested, he couldn't eat, so he learned to build up a stash for emergencies.

He didn't have toys; they were for 'queers' according to Mama. He did find an old tennis ball at the back of the house which he used to play with, just to ease the boredom. It was his secret toy. She never found it.

It wasn't like they didn't do stuff together, he and Mama. They did things as a family periodically; it was Mama who helped him kill his first squirrel. She ate the thigh meat raw. She was off her tits on crack at the time, but he didn't know that. He supposed he got his 'specialness' from her. Anyway, she killed herself by jumping out a window onto some railings. He was there, and he only helped her a bit. Surely any son would have? He was giving her what she wanted. It was a mistake because he realised that he then had to survive on his own and at fourteen that was a difficult prospect. He left before the cops arrived, kissing his dead mother on the cheek as she hung lifeless on the railings that pierced her abdomen. No-one was around. It was 3.30 in the goddamn morning.

He had always been reasonably intelligent though, at least to some extent, street smart you would call it, and he had thought carefully about finding a way to burgle houses knowing that he would not be disturbed by the occupants. He was too small to fight his way out of a paper bag. Then it came to him when they buried Mama. Funerals. He would check the newspaper in the café every day and see where the local funerals were, and burgle the house. It was just added juice that they would come back and see the mess he had made at their time of most profound sorrow. He could extend the grief even beyond that of mourning a dead relative. That was special. Sometimes he would wait near to the house and listen for the scream of discovery. It always came if it was a woman. Then he thought about that scream and how he had made it happen, and he could do that whenever he wanted. He was sixteen by now and still hadn't had sex, so why not combine his desires? The love of the scream, the want of sex, the control and the fascination with death. He needed to change his ways of working on getting to that haven.

Sticking with the funeral theme, he would seek out male obituaries, and if he liked the look of the widow, and sometimes if he didn't, he would visit them late at night. They were so frightened of him, even though he was only ten stone wet through at that time, just a young kid. It was the context they were frightened of, not him as such, but it empowered him in any case. Then he would fuck them. That was back in the day, before the killing started, and all that craziness. Happier times, really. Then the killing began. His psychopathic mania came in ever more violent stages, year upon year, and now he was one of the most wanted men on the planet.

He hadn't been in England long but, man, he was so close to getting caught back in the States, he had to jump ship quickly.

He'd had a long run in his home country, and by moving county lines, and then travelling across different States it was easy to avoid capture with the way the police worked back home. The cops were so inward-looking they thought shit didn't happen outside the county line, and if it did, what had it to do with them? A country that holds a 'world series' of baseball, consisting of only American teams, shows how limited their horizons are. It is such a huge country that the vast majority of people never leave its shores. It is inward-looking at the county level, state level and even nationally. So this killer, and many like him were able to evade justice merely by putting distance between him and his last offence. That was before the Feds got involved, and he felt their breath on his neck. He needed a new identity and to get the hell as far away from home as was possible.

This was how he found himself outside of 64 Watnall Road, Hucknall, Nottingham, with a knife in his hand, at midnight. The hot summer and the disorientation of the recently bereaved victims had meant that it had been too easy, so far. Windows left open made it simple.

He was inside the house in seconds and went straight to the fridge. He was so thirsty; he had been hanging around for hours waiting for Aunty fucking Dot to piss off. He must have smoked ten cigarettes through boredom, careful to put the extinguished butts in his pocket. He would come and go, back and forth to the bungalow, waiting for the stillness. He had entertained himself by playing with his tennis ball and listening to some of the conversations through the open kitchen window; even the one where Sandra had said, 'he can murder me tomorrow, I'm too tired tonight.'

That was classy. Funny. It made him smile, and he gave her the courtesy of waiting until midnight to oblige. It just gave it a nice little story for the papers. He could imagine a crying Aunty Dot telling the press what she had said, and it would give the story legs. He couldn't wait to read all about it.

He was pleased to see two things in the kitchen; one being that there was some soda to drink, and the second was that she had an expensive block of kitchen knives readily in view. He folded his bowie knife up and put it in his pocket. He preferred to use the householder's knife if they were well made. You had to be so careful not to break it if you hit a rib, for example. That's why he always had a back up in his pocket.

As with many psychopaths, his confidence often outweighed the reality of the situation, and this was a potential downfall. He felt invincible, but of course, he wasn't. Formidable, yes. Invincible, no.

He padded through the living room and halted when he heard a noise in the bedroom to his right. The kid was talking in his sleep. That was freaky. He smiled.

It never occurred to him that a man holding a carving knife and a tennis ball tip-toeing through a living room at midnight might be a bit more 'freaky' to a casual observer. He had a look at some of the paintings and photographs on the walls and tables. He didn't want to rush. He liked to savour the moment. He sat in the armchair for a couple of minutes just looking around, acclimatising to the room and the darkness. He pulled his gloves tight and went over the preliminaries in his mind. The first three seconds were so important. He got up and walked over to the bedroom door. It was ajar, and he slowly pushed it open. He watched. Her room was darker inside, and it silhouetted him in the doorframe. There was no rush. He watched for a minute or so. He could feel the rage brewing, simmering up to boil; once past the point of no return, there would be no stopping him.

In the stale heat of the summer night, Sandra had pushed the sheet down, and her nightdress had rolled up to show a pretty hairy, if not unkempt bush. Nice legs. He was starting to get excited, and his breathing increased. He could smell her sweat and began to walk over, exceptionally slowly.

He now stood at the side of her and observed her face; her eyelids were flickering with dreams. He gently moved a length of hair away from her face. He was ready.

The killer took a deep breath and made his move. He held the knife just under her nose; he did this so she could both see and feel the knife. Keeping it to the throat was too risky; they can't always fathom what is happening; they don't realise it's a knife. Her eyes flashed open wide, and she tried to sit up, but he held her down and reinforced it with a growled 'Don't fucking move.'

As her mouth opened to scream, he forced the tennis ball in, causing her to choke and cough. Most of the ball was inside the mouth, and some still visible. Her lips were pulled back over her teeth, and her nostrils flared as she tried to draw in air. The bastard had squeezed it to get it in the mouth cavity, and when released, it forced her jaw outwards. It was uncomfortable and disorientating, precisely what he wanted to achieve.

'Listen to me.' She was still trying to thrash about. He would have to give her a pacifier. He punctured her cheek with the knife and had to hold the tennis ball, still inside her mouth, to withdraw the blade.

'Listen to me, Ma'am.' He repeated calmly.

She nodded.

'If you are going to survive this you have to do as I say, understand?' Of course, she was already as good as dead.

She recognised the accent to be American. 'I'm happy to kill you and Toby, but he can live if you do exactly as I say. I kinda like the kid. Do I make myself clear, ma'am?'

Her eyes were wide, and saliva was coming out the side of her improvised gag and merging with the blood from the pacifying cut. She nodded. Her breathing rate was through the roof, and her heart pounded in her chest cavity. It felt like her jaw would dislocate with the pressure of that fucking tennis ball.

'I'm going to wait a minute while y'all just calm down.' He spoke calmly, his voice was not raised, but it was assured and menacing. He whispered his instructions.

Sandra closed her eyes and tears joined the saliva and blood, stinging her wound.

The man dropped his tracksuit bottoms and exposed his semi-erect penis, which he massaged. She opened her eyes and turned her head away. He grabbed her hair.

'Open your eyes, bitch.'

She complied.

'Slowly now, get on all fours. You know how this works.'

Sandra couldn't move at first. She physically couldn't control her limbs; her mind was objecting.

The killer placed the knife back in the cheek wound and ripped back towards the ear, and she made a subdued scream with pain. A fragment of torn flesh from her cheek landed on the pillow. It jolted her enough for her to do as he said, and she slowly got on her hands and knees on the mattress, with her backside facing him. She stretched her arm back between her legs and put her hand over her privates, as she felt so embarrassed. She felt so ashamed.

'Back up closer to me. Move your fucking hand!' He knocked her arm away. She was whimpering.

Sandra inched her way backwards, and he threw the nightdress further up her back.

'That is one hairy pussy.'

She jerked as he entered her, and her head fell to the mattress as he hammered away aggressively. The sick bastard pulled at her hair, and she gave a muffled scream. He groaned as he ejaculated into her and she fell forwards on to the bed, with his weight pressing on her back. There was some jerking as he emptied himself into her. She was crying.

He was gasping for air, and his heart was beating fast. They lay there entwined for a couple of minutes. Neither said a word. There was silence other than Sandra's muffled sobs.

As they lay quietly in hiatus, all sorts of plans began racing through Sandra's head, but the truth was she was far too scared to do anything but submit. He pulled his penis out and wiped it against her buttocks before pulling his pants and tracksuit bottoms up. She was still lying face down. Mucus had come down her nose as she had struggled to breathe because the tennis ball constricted hardly any air entering and leaving her mouth. She wiped her nose on the sheet by moving her head from side to side. It was as though her hands were tied, but they weren't. The power of the threat were her chains, and the thought of little Toby being killed, destroyed any cogent thoughts of making a move to escape.

Suddenly there was a noise at the door. 'Mummy?'

Sandra made a noise of desperation.

'Why, hi little fella, remember me? We played ball.'

'Where's Mummy?'

The man put his finger to his lips. 'Ssh. She's sleeping. I'm mummy's friend. Come on back to bed; there's a good kid.'

The killer walked out of the bedroom with Toby in front. The pervert put the knife down the back of his tracksuit bottoms, and he turned when he reached the door. He spoke quietly.

'You put one foot on the floor, and I'm gonna slit his throat.'

With that, he was gone. Sandra shuffled to the edge of the bed, listening. Could she get to the kitchen and get a knife? Could she ring for help? The phone was in the living room, and he would hear the first number she dialled. Could she scream? None of these seemed to fill her with confidence, and he could be back in a second, he was strong. Very strong. Do as you are told, she thought. He's had his way; maybe he will just go. If anything happened to Toby because she had tried something, she would never forgive herself.

She could hear the man talking. What the hell? He was reading Toby a story. Maybe he would leave when he had finished if she stayed quiet. Should she take the damned ball out of her mouth? She took hold of it and loosened it a little to make it more comfortable. Was there a weapon she could hide somewhere? As a last resort, perhaps?

The talking had stopped. There was silence. It sounded like Toby had gone back to sleep. The man came walking back. He stopped in the door frame.

'He's a good kid.'

She nodded.

'I love the hairy bush, Sandra.'

'Listen, I hate to leave the kid without a mother, but, I never leave witnesses. It's company policy I'm afraid.' He sniggered. 'He's too young, so...'

Sandra shook her head and tried to say 'no', but the ball stopped the plea. It would have been futile anyway.

He moved towards her as she backed away, but he was too quick, and he grabbed her hair, jarring her head backwards, exposing the neck. Her eyes were wide and fearful; pleading. She was shaking her head. Her hands went to his arm, to try to stop him, but they made no impact. He rammed the knife into her throat and began cutting along her gullet. She screamed through the tennis ball, but he kept sawing. He waited a moment to listen to her gurgle as the blood went down her airway. He paused, sensing the jugular, and with one last rip, it sprayed. He let go, and she fell off the bed, on to the floor.

He watched as she tried to block the blood with her hands momentarily. He laughed because she was trying so hard, and there was no point. None at all. He leaned over her as her movements slowed; through her misting vision, she saw him peering over her. He was waiting, waiting for that special moment. Then her eyeballs glazed over, fixed, unseeing. Her face relaxed from pain. There it was. She'd gone.

6

'Of all the things my hands have held, the best, by far, is you.'

Unknown.

Toby had awoken at his usual time, just before 6.30 am. He couldn't hear his Mummy in the kitchen, so he decided to play in his room for a while. It had taken almost his whole five years for his Mummy to get him to do this. It was bliss now that he finally did. The house was still.

Little Toby loved his matchbox cars, and he had a plastic mat which had roads printed on it. He had picked up different figures that he would place around the track and also a couple of little trees from a lego set he had. Toby noticed the book on the floor which the nice man had read to him in the night. He smiled warmly at the memory. The man seemed nice. Maybe he is still here? The man said he would leave his tennis ball for Toby to find in the morning. Toby liked him. He couldn't see the ball anywhere in his room, however.

After twenty minutes, or so, he was getting hungry, and he wanted his orange juice as he was thirsty too. He stepped out into the living room and pitter-pattered across the wooden floor towards the kitchen. His pyjama bottoms were getting too short for him; they were above his ankles. He grew at such a rate, Sandra couldn't keep up with him. He got to the kitchen—still, no Mummy anywhere to be seen.

Toby then went running over to her bedroom and burst in the door and halted abruptly. Mummy was asleep on the floor. Something wasn't right. Toby was transfixed and put his finger in his mouth, nibbling at his fingernail. She looked funny. It didn't look like her, but it was her. He slowly moved closer and saw all the red stuff around her neck. She can't be asleep because her eyes are open.

'Mummy?'

He jumped on her stomach. 'Mummy, wake up, lazybones.' He began to giggle and tickle her tummy. 'Mummy did a trumper.' He said excitedly.

There was no reaction. She felt stiff. Why wouldn't she wake up?

Toby looked at his mother and noticed the tennis ball in her mouth. He had seen it straight away, but it hadn't registered. Toby's mind had edited it out to protect his sensibilities; he didn't like it. He felt scared. Toby stood and moved slowly back towards the door frame, turning slowly to glance back. 'Mummy?' Still nothing. He could smell something strange. It wasn't very nice. He decided to go back into the living room and wait for a bit. He had learned how to put the television on, and he flicked through some channels to find a cartoon. Mummy would come in when she felt better, probably. Might Daddy be home today? Daddy would be able to wake Mummy up. There was no point trying to get orange juice, he could just about reach the fridge door but didn't have the strength to pull it open, so he would have to wait for now.

After so long, he returned to Mummy's bedroom and peeked through from behind the door somewhat tentatively. It felt like something was wrong. She was still in the same position. This time he decided to close the door behind him as he went back to the living room; there was such a horrible smell. What was it? He couldn't understand that it was his mother's rotting carcass.

Toby decided to try to get some juice. Maybe if he climbed onto the work-top, he could reach around and get the fridge door open? He tiptoed into the kitchen and stood, looking at the giant fridge-freezer. It was like the cliff face of a mountain to young Toby.

Without warning, there was a loud banging on the kitchen door behind him. It made him jump. A man's voice gave a questioning greeting. 'Hello?'

Toby stood looking at the outline of the big man in the frosted glass of the door. He thought he had seen him before, but he was rooted to the spot in fear. Toby felt like he wanted to cry. He gulped air, and his bottom lip started to curl and tremble.

A face appeared in the window. It was a man with unkempt greying hair and a weathered, tanned face. 'Here, your window is open. Oh, hello, little fellow, is Mummy or Daddy in?'

The boy didn't reply but started to suck his thumb and twist his hair. Sandra had been trying for weeks to ween him off this habit. The children at nursery were teasing him about it.

'It's alright, little one. I'm the milkman. The man who brings the milk.' He raised a bottle so the boy could see it. 'Is Mummy there?' The man peered beyond Toby into the living room but could see no movement.

'Mummy's asleep.' Toby mumbled.

'Is she now? I need to give her this, it's payday today, little one. She's three weeks behind.' He realised none of this would make sense to the child. 'Will you go and get Mummy for me? There's a good lad.'

The boy turned and ran into the living room but stopped dead after only a few steps. He began to cry. 'I don't want to.'

'Alright, alright. No need to cry.'

'I can't wake her up.'

'Alright, don't get upset, little one. Let me leave this bit of paper on the sink for her.' He reached through the window and put it on the sink drainer.

'Make sure she sees it, won't you? Bye then.'

The boy was still sniffling as the man headed back towards his electric float. Toby didn't move; he just kept staring at the window. He suddenly felt very alone, and his tummy was hurting. The boy could hear the clink of bottles as the milkman put the empties on to the wagon. Then there was quiet again until he heard footsteps approaching once more. Toby hid behind the side of the fridge and peeped around as the milkman's face reappeared in the window.

'Hey, there little fellow. You know when you said you couldn't wake up Mummy. Is she okay?'

'She looks funny.' Toby sniffed.

'Mmm.' The milkman rubbed at his chin. He had a concerned look on his face. 'Here, what's that awful pong?'

Toby shrugged.

Then it dawned on him. He had been a milkman long enough and delivered to enough older people over the years to recognise that smell. He sighed and shook his head. 'Do you want me to check on her for you?' Eric had been delivering this round for over twelve years, and everyone knew him, and he knew pretty much everyone in return, even if it was just to say "good morning." He knew Sandra quite well, she was a talker, and she was always up and about at this time of the morning. She would want him to help if he thought something was wrong, surely?

Toby didn't say anything but nodded as he sucked his thumb.

'I'm going to get the bloody sack for this,' Eric muttered, as he pulled himself up into the window frame. He wasn't as nimble as he used to be and after much puffing and panting, he somewhat clumsily pushed himself forward on to the draining board, catching his trouser pocket on the metal spigot of the window frame. He fiddled around and cussed until he was free enough to inch through. Eventually, Eric managed to swivel around and found himself sitting on the metal drainer next to the sink. 'I'm getting too old for this.'

He slid his feet down to the lino floor. The smell was even worse inside the house; he winced and covered his nose. 'Show me Mummy's bedroom; there's a good lad.' Toby pointed at the door but didn't follow the milkman, he merely watched, as the man approached it somewhat tentatively. He knocked on the bedroom door. 'Hello? Everything alright?'

There was no response. Eric turned around and saw the look of concern on the young boys face; it matched his own. Eric pressed down the handle of the door and slowly opened it. He allowed a second or two, for his eyes to take in just what he was seeing.

'Oh, my Jesus Christ!'

'Is Mummy awake?' Toby asked.

Eric quickly closed the door. He turned and blew out a lung full of breath. 'Where's your phone?'

Again Toby pointed to the phone on the window sill, next to the armchair. The milkman walked over leadenly and sat on the chair, putting his head in his hands. 'Oh, my lord.'

The boy started to head for his mother's bedroom again.

'Oi, young un, come here a minute.' Eric was gasping, short of breath, as he shouted over. Toby headed towards the man and stopped a few feet short. The boy was still wary. Eric's mind was racing in tandem with his heart.

'Why don't you, erm, go and get me your favourite Teddy bear, I want to see it.'

'Okay.' Toby ran over to his bedroom.

Eric put the phone to his ear and dialled the three numbers as quickly as he could. The woman answered wearily. 'Emergency, which service do you require?'

'Police, please. There's been a...' He could scarcely bring himself to say it. '...there's been a...murder.'

*

It is inevitable for all of us that despite our endeavours in life to make an impact and even leave a legacy of sorts, the outcome is that we merely become a foul stench in someone's memory.

Detective Inspector David Stark and Detective Sergeant Alan 'Nobby' Clarke stood at the side of Sandra Teversall in her bedroom. It was still fairly dark in there. Nothing would be touched. The investigating officer needed a one-way route in to see what they were dealing with first, and then get out of the way for the forensics to start their all-important work using the same route in and out. The detectives wore no forensic gear as was the protocol of the day. They had briefly checked the other rooms and saw no sign of a disturbance in them. Then they got to this horror scene.

A uniformed policewoman had taken little Toby, along with his favourite teddy bear, over to social services, as soon as they arrived on the scene.

Steve Aston and Cynthia Walker were speaking to Eric, the milkman, outside, away from the smell. A uniformed cop was outside the door, logging everyone's movements, and other officers were attaching blue tape around the hedges of the curtilage of the property. It was futile as there was no-one around; it was all part of the circus, however. The police were not short of protocol, but sometimes this overrode common sense.

Stark spoke. His voice sounded louder than he intended, as they took in the grim scene. 'There's your answer, Nobby.'

'Yep. Mole is going to be pissed off.' Nobby shook his head. He was holding a briefcase, which he wished he'd left outside the bungalow as it suddenly felt cumbersome.

'He sure is, but I wish we'd been wrong. This poor soul wouldn't have suffered like this.'

'It was never going to be Paul Masters.' Nobby was tucking his shirt in, and as he pushed it in his trousers, as he drew his hand out, the shirt came with it. Only he could make something so simple seem difficult.

'Poor kid, finding his mother like that. It's going to destroy him.' Stark winced at the thought.

'He'll be fine.' Nobby said, not believing it. 'The tennis ball thing is something I've not come across before have you, boss?'

'No, I've seen masking tape, and socks and knickers rammed in mouths but not a tennis ball, that's a first. He's either a first-timer or he's new to the area.'

'I've not heard about it anywhere in the country though, have you?' Nobby scratched at his head.

'No, it's special, that is for certain. I'll get Jim to research it.' Stark looked around the room and then leaned in close to Sandra's face. 'Looks like he's given her a softener, maybe?'

'The cheek wound, you mean? Yes, I can't believe he's chosen a house with a kid in it, though, can you?' Nobby leaned in also, to get a closer look. 'Why take on that added complication?'

'Unless he didn't know.' Stark observed. 'It's all taken place in this one room, by the looks of it.'

'Where is the point of entry, do we know, boss?' Nobby asked.

'According to the radio dispatcher, the milkman said the kitchen window was open, that's how he got in. He had to climb through it to check what was going on.'

'I bet she's left it open because of the heat. Milko will have rubbed all the forensics off as he's clambered through, I bet. You don't think it could be him then?'

'Who, the milkman? Nah. No chance.' The two moved over towards the bed. 'There's is a little bit of blood on the pillow, Nobby.'

'Softener?'

'Yes, probably.'

'There's spunk on the sheet here by the looks of it.'

'I think the word you are looking for is semen, Nobby.' The DS shrugged. Stark continued, 'Let's see, it looks like, she's asleep, and he gives her the softener, rapes her on the bed and then finishes her off on the floor. No hang on, there is quite a bit of blood on the end of the quilt, look. He's slit her throat on the edge of the bed, and she's fallen to the floor.'

'Does it matter?'

'Yes, because when we interview the bastard, and he coughs it, he needs to explain what happened so we know it's a proper cough and not a Paul Masters style admission.'

'Fair enough.' Nobby said.

'Come on let's go and get a smoke. It bloody stinks in here. Let SOCO do their job.'

Stark waved to his two DC's talking to the milkman near his vehicle as they stepped outside. He squinted in the bright sunlight.

DC Steve Aston walked over to his Detective Inspector. 'Morning, sir.'

'Morning, Steve. What's the news?'

'Not a lot. He's been on the round twelve years, saw the kid upset and thought he'd better get involved. That's it really.'

'No strangers knocking around, I assume.'

'No, I'm afraid not, sir.'

'We will need a formal statement off him, for continuity, describing the scene he saw, the conversation he had with the kid, erm, also, any background, any visitors and all of that. Anything unusual recently when he's delivered to the house, you know the routine, Steve.'

'Yep, no problem, sir. We will take him back to the nick in a minute; we're just getting the first account. He's wittering about finishing his round.'

Nobby chimed in. 'Fuck that; he goes with you.'

'I've already told him that, Sarge.'

'When you get him back to the nick, you need to tell him we need his clothes as well.' Stark said.

'How come, sir?'

'He's climbed through the window so there may be a transference of fibres from the killer. Come on, Steve.'

'Oh, yes.'

'Oh, yes, indeed. Keep me posted if anything is startling, will you? In fact, no, tell Nobby instead.'

'Will do, sir.' Steve turned and headed back towards Eric and Cynthia. Stark shouted after him. 'Steve?'

'Yes?'

'Shoes as well.'

Steve gave him a thumbs up.

Nobby sat at the patio table, and Stark joined him. They both lit up a cigarette and cigar, respectively.

'Do you think it will be a problem if I put the kettle on, boss, I've got a mouth like the bottom of a budgies birdcage?'

'Best not, Nobby.' Stark put his sunglasses on and sucked at his small cigar. 'It's a bit out the way, isn't it?'

'Yes, he won't have come this far down the garden.' Nobby put his sunglasses on also not to be outdone.

'I didn't mean that.' Stark said.

'What, the bungalow, you mean?'

'Yes. The drive must be 200 yards long. I wonder if it used to be a farmhouse or something? It is pretty secluded. I doubt there will be any witnesses. No house-to-house needs doing, that is for certain. Not here, anyway.'

'There is a footpath that runs over the back to Misk Hill Farm.' Nobby offered.

'Who's talking to the kid? What's his name, Toby?' Stark asked.

'Yes, Toby. Steph says she will do it, and she's the best for that type of job. She's got the experience.'

'Steph? What is she doing at work? Her Dad's just popped his clogs, hasn't he?'

'Don't have a go at me, boss. Steph insisted; you know what she's like, she lives for the job. I told her to take time off, but she wouldn't have it.'

'Let's keep an eye on her, then, Nobby. If she gets a bit flaky, tell her from me that she needs to take some bereavement leave.'

'Of course. I have told her all of this myself.'

Stark moved to the edge of his seat. 'Right, how are we going to play this one? Let's think about what the priorities are. Get your pen out Nobby.'

Detective Sergeant Clarke opened his briefcase and took out a pen and a note pad. He had learned from his finite bit of paper at the Paul Masters scene. Nobby also took out some reading glasses. He took off his sunglasses, put his reading glasses on and then tried to put his sunglasses over the top of them. They fell, the arms pivoting on his cheekbone and the lenses over his mouth.

'What the fuck are you doing, Nobby?'

'It's bright in the sunshine.'

'We're in the shade.'

'Yes, but it's bright all around. Fine.' Nobby put the sunglasses on the table and squinted down at the glaring white sheets on his pad.

Stark shook his head. 'Ready, darling? You don't want to juggle some fucking batons or ride around the garden on a unicycle before we start?'

'Ha ha, no, crack on, boss, I'm ready. The pen is suitably poised.'

Stark leaned forward and closed his eyes in thought. 'Okay, SOCO and forensic results. Post Mortem and results. Who and where is the kid's father? Send the teleprinter message to all forces, get a witness statement from person finding the body and his clothes, arrange an ID of the body before the post mortem.'

'Hang on, boss, give me a chance.' Nobby said. He was sweating in the baking heat.

Stark paused a second before continuing. He was in full flow. 'Press release, but we will hold back the tennis ball aspect, we won't let the press know for now. Waggy can do that, hopefully.'

Stark took a chuff on his cigar to let Nobby catch up with his notes, before resuming his download. 'Interview little Toby, debrief Wagstaff, erm what else? Paul Masters – speak to him in person in prison. We need to do some research to see what can we find out about the tennis ball - is there anything unusual about it? Where was it brought, all of that? House-to-house at all points of entry to the grounds.' He paused again. 'Christ, Nobby. what are you doing, writing in bloody calligraphy?'

'I'm not rushing it, boss, I've rushed it in the past, and then got back to the nick and I can't read the damned thing.'

Stark sighed; he was itching to get cracking. 'Ready?'

'Ready, boss. All good.'

'Right, consider how or why the victims are chosen, are they random? We need to try at least to anticipate the next victim because this bastard ain't going to stop.' Stark pinched the top of his nose, forcing his fingers into the edge of his eyes, balancing his sunglasses on the top of his fingers, as he did. He was trying to focus, trying to bat off the swirling demons of thought all vying for attention. 'We need to arrange a fingertip search of the house and grounds, and we can use Special Ops to do that. Coroners report. Notify relatives, and find out if any of them has got any information? Get the body formally ID'd. I think that's about it, for now.' Stark tapped at the patio table. 'We are doing the milkman, so he's sorted. That'll do for now, Nobby. Turn them into actions for the team and put it on the HOLMES computer system. Pick up any snippets from the SOCO and the search team.'

'No problem.' Nobby was still writing.

'Put me down for speaking to Paul Masters. I'm going to head over to see Steph and young Toby. Which social services is she at?'

'Sherwood, I think. What was the last one again, boss?'

'For fuck's sake, Nobby, keep up, will you? What is the matter with you?'

'I'm worried about, Steph, aren't I? Tell her I'm thinking about her, boss when you see her.'

'Seriously?'

Nobby looked serious. 'If you don't mind.'

*

Steph was standing outside the social services offices smoking a cigarette as Stark pulled up in his black Vauxhall Cavalier. She had a flowery low-cut summer dress on which accentuated her figure. Stark was smiling as he got out of the car. Even Steph thought he looked quite tasty as he walked over in his shades.

'Hard at it, I see.' Stark said with a smile.

'As always, sir. You have to pace yourself.'

He hugged her; she extended her fingers, holding the cigarette behind his back as they embraced.

'Sorry about your Dad, Steph.'

'Thanks, sir, he had a good innings as they say.'

'I know, but it's still a shock. Let me know if you need any time off, won't you? Or if you're struggling to be as excellent as you always are.'

'I will; Nobby has said the same, but, honestly, I need to work, it occupies my mind. I'm fine, honestly.'

'Okay, Nobby is freaking out worrying about you. He sends his undying love, of course.'

'Poor Nobby, he fusses around me too much sometimes, I know he means well, but he can't seem to grasp, oh I don't know, anyway, I'm fine.'

'I'll be guided by you, Steph, you know how you are feeling. How have you got on with young Toby?'

'Not brilliantly. He is only five years old, bless him. The social worker's a waste of space, though she just sits there like cheese at fourpence.' Stark laughed as Steph continued. 'I don't think the boy's seen the murder take place, thank God.'

'That's a blessing.' Stark lit up a cigar. He always smoked more heavily when the heat was on. 'What *has* he seen, anything?'

'It might sound weird, or he's confusing things in his mind, but he reckons a man read him a bed-time story last night.'

'What?'

'Yes, he says he woke up in the middle of the night, Mummy was in bed, and the man was there. He said he tucked him in and read him a story.'

'Could be she knows her attacker then?' Stark mused. 'Maybe someone she hooked up with? We don't even know who the father is; it could be as simple as that. A domestic.'

'Could be. Like Paul Masters, you mean?'

'No, I don't mean that. I'm just thinking aloud, and the truth is we don't know much about the mother at all, yet. It puts a different emphasis on the enquiry if Toby is right; surely a murderer ain't going to stop mid-attack and put the kid to bed?'

'I wouldn't have thought so. Unless, no, that's daft.'

'No, go on, Steph, unless what?'

'Unless he was trying to get us to waste time thinking that.'

Stark ran his fingers through his greying hair. Sweat was appearing in the hot sun, despite the fact they were standing in the shade. 'We're going to disappear up our backsides if we start hypothesising too much, but I take your point. Is it worth me having a go with the kid?'

'Maybe, if you fancy it. I'm not precious, boss, sometimes kids, especially boys, relate better to men than women. I don't see what we would lose. Gently does it, though.'

'Of course. I have got kids, you know, Steph. Come on let me give it a go. I want to know more about this bedtime storyteller.'

'If he exists.' Steph said guardedly.

'If he exists, granted.'

The two threw their roach ends to the floor and trod on them before entering the building.

Stark put his smile on as they walked in. He didn't barge straight up to the boy but ambled and appeared relaxed. 'Hiya, Toby, my name's David.'

The boy was sitting on the floor playing solemnly with some toys; a couple of cars, like the ones he had at home. His soft toy that he had brought from home was still on his lap. Toby looked up briefly but said nothing. The social worker sat on a soft play bench next to the child. She had curly hair, wore large 'Deirdre Barlow' glasses and had an expression like she was chewing a piece of shit she'd mistaken for chocolate.

Steph hung back, and Stark went to sit on the playmat with Toby. He remembered seeing the cars and race track in Toby's bedroom. 'Oh, I love cars, when I was little like you I had a mat which had a race track on it, it was great.'

'I've got one of those!'

'Have you? Hey, we like the same things. That's great, isn't it?'

'Yes.'

'Can I play, please?'

'Yes.' Toby gave him a blue matchbox car.

'Thanks.' Stark began making engine noises, and Steph raised her eyebrows. This was a first.

'Let's see if they crash, I'll go over here and let's roll them at each other.' Stark said.

'Okay.'

'Ready, brrrm, brrrm, steady, go. Oh, they missed. Try again.'

After a few minutes, Stark noticed a book at the side of the toy box. Throughout his 'play' session with Toby, a thousand thoughts kept invading his mind. What needed doing. He was desperate to get back to the station. There was so much to sort out. But this was vital; Toby was the only person they knew so far who had seen the killer and survived.

'Hey, I'd like to read a story. What do you think, Toby?'

Toby was quite relaxed and enjoying the fun. 'Me too.' Stark crawled on all fours to get the book and sat cross-legged as Toby joined him and leant on his legs. 'Great, it's about a fox!' Stark said. 'Whoopee.'

'Yay.' Toby said, smiling.

'I know, let's play a guessing game first.'

'Okay.'

'Let's think of a question. Erm, who was the last person to read you a story?'

'The man.'

''Okay, a man. And his name is?'

'I don't know.'

'Was he naughty?'

'He was nice.'

'Great. He sounds nice.'

'He had a funny voice.' Toby said.

'I wondered if he did. What was funny about it?'

Toby shrugged. 'Just funny.'

'Did he have trouble saying words?' Steph coughed and shook her head. Stark realised he was leading the kid. 'No, forget that, what was it?' He was getting himself in a mess.

Toby put his hand on the book on Stark's lap. 'Fox.'

'I know I like foxes; they're one of my favourite animals in the whole wide world.'

Steph looked puzzled, was this the man who fought with knife-wielding maniacs and feared neither man nor beast?

Dave read the brief story aloud, including putting on voices for the various characters, and Toby listened intently, laughing when the fox got stung on his nose by a bee. Stark had used his fingers to move around like the bee, 'buzz buzz buzz – ping!' And he nipped Toby's nose.

Once the story was done, the detective inspector was running out of ideas, and so he rummaged in the toy box and picked up a plastic gun which clicked when he pressed the trigger.

'The man had that.'

'This gun?'

'Yes.'

'Did the man have a gun then?' Steph coughed again, but Stark ignored it.

'No, silly.' Toby giggled.

'When was this?' He almost asked what time but realised that would be futile.

'After Mummy had put me to night-nights.'

'How do you know he had one of these guns, Toby?'

'The click, click.'

'This clicking?' He pressed the trigger a few more times, and Toby nodded. 'Did he make the noise inside the house, or outside, Toby?'

'Outside.' He suddenly became more solemn. 'I couldn't wake mummy up.'

'I think we'd better have a break.' The social worker spoke for the first time.

'Okay, I agree. Are you going to give me a big hug, young Toby?'

The two hugged, and Stark tapped his nose. 'Thanks for playing with me, Toby, it's been great fun. Be a brave soldier, huh?'

Toby nodded exaggeratedly.

'Will you come back?' He blurted out.

'Me? I don't know if I'll be able to. We'll see. Maybe play with Aunty Steph in a little while, huh?' Steph nodded and waved from behind Stark.

Toby nodded. He turned to the social worker. 'Can I go to the toilet, please?'

Stark and Stephanie reconvened outside, automatically reaching for tobacco.

'Any thoughts?' Stark asked the Detective Policewoman.

'I should congratulate you on your interview style, very impressive.'

Stark laughed. 'I just like playing with toy cars.'

'What man doesn't?'

'Thoughts generally?' Stark asked.

'A couple of interesting snippets about the killer, well, the guy we assume is the killer.' Steph observed.

'Who else could it be?'

'I don't know, it just seems a bit of a funny one, that this maniac would take time out to read the kid a story.'

'Strange, isn't it?' Stark drew on his cigar. 'If we can believe young Toby, the killer has a funny voice, or a stammer, something like that. And then there is something about clicking outside the bedroom window. That might be a red herring though, do you think?'

'Could be, sir, you have to take what they say with a pinch of salt. He volunteered it, though, didn't he? It's something to throw in the pot. Just don't take it as gospel.'

'Okay, will you do some more work with Toby on the offender's appearance and clothing, and all that, please? I need to get back to the nick, sharpish.'

'No problem.' They hugged again. Hugging wasn't a normal way for them to meet and depart but, under the circumstances, with her father dying, it felt right. Stark walked over to his car and turned to wave to Steph.

'I'll tell the lads about your playgroup skills, boss; they will be really impressed.'

'Don't you bloody dare.'

7

'The final forming of a person's character lies in their own hands.'

Ann Frank.

Detective's Cynthia Walker and Steve Aston sat on the settee opposite Dorothy Westwood. They had been unable to break into the sobbing and wailing. She was so distressed.

It was a cosy home if a little old fashioned, with a display cabinet of ornaments and chinaware. There was a pleasant smell of baking bread, giving an incongruous backdrop to a moment of extreme sadness. It was heartrending to see the lady's distress. 'Aunty Dot' must have been close to Sandra.

Cynthia sat back and allowed Aunty Dot's grief to come out. The moment would come when she felt able to converse.

'That poor boy.' Mrs Westwood kept saying, her mind fixed on young Toby. 'I want him here, he's not going in any home, not if I've got anything to do with it. Over my dead body.' More tears rolled down her cheeks. Dot kept reaching for the tissues on her coffee table and had gathered a loose pile which balanced precariously on her lap.

'Whereabouts is his father, Mrs Westwood?' Cynthia asked.

'That's the tragedy; we only buried him yesterday.' She began sobbing again.

'Oh, I'm so sorry, I didn't know.' She glanced at Steve.

'I want that boy here where he's loved and will be looked after. Not with strangers.'

'We will help with all of that Mrs Westwood, don't worry. I can't see a problem.' Cynthia said reassuringly.

'Thank you. I knew he was trouble.'

'Knew *who* was trouble, Mrs Westwood?'

'Him. The lad on the bike.'

Cynthia leaned forward and opened her notebook on the same coffee table that Dot was pulling tissues from a box.

'Did you see someone then?'

'Yes, I told Sandra about him, but she just laughed it off. Oh My God.'

'What?'

'Oh, Lord, she even joked that she was so tired that if he was a killer, he could "murder me tomorrow." That's what she said, "murder me tomorrow", can you believe it? What she must have gone through with that monster.'

Cynthia had begun scribbling notes. 'I appreciate it's upsetting, but can we just rewind a little; when did you first see this person?'

Dot was recovering a little, now that her mind was focussing more on events, distracting her from her sorrow.

'It was the day of Mark's funeral, and close friends and relatives came back for an hour. Not here, to Sandra's, I mean. I stayed even longer, after they had all left, just to make sure she was okay and to help with the tidying up, that sort of thing.'

'This is her husband, Mark? The funeral?'

'Yes, poor Mark, far too young. He had a brain embolism, totally out of the blue. Completely unexpected, it was. And now this. It beggars belief.' She sighed, and another tear fell.

'Were you with Sandra when you saw the man?' Cynthia asked.

'Yes, as I said, we spoke about him, it would be after everyone had gone, so maybe around half six, or seven o'clock. Yes, it must have been then, as I was conscious it was getting close to Toby's bedtime. You can overstay your welcome, can't you? Plus, I knew she was shattered, bless her.'

'Where was this man, in relation to the house.' Cynthia enquired.

'He was just hanging around. I saw glimpses of him maybe two or three times from the kitchen window. I nearly shouted at him. I wished I had now, but you have to mind your business to some extent. They were fleeting glimpses, as he was quite a distance away, or zipping past on his bike. No sooner did I see him than he was gone again.' Dorothy padded at her eyes with the tissue.

'Can you describe him at all?'

'Oh, blimey. I didn't see the man's face because he had a jogging-top thing on, with a hood over his head. I mean, that is suspicious for a start, you know how hot it was yesterday, and he was wearing that jogging top.'

'What colour was it?' Cynthia paused the pen as she asked.

'You know the sort of thing I mean, with a hood.'

'Yes, I know, quite a few of the young ones have started wearing them. So, what colour was it Mrs Westwood?'

'Grey, a light grey, it had got those white things hanging down, where the hood was.'

'Were they like shoelace strings, which you pull to tighten the hood?' Steve asked, rubbing his fingers through his ginger hair, adding to its unkempt appearance.

'Yes, that's it, you've got it.'

'How tall?' Steve continued.

'I couldn't tell you, I'm afraid, normal size, I suppose.'

'Colour?' Steve asked.

'As I said, it was light grey.'

'No, sorry, was he white or black?'

'White, we don't get many…' Her voice trailed off as it dawned on her that Cynthia, of course, was a 'half-caste.' Cynthia kept scribbling and didn't look up.

'What else was he wearing?' Steve asked.

'I couldn't tell you.'

'What did the bike look like?'

'Just a bike. I don't know.'

'Was it a Raleigh Chopper, a racing bike, or a BMX?'

'Don't ask me, I've no idea, I'm afraid. I'm not up on all that, a bike is a bike to me.'

'Would it be helpful to show you some pictures of different styles of bicycles?' Cynthia asked with a smile.

Dot nodded. 'Yes, I think I would know if I saw it. It was orange. I can tell you that.'

'Quite distinctive then, what about age?'

'It looked quite new, not very old.'

'Sorry, my fault, how old was the man, would you say?'

'Oh, I see. I thought he was young at first but then maybe older, 30's.'

'30's riding up and down on a bike?' Steve seemed surprised.

'Maybe he was younger then I don't know.' Dot said. 'I couldn't say with any degree of certainty. I'm not doing very well, am I?'

Cynthia smiled. 'You are Mrs Westwood; you really are, given the circumstances; this a terrific lead. This information will be a big help.'

Dot smiled briefly. 'That's something at least.' She became distant momentarily, as if in a trance.

'This is a sensitive question, I'm afraid. Did Sandra have any, erm, other men friends that, she…' Cynthia decided just to say it. 'Was she seeing anyone else?'

'Don't be so bloody ridiculous! She buried her damned husband that day. What an awful thing to ask.'

'I'm sorry.' Cynthia grimaced. 'Please forgive me; I have to ask because sometimes there are other people we need to speak to, Mrs Westwood. I don't know Sandra. I don't know anything about her husband. My intention was not to upset you.'

'Well. Imagine such a thing. At a time like this. What a crass thing to suggest.'

'Mrs Westwood, I wasn't suggesting anything, I promise you. I didn't mean to upset you, but it is a question that has to be asked, I'm afraid. I know it is upsetting. I'm sorry. I understand how awful it must sound.'

Aunty Dot looked over to the window and very gently shook her head. She sighed.

Cynthia glanced at Steve. The conversation lulled for a moment before Aunty Dot broke the tension. 'Anyway, the less said about it, the better. What about young Toby? I need to have him here. I don't want the poor lad in a children's home, not even for one night. It's not fair on him. I couldn't bear the thought of it.'

'We can arrange all of that with social services, but first I'm afraid I have to ask something else that is rather unpleasant.'

'Oh, dear Lord. What now?'

'I have to ask if you would be good enough to identify Sandra's body for the Coroner?'

'I can't do that; I couldn't face it, I'm sorry.' Dot was shaking her head. She seemed resolute.

'Is there anyone else that could do it?' Steve asked.

'Couldn't a friend do it, or something like that.' Dot held a tissue up to her nose. She was alarmed at the prospect.

'Are there any friends or family you could suggest?' Cynthia asked.

'I wouldn't want to put them in that position. It's not for me to suggest them, I wouldn't feel comfortable doing so.'

'Okay. Leave it with us,' Cynthia said, 'the milkman who found her, knew her, so maybe the Coroner's office will accept that as a formal identification. I will give them a call later.'

'I just need to get Toby safe. That's my main priority. I don't like all of this, police and social workers. We're not like that as a family, we've never had any trouble like this.'

'I know.' Cynthia smiled reassuringly. 'We will get him here for you, don't worry about that.'

'Thank you. I'm sorry if I was a bit abrupt earlier, but I am so angry at…at what has happened, angry at that man. To do this to Sandra, to us all, especially little Toby, God bless him. It is despicable it really is. It's pure evil.

'I know. It is evil. You're right. And as for getting upset at the question, I asked you. I probably would too, if it was someone close to me. We have to ask it because people do have their secrets; it is a fact of life, it's nothing personal, we don't know anyone involved. Please, rest assured that we are doing our utmost to find this maniac even though it is probably little solace for you at the moment. We will get him and hopefully soon.'

*

While the team were busy sorting out the preliminary actions, notably around the Coroner and piecing together a chain of events, Wagstaff had very kindly let Stark take the initial press conference while he rode shotgun. It was in the training room of the police station; the largest room available. The two senior detectives sat at a table with a crowd of journalists in rows on plastic chairs opposing them. Various cameras and microphones had been set up in front of, and indeed on the desk. The table cloth was blue and hung over the front, displaying the force crest.

Superintendent Wagstaff's gesture to lead the press conference was a simple courtesy to Stark, but, of course, it had triggered his anxiety, and he was sweating profusely; his vision blurring. He could not make out the faces of the crowd of journalists, and he was on auto-pilot, just trying to get it over; saying the words out loud. Stark kept taking large gulps of air and coughing inexplicably, causing one or two puzzling looks between those assembled.

Thankfully it was drawing to a close; he was nearly there. 'We cannot disclose anything further at this point I'm afraid, but rest assured that we will...' Stark had been tapping his leg throughout but to no avail. He was getting increasingly anxious. This stupid technique that Linda had given him clearly didn't bloody work. His hands were trembling now. He reached for his pad and knocked the damned glass of water over next to him. Thankfully he had been guzzling a lot of it, so only a quarter of it remained, but it seeped into the white table cloth slew over the bench table. '...Oops, let you know if we have any major developments, through the press office.'

'Any leads? 'Any suspects?' 'Was the woman raped?' 'Where is the boy?' These were the myriad questions, from the press pack, but Stark and Wagstaff were already standing. There would be no reply. 'Thank you, everyone.' Wagstaff cheerily said as they left the table.

Stark led the way outside and across the concourse to his office with Wagstaff in tow. Wagstaff had started limping. 'Are you okay, sir?' Stark asked, his rapid breathing already starting to slow a little.

'Not really, my bloody hip is on it's way out. It's giving me all sorts of gip, that's why I asked you to lead the press conference for me. I hope you don't mind, David?'

'Me. No. No problem at all.' He wiped the sweat from his brow. 'Do you need an operation do you think?'

'Maybe. It's a long time to be off work. I will see how bad it gets. I've not got that much longer before I retire, David, and I'm on my bike.'

'Not literally.' Stark smiled.

'No, perhaps not, at this rate.'

Wagstaff paused at the entrance door and rubbed at his hip. He seemed to have something on his mind. 'You know when I was younger, David, probably your rank, I used to get the fuzzy-wuzzies when I had to do the public speaking bit.' He lied.

'The fuzzy-wuzzies?' Stark laughed.

'I got myself into a right state about it. I would have the shivers and the shakes, all sorts.' Stark was beginning to feel a little awkward. He knew, didn't he? His Superintendent continued. 'The thing is I just forced myself to do it, and eventually, it passed, just like that. Sometimes you have to plough on. You know?'

'I'm glad it worked out for you, sir.' Stark smiled.

'Most things do.' There was a brief lull, and Wagstaff patted Stark on the shoulder. 'Anyway, let's go and get a cuppa, shall we?'

'Sounds like a plan. Thanks.'

'Thanks? I don't know what you are thanking me for; you're making the coffee.'

They settled in Stark's office, and each gulped at a hot coffee, once Ashley had made it, at Stark's instruction.

'I need to see Paul Masters, sir.' David said as he sat behind his desk. His shirt stuck to his back with sweat.

'You're right, you do.' Wagstaff agreed. 'It is starting to look like you were right about him. I had a daunting feeling that you might be.'

'It's looking that way, but Masters still admitted his involvement, albeit in a manner of speaking, and there is the forensic yet to come. So, while there is a question mark, it becomes tricky just to release the guy merely because we have had another murder on the patch, even with the distinctive M.O.'

Wagstaff twiddled his moustache. 'Mmm. It is an unusual one.' Wagstaff glanced at Stark, before continuing; 'What we don't want is an unsafe conviction, and for all this to come out after the fact. We need to be straight, upfront from the get-go. Maybe I should talk to CPS.'

'I think that is wise, sir. No point making a bad situation worse. Can I ask that you do that once I have seen Paul Masters? At least then I can take a view on what is happening with this guy and why he finds himself locked in a cell. It should give you more to take to CPS, I'm hoping.'

'Seems perfectly reasonable to me. When are you seeing him?' Wagstaff sipped at his coffee, his little finger raised as he did. An observer might have thought he was sipping from a bone china coffee cup rather than a mug with Nottingham Forest plastered on the side of it.

'I'm going to take Steph up to the prison with me this afternoon. I can get an emergency visit ordered. I'll do a one-on-one.'

'I think they will need a bit more notice than that, David, for a one-to-one conversation. They are picky about it, you know, at the prison. It is a regimented regime; they don't like having to change their routine, you know that.'

'I know, but, come on, for something like this they can make an exception. I know the deputy governor, anyway. I'll get it done today, don't worry about that.'

'That would be good. I know it will take us into tomorrow before I can see CPS, but it can wait another day while we try to get a complete picture. It is the right thing to do.' Wagstaff crossed his legs a bit too high up for David's liking. The motion also showed a sliver of the white chicken leg above his sock. It wasn't a good look.

Stark opened his notebook. 'Have you got time for me to update you on this latest one, boss? While you're here. Topline?'

'Absolutely, there's nothing more pressing than murder.'

'In my view, this is the same guy as the Master's murders.'

'Okay, because...?'

'Because...well a few things, to be honest, but the tennis ball for one. In both cases, a tennis ball has been stuffed in the mouth of a victim, as a gag. I mean, come on, this is a unique M.O.'

'It certainly is, could it be a copy cat of the first one?'

'No. It's the same guy. In any case, no-one knew about the tennis ball. It was never released to the press.'

'What else do we know?'

'A relative was with the mother, the afternoon of the killings. Aunty

Dot.'

'Good old Aunty Dot.' Wagstaff smiled as the sweet coffee smell wafted his nostrils and prompted another sip.

'Aunty Dot says that she saw some bloke hanging around the bungalow and warned Sandra about him. This would have been around 6 or 7 o'clock, though, some hours before the attack.'

Wagstaff winced. 'Quite some time before, then. There is a big gap there.'

'Yes, but he was seemingly checking the place out, according to Aunty Dot. The victim, Sandra, had buried her husband that day, and she couldn't care less about the bloke, by the sounds of it.'

'Unsurprising. How awful for the little one, though, to lose both parents like that.'

'Exactly.'

'How did the father die, incidentally?'

'Natural causes, we think, an embolism. We will clarify it, but there is nothing sinister about it.'

'Prints?'

'None, he was wearing gloves.'

'Bugger.'

'He's an inconsiderate murderer, isn't he?' Stark grinned, ignoring the clamminess of his shirt still sticking to his back from the torture of the press conference. He ploughed on regardless.

'Description?' Wagstaff asked.

'White male, possibly thirties, wearing a grey hoody and riding a bicycle.'

'Riding a bike? In his thirties? Sounds as though he could be a bit retarded to me.'

'I don't know about that, not everyone can afford a car, but he is one psychotic bastard, I can tell you that.' Stark said.

'He's slit her throat, hasn't he? What did the postmortem tell us?'

'It's more than a slit; he has carved his way into her neck; the cut is deep, three inches at it's deepest.'

'He meant it then. Pretty much down to the bone.'

'He meant it all right, sir—nothing much else from the PM, apart from all the rape residue. We have semen; so once we have a name, we can crucify him at court, if they are doing sampling by then. It's still very much in its infancy this DNA business.'

'It could be a good one to start them with, serial killer, rapist. What could be better?'

'What could be better, indeed? What has the boy said?' Wagstaff asked.

'He's only five, so we have to be a bit cautious with what he says. He heard a clicking sound.'

'A clicking sound?'

'Don't hold me to this, because kids can get very confused as you know, sir, but he also reckons the killer read him a story.'

'How bizarre. In fact, this whole thing gets bloody stranger by the minute.' Wagstaff observed.

'Doesn't it just. And the lad, Toby his name is, says that he heard this clicking noise outside his room, as he was going to sleep. It may be nothing. Who knows?'

'At least it is something to go on.'

'It is something to bear in mind, and he said the man who read him the story spoke in a funny way.'

'Did he elaborate?'

'No, did he hell, but maybe it's a stammer or something like that.'

'Or an accent? Scouser or Geordie, perhaps?'

'Could be. If we get a potential suspect, then it could strengthen the view if they have something distinctive about their voice.'

'And if they don't?'

'I don't think we should discount anyone, it is too flimsy, and he is only little. Let me have a think to see if we can turn these snippets into something more positive.'

'Who's with the lad, is it Steph?'

'Yes.'

'That's good. Is there any connection between the two women that we know of?' Wagstaff uncrossed his legs, much to Stark's relief, it looked painful.

'Not as far as we know, it's a bit early, I will have a look later if I get a chance. I will ask Jim to do it.'

'Get someone doing common denominators on them, David. Maybe use someone at the Force Intelligence department if Jim is busy.'

'Of course. It's going to be one of those where we will have no problem proving it, once we know who the hell he is.'

'Yes, there's always a snag, isn't there? We've got everything apart from the offender, and unfortunately, that's the difficult bit.' Wagstaff slurped at his coffee as he stared at Stark with a twinkle in his eye.

'You know what I mean, though.' Stark could feel Wagstaff's gaze cutting through him.

'Of course, I do. I get it, David. What is going to take us to him? What is the journey to the killer?'

'Potentials are the tennis ball and where that came from, maybe the bike, he can't live that far away if he's on a bloody bike. I mean, not the other end of the country in any case.'

Wagstaff ruminated for a moment. 'Let's see what Paul Masters says later on, and get the lads to do some localised enquiries on this bike and all the regular stuff. Someone is going to know him in the locale, surely?'

'You would think so. There is quite a bit we can drip feed the press with this one, sir, but I think we should hold back releasing this weird tennis ball bullshit.'

'Agreed.'

'We could put out an artists impression of him, and a picture of the bike when we identify what type it is.' Stark suggested.

'Do it, but let's not put it out to the press just yet.'

'Really?'

'Don't force it, David. Let's see what Masters says; for all we know, this prat on the bike might not be the killer. It was some hours before the attack, at least, when Aunty Dot, saw him, by the sounds of things.'

'Okay. Fair enough, but we need to trace and eliminate him, even if it transpires he isn't the killer. He's the best we've got at the moment.'

'He is, and the clock's ticking.' Wagstaff smiled unnervingly.

'It starts the second after the previous murder, as you know, sir, with a serial killer, the question is always who will be next, and when?'

'I meant the overtime bill, but you're right.' Wagstaff smiled.

*

DC Charlie Carter and Jim McIntyre strolled along the footpath which leads from the bungalow to Wighay farm.

'Hang on, Jim, what's the bloody rush?'

'Och. Piles playing yae up agin, Charlie?'

'I've got an arse like a blood orange, and the heat doesn't help.'

'You need to get them sorted, bonnie lad.'

Charlie ducked and thrashed out at a seemingly invisible foe. 'What the hell was that thing?'

Jim laughed. 'It's a dragonfly, Charlie, it'll nae hurt you.'

'Fucking buzzing creatures, midges, flies, beeky-bobs, what a bloody hell-hole this is.'

'It's the countryside, Charlie. D'ya ken, it's not even that, it's just a footpath, man, what's wrong wi yae?'

'There should be a health warning. All these bugs and shit, it's nasty.'

'Yae'll get over it, although, I don't know how we ended up with this action, the youngsters should be doing this, we did all this shite when we were young DC's. Nobby's taking the piss, isn't he?'

Charlie stopped and lit up a cigarette. He thought it might help ward off some of the insects swarming around him. He blew out some smoke and wiped at his brow. 'He's a bit distracted with Steph, I reckon, Jim.'

'That needs sorting as well. It cannae be right that the sergeant is shacked up with one of his DC's.'

'They're not shacked up, Jim. They are just fucking each other. Now, where's the harm in that?' Charlie laughed.

Jim shrugged. 'Well, yae say that, but it's cock ruling head if yae ask me.'

'You would, though, wouldn't you?'

'Steph? Och, Christ, aye, who wouldnae?'

They began to walk again. There was a haze ahead of the detectives and dust thrown up behind them as they moved along at a snail's pace, puffing and panting as if they were traversing the jungles of Borneo. They were only a couple of hundred yards from the road.

Jim sneered. 'This is garbage, isnae it? Nobody can see anything this far up the path. Let's gae back.'

'No. Come on, Jim. We do the action as instructed.' Charlie took the flimsy self-carbonated piece of paper from his pocket and unfolded it. He squinted as he read it. *'Walk the length of the footpath at the rear of the bungalow to Wighay Farm. Identify any likely buildings for enquiries or regular users of the pathway. Did they see anything suspicious?'*

'It's bloody miles, man. There's nae sign of man nor bloody beast.' Jim observed.

'That's where you're wrong, look at this.' Charlie pointed down the path, and in the distance, they could see a man in full cycling gear heading towards them. Charlie pulled his wallet from his hip pocket and held it out in front of him, displaying his warrant card. As the cyclist got closer, Charlie shouted to him. 'Can we have a word, my friend?'

The cyclist slowed and eventually drew to a stop, the brakes squealing as he did, with Charlie's warrant card now hovering in front of his face.

Jim spoke. 'I think you're a bit lost, kid, the Tour de France starts in Paris. I think yae turned left at the wrong traffic cone.'

The cyclist didn't see the funny side, and it set them off on the wrong foot. Charlie tried to resurrect it. 'Sorry to stop you in mid-ride, we're from the CID, and investigating the murder of a woman back along the pathway, do you ride down here regularly?'

'Every day come rain or shine.' The man seemed pleased with himself. He was breathing heavily, and sweat was evident on his brow with droplets falling periodically.

'I take it you draw the line at wind and snow.' Jim said.

'It would be a couple of days ago, afternoon time. That's when we are interested in.' Charlie said.

The information was sinking into the cyclist's shiny helmet as was the sweat in his lycra shorts.

'Oh, you mean the bungalow. That's awful; it's just been on the news, funnily enough, yes, I did see something, it is probably nothing because there are often kids on bikes and walkers, I see all sorts of weird and wonderful people on my travels.'

From his demeanour and the way he spoke, Jim had the cyclist down as a middle manager on his day off. 'What caught your eye?' He asked.

'It was a bloke in a hoody top. He had a bike, but he wasn't riding it, he had it propped up against the hedge just up from the bungalow. I don't know, maybe fifty yards this side of it.'

Charlie glanced at Jim. 'What did the bloke look like?'

The cyclist dismounted with a groan as his backside peeled off the saddle. 'You'd be nae good on one of those, Charlie.' Jim cracked. Charlie ignored the comment.

The cyclist stretched his back. 'That's better. He was a white bloke, not a kid, maybe late twenties something like that.'

Charlie led the questioning. 'What colour was the hoody?'

'Grey. Light grey.'

'Any logo?'

'Not that I could see. I don't think it was an expensive one, it had a drawstring on the hood, but it was frayed. He looked a bit dirty. One of the great unwashed by the looks of him.'

'What about trousers or shorts?'

'Jeans I think, I didn't really notice. Just the hoody, really, and the bike.'

'What about the bike? What did that look like?'

'It was a mountain bike, a dirty orange frame, and it looked like he might have sprayed it himself. No mudguards, erm, that's about it for the bike. It was only a glimpse as I went by. I think there might be something wrong with him, to be honest.'

'What makes you say that?'

'Well, as I say, he was maybe 30 years old, but he was bouncing a tennis ball. That's not normal, is it?'

'No, I suppose it's not.'

Charlie took the cyclists details and agreed that someone would be around to see him for a written statement later in the day or this evening. As he mounted the bike and cycled away, Charlie gave him a wave as he continued down the dusty path.

'There you go, Jim. Not a waste of time, after all.'

'It's not anything we didn't know before is it, really?'

'It is mate; this info has him with the tennis ball outside the property. It's his. He brings the tennis ball to the scene. Come on, only another mile to go.'

'Don't forget the 2-mile walk back.'

'I'd put that to the back of my mind, Jim.'

'Maybe that cyclist will give you a croggy on his way back?'

'I think I'd have to pass on that one.' He grimaced and clutched his buttocks together. 'Ouch, ya bugger.'

They continued their stroll along the dusty path with Charlie flapping at all the midges and Jim running a couple of feet and dodging around like a boxer on the ropes, as a bee decided to pick on him. They looked a comical pair, but they had got another snippet, another tiny piece to slot in. It all counted.

*

Ashley drove, and Nobby chuntered and sweated in the passenger seat of the CID car. 'Yes, boss, no boss, of course, boss. Yes, I will allocate all the actions, boss, no problem, you just swan off and go and play fucking choo-choo's or whatever with a little boy, while we do all the work.'

Ashley was chuckling. 'I think he was desperate to speak to the kid because he'd seen the killer, Sarge.'

'I get that, but you can't do everything yourself, you have to trust others. Steph had got it all in hand, but no, he has to go over there and stick his oar in.'

'Ah, now I see.'

'What's that supposed to mean?'

'Nothing, Sarge. Where is this pawn shop?'

'Just keep going it's half a mile down here on the left. You should get in the bay at the front with a bit of luck.'

'What did Special Ops find when they searched the house, then?' Ashley asked.

'It was a receipt for some watches that she had sold at the pawnshop.

Gents watches, three of them. It was only three or four days ago.'

'I'm tempted to say "so what"?'

'It is just a case of understanding her movements, Ash. It won't take much doing, it's a recent movement by the victim, and if it turns out she's been in the Pawnshop with a fella, and we haven't checked; we're going to have a great dollop of egg on our faces. Know what I mean?'

'Got you, Sarge. Once we get the postmortem results and SOCO findings through, we will have an idea where we are, won't we?'

'I hope so. We might as well do some of these bits and bobs until we know more. Stark will brief us later, once everything is in. This little job is just to find out a bit about her before we can find a groove and get some bloody structure to the enquiry.'

'The problem is, at this point we don't know what we don't know.'

'That's a good way of putting it, young Ashley.'

'Thanks, Sarge.'

'Just in here on the left, look.'

Ashley pulled into the bay and ratcheted the handbrake up.

Nobby gave him a word of warning. 'Now the guy that owns this place is a little, how can I put it? Different, shall we say.'

'In what way?'

Nobby grinned. 'If it's the same guy who was here a couple of years ago, he's...well, it's best you find out for yourself. It'll be fun.'

'It doesn't sound it.'

The two detectives got out of the car and approached the pawnshop. It had rusty bars at the window, and beyond the glass façade was an untidy mess of stock of all manner, from china plates to roller skates. You couldn't see anything beyond the window 'display.' Strangely, despite it being the height of summer, there was Christmas tinsel stretched around the inside of the window.

The bell chimed on the door as Nobby pushed it and the two cops walked in. It smelt of old items, ageing, and dusty, with antiquated books and a general fusty feel to the whole place. It made Nobby feel itchy straight away. 'Thank Christ, somewhere cool.' He said.

The man emerging from behind the black curtain was chiselled from granite. He was big and had arms like legs. The guy was skin-bald and smeared in tattoos over arm, neck, head and face. He gave a mock grin which displayed a gold tooth just off centre. His eyes were dark and unforgiving.

The shopkeeper's voice was deep and was more of a growl, its resonance so low that it was almost beyond the spectrum of the human ear.

'No bent gear,' was all he uttered.

'We're from the…' Ashley began. Nobby interrupted him. 'I think he knows that, Ashley. I'm Detective Sergeant Alan Clarke, and this is my colleague DC Stevens, your name is?'

The man hadn't blinked yet and stared straight into Nobby's soul, his eyes black and unforgiving. Nobby put his hand out to shake the man's hand. It was rebuked, the owner choosing to spit some gum into a brass coal bucket next to the counter which gave a pleasing 'ding' sound. The man threw another piece of fresh chewing gum into his mouth immediately.

'Get your sales book out.' Nobby said.

'I think you mean please, don't you, kid?' Mr Granite said.

'Ashley, go and put the closed sign on the door.' Nobby instructed.

'Here, what's your fucking game, you can't do that.' The owner protested.

'Can't I? Just watch me. Now unless you wind your neck in a couple of notches, and lose the attitude, I'm going to get a fucking great truck to clear this shop and take the next year checking every piece is not stolen. Does that make sense to you, Mr fucking, no name?'

'You wouldn't dare.'

'Try me. Now, what's it to be?'

'Gerald Swan.' The man sneered.

'Thank you, Mr Swan.' Nobby gave a roguish grin which he dropped as quickly as he formed it.

Suddenly a skinny young man in hot pants came tripping through the curtain behind the counter. He had a pink Mohican haircut and was very, as Nobby would describe, 'light on his feet.'

'I'm off, now Mr Muscles…oh, customers.'

'It's the Feds, Jason.' Gerald said morosely.

'Oh, very butch, I'm sure.' He looked Nobby up and down.

Jason kissed Gerald on the lips, and they tongued each other. No doubt for effect. Ashley looked confused.

'Be a good boy for me, won't you, Jezza?'

'We need milk.' Gerald said stony-faced.

'I'll bring your favourite back as well.' Gerry glanced at Nobby. 'He just loves Jelly Tots, don't you, big daddy.'

'Er, yeah, they're pretty fucking fruity.'

'Let's face it, Mr Swan, they aren't alone, are they?' Nobby said.

The slightest flicker of a smile traversed big butch Jezza's face.

'He crams them in his cake-hole ten at a time don't you, Mr Grumble tum?' Jason tapped at Gerald's stomach.

'Do I?'

Jason started to camp it up even further. 'Ignore Mr Grumpy. He's always miserable because he can't stand queers, can you?'

'No, I fucking hate them.'

Ashley raised a finger as if to ask a question, 'But. Aren't you, it doesn't matter. Forget it.'

Jason scrunched up his nose and rubbed it against Gerald's nose, Eskimo style. 'Who's a sour old cow, then, eh?'

'I'd rather be a cow than a sow.'

Ashley could hardly believe what he was seeing.

Jason squealed. 'Meow, Bitch! He's such a tart. That's why I love him.' He gave Gerald a peck on the lips and stumbled out in what appeared to be female high-heeled shoes. Jason winked at Nobby as he trotted past him.

'Don't forget the milk.' Nobby said grinning. The bell of the door tinkled as Jason walked out, blowing a kiss.

'Queer bastard.' Gerald shouted after his lover. It was all terribly confusing for Ashley, who stood there with his mouth agape.

Gerald leaned on the counter and sighed. There was a silence only interrupted by the fading resonance of the chiming shop doorbell.

'I'll get the sales book.' Gerald announced.

'Thank you, Mr Swan, we just want to check you had a visit from a Mrs...'

'The woman who got killed. Yeah, we did. I bought a couple of watches off her, as memory serves.'

'Excellent, was she alone?'

'I think she had a kid with her, a little boy. She said her husband had recently died, and she only wanted one of the watches as a keepsake, but she was selling the rest. Something like that.'

'Was there anything unusual said, or anything of note, Gerald?' Nobby asked, the tension now easing.

'No, she was an attractive woman, if you like that sort of thing.'

'Not so much when I saw her, I'm afraid, Mr Swan.'

'No, I can imagine. She got a little tearful when she sold the watches, but it's understandable. That poor kid; losing his Mum and Dad so close to each other. It's a crying shame.'

It seemed that Jason had broken the pretence of Geralds hard-man image and he was being quite accommodating now.

'Absolutely.' Nobby agreed.

Ashley spoke up. 'The boy wasn't playing with a ball or anything like that was he?'

'A ball?'

'Yes, a tennis ball.'

'No, I don't think so.' Gerald smiled somewhat warmly at the handsome young detective.

'I'll just need the details, time and date and all that please, Gerald.' Nobby said.

'Sure, the book is in the back.' He half-turned and then paused. He turned to Ashley. 'Did you want to come and have a look with me?' He asked DC Stevens.

'Erm, I…no…no need, just bring it out.' Ashley had gone red.

Gerald winked at Nobby who grinned. 'Go on Ashley, Gerald will look after you.'

'Nobby! No. I'm good thanks.'

There was a skip in Gerald's step as he blazed through the curtain. He loved to flirt with the young bucks.

Ash was shaking his head. 'This ain't funny, Sarge.'

'It's fucking hilarious; you should see your face. Lighten up, Ash, it's only a bit of fun.'

'Can we just get the details and go, please?'

'Are you sure you don't want to stay for tea with big daddy G?'

'Erm, no, I think I will pass. Thanks for asking.'

'Please yourself.'

8

'Every thought you produce, anything you say,

any action you do, it bears your signature.'

Thich Nhat Hanh

Detective Inspector Stark and DC Steph Dawson sat in a vast room full of small tables. It was the deserted visiting room of Lincoln Prison where Paul Masters was spending his remand pending a trial. The two detectives sat alone at the middle table. It could be mistaken for a large classroom apart from the bars at the windows. It was echoey as Stark spoke. 'If Toby hasn't any more to say for now can we get him with Aunty Dot, Steph?'

'I will go back and see him in a week or so, but it is already sorted for Aunty Dot to have him. He's probably there now, sir. It looks like Social Services are going to let her look after him and formulate a more permanent solution after that. At least that's what old sourpuss the social worker told me.'

'She was a barrel of laughs, wasn't she? I bet she'll end up having him. Aunty Dot, I mean, not old Deirdre specs.'

Steph laughed. 'Probably.'

They paused, and Stark glanced at the door in the corner of the room. There was still no sign of Paul Masters. It was probably quite a hike through the prison corridors to get to them.

'Always grim coming here, isn't it?' Steph said.

'Just a bit. It always has the feel of a comprehensive school for grown-ups. "No running in the corridors" vibe.'

'I see what you mean. It's desperate; I know that.' She pulled her dress down over her knees.

'It gets the senses tingling,' Stark said, 'every single person here doesn't want to be here. Even the guards.'

'As I said, fucking grim.' Steph laughed. 'And in the middle of it is a decent bloke put here by the arrogance of that piece of shit, Lee Mole.'

Stark shook his head. 'It makes you wonder how many Lee Moles there are knocking around.'

'Not many. I don't think, do you?'

'No, not really. You scarcely come across it. One is one too many.'

'However, he got to the rank of DI I'll never know.'

'Probably got someone out of the shit and got his payback.' Stark said cynically.

'Maybe.'

Stark heard a door banging and craned his neck to look over the windows into adjacent rooms, but there was still no sign of life. They sat in a few seconds of silence. Stark could see that Steph had a far-away look in her eye; she looked tired. Stark reminded her, 'I meant what I said in the car about your Dad, and having some time off. I would if I were you. The world won't end, you know.'

'I know, sir, thanks, maybe I'm weird, but I know what I will be like on my own at home. I will go insane, trust me. Maybe I will have a bit of time off in a few days, for the funeral. We'll see.'

Stark nodded. 'The offer is there. Grief is a funny thing, you know, Steph; sometimes it pounces on you from behind, it comes out of nowhere, and all of a sudden it overwhelms you. Anyway, enough said, you know you only have to say the word.'

'I know, and it is appreciated.'

'Is Nobby still mithering you?' Stark smiled.

She sighed. 'Nobby means well, boss, you know what he's like; he wants to protect me, but sometimes it's too much, you know.'

'Don't be too harsh on him, Steph, he's got a heart of gold underneath all that hard exterior. He'd run through a wall for any of us.'

'He actually would try to do that if he thought we needed him.'

'Sometimes I wish he'd just walk around it.' Stark grinned.

In the distance, there were bangs and shouts and unexplained noises. It seemed like every action by the guards was done noisily. Every task is done offensively, as a statement. There was no room for subtlety or nuance, just bluster and survival for all in the zoo. The prison officers slammed the doors as an emphasis, to underline the difference, where the power lay. It shone a light on the raison d'etre of the whole establishment. It seemed a thin veneer.

Stark reached down the side of his plastic chair and picked up his briefcase. He clicked it open and took a wad of papers out. He gave some blank interview notes to Steph. 'You will need these, you being the scribe.'

'Thanks.'

'I will need the 999 transcript and Lee Mole's notes. I'm curious to hear what Paul has got to say about, ah, here he is by the looks of it.'

Paul entered with one rather tall and skinny guard who stood near the door as the prisoner approached the detectives in his boiler suit and black plimsolls. Both detectives rose to greet him and shook Paul's hand. He looked pale and gaunt. There was not much spark to him; he looked a broken man, unsurprisingly.

'Hello, Paul. I'm David Stark, detective inspector, and this is detective Steph Dawson.' Steph smiled at him and shook his hand.

Paul was immediately on the defensive. 'I'm telling you now that I'm not saying any more, I know you lot are trying to fit me up here. You took advantage of me last time, and I'm putting a complaint in now that I've got a solicitor.'

Stark raised a hand to stop him in mid-flow. 'Hang on, Paul. You know it wasn't us that interviewed you at the police station, don't you?'

'I know that. I know there wasn't a woman there, anyway, but you lot all gang up on someone like me. What do you even want to see me for?'

'Paul. Listen. I know the officer that interviewed you, and he and I work very differently. I want the truth, and let me tell you something, are you listening?'

Paul nodded.

'I know you haven't done this.'

'*Haven't*, did you say?'

'Yes, I know you did not do those things to your family, and I want to catch the person who did.'

Paul started to well up, and tears came into his eyes. 'You're not messing me about are you?'

'I promise you; I'm not. You will know sure enough when we begin the interview what my thoughts are, and I am happy for this officer to write them down as I say them. I understand you will be wary but, trust me, there is no need to be.'

'I don't know.'

'Let's make a start; we don't have much time; I've had to pull a lot of strings to get to see you at short notice. I am trying to sort this out, Paul. I want you out of here.'

Stark lit up a cigarette and offered one to Paul, glancing over to the guard who nodded consent. Paul took it, and the DI lit it for him. 'Just tell us everything you remember about that night, Paul.'

'Some of it has come back to me. I was in shock when that other copper spoke to me. I didn't know what was going on.'

'I'm not surprised, Paul.'

Steph had begun scribbling away. 'Do you want a solicitor present, by the way?'

'No. I will tell the guard if I've had enough, anything to get out of the cell. That's how it works here. I've never looked forward to mopping floors so much in my life.'

Stark smiled reassuringly. 'I can imagine. It is just a few questions, that's all. What do you remember about the night?'

'I've done nothing but think about that night. It has been on my mind every single hour that I've been banged up in my cell. I remember a lot more than I did the day I was arrested, I can tell you that. I remember I was exhausted; we'd buried Ella's father; we were both tired physically and emotionally. My daughter, Jemma, was already in bed, or in her bedroom at least. I went in the kitchen to make Jemma's sandwiches for college the next day, and that's where all this confusion about the knife comes in. I wiped it because it had tomato juice on it, not blood. I'd done her chicken and tomato sandwiches; it's her favourite.' Paul began to get emotional and sobbed a little. 'Sorry. It just wells up. I can't stop it.'

'It's okay. Take your time, Paul.'

He wiped the tears from his cheeks with his hands and sighed heavily.

'Do you want a hankie?' Steph asked.

'No, I'm fine. Thank you. Where was I? Oh, yes, the kitchen. I opened the window, because, huh, it doesn't matter now, but I had started smoking again, and Ella disapproved. I wanted to keep it a secret because I intended quitting. I saw it as a temporary lapse, you know.'

'I've been lapsing for ten years, Paul.' Stark said.

'Anyway, I went back to the living room to watch telly.'

'What were you watching, out of curiosity?' Stark's mind went back to the scene and Nobby turning the TV on at his request.

'It was a video, Fawlty Towers, I think.'

'But what channel was it on? The telly, I mean.'

'I don't know. Probably BBC news. I'm not sure. Why?'

'No particular reason, Paul.'

'Anyway, I dozed off and woke up in the early hours. I went in the kitchen and immediately saw that I'd left the bloody window wide open, like a fool, from when I had the cigarette. That's why I said it was "my fault" to the police. I didn't mean I'd bloody done it. I was wracked with guilt for leaving the window open for a damned cigarette. I felt as though I'd let everyone down. I still think it's my fault.' Tears began to form again, and his face contorted with grief. He was trying hard to hold it all in. 'This is what it's done to me.' He uttered.

'Paul, the bloke would have got in, if he wanted to, don't blame yourself. We've all left windows open and doors, we've all done it mate.' Stark said sympathetically.

Paul went quiet and swallowed hard. 'Thanks. But when something like this happens, it's just…' He didn't finish the sentence but closed his eyes for a moment and shook his head.

'Then what did you do?' DC Dawson asked, pen hovering above the notepaper.

'I went to bed. I know it sounds bad that I didn't notice what had happened, but it's true. Ella was fast on. Well, I thought she was. I don't touch her or kiss her or anything like that, not if she's asleep. It's not fair. Why risk waking her up? We're not teenagers.'

'All quite normal, Paul.' Stark smiled reassuringly.

'And then...' He sighed. 'And then, in the morning. I woke up and had got blood on my legs. I saw what happened to Ella and ran into our Jemma's room, and I can't say what I saw. It was the most horrific image. I will carry that around with me for the rest of my life.'

'Did you have pyjamas or underpants on?' Stark asked.

'No, I don't sleep in anything. I never have. Why do you ask?'

'It's alright, I guessed as much. There is a pubic hair on the carpet, which is yours, and that explains how it got there.'

'I vaguely remember those other officers mentioning something. I was completely out of it by then. Normally I would put something on, obviously, but with the horror of it all, I just reacted and wanted to check on Jemma.'

'Sorry to have to ask this, but it is important, Paul. The tennis ball is it from your house?'

'No, we don't have one, she's a bit old for all that now.' Paul went quiet as the misuse of the present tense hit home.

'Could it have been an old one, perhaps?'

'No, no way. It's not ours.'

'Okay, thank you, Paul, let's leave that subject. Going back to when you discovered Ella, was she already on her back?'

'Lying on her back?'

'Yes.'

'No. Ella was on her side, facing away from me, and I tried to wake her by pulling her shoulder, and she just flopped onto her back. It was just horrific. More than anyone can imagine.'

'What about all the comments you made on the 999 call; "What have I done?" and "This is my fault." That relates to you leaving the window wide open, does it?'

'Yes, obviously.'

'Not obviously, Paul, if you were to listen to it, you would see why there was a supposition that you were talking about…what had happened. No window was mentioned. Incidentally, when did you close it?'

'When I saw I had left it open in the early hours after I woke up. Well, I did have a cigarette first and then closed it.'

'What time was it, do you know?'

'Something like three in the morning, I think.'

'And you shut it then?'

'Yes.'

'So, it's happened between…what? Midnight and three in the morning.'

'I would say between 11 and 3 in the morning. The bloke who broke in might not have even known I was there for all I know.'

'Why did you go into the kitchen when you woke up?' Stark asked as Steph scribbled the notes at a high rate of knots.

'To get a drink. I was gagging for one when I woke up and so I had another cheeky cigarette.'

'Where were the cigarettes then, if it was a secret from Ella?'

'In the utility room under the sink, there's a cupboard blocking it. Check it out; the cigarettes will still be there.'

'Thank you, Paul; I will do that.' Stark knew they would be there, but he made a note in his jotter, to get one of the lads to do it. It gave Steph a chance to catch up with the formal notes, by Stark pausing to write it down. 'Why did you admit it to the officers, Paul?'

'I don't remember too much about that interview. I don't think I said I'd done it, as such. Not in any great detail. Those coppers were messing with my mind. Taking advantage.'

Stark read out the final paragraph of the notes to Paul where he admitted "fancying" his daughter and wanting to "fuck her".

'That is sick. It's a setup. I never said that, I mean, come on, I wouldn't. It's just ridiculous. It doesn't even sound like me. I don't even talk like that.'

'Let's be honest, Paul, I don't think it is you. I think that was added later in the half-page gap above your signature. It does leave us with a problem, though. A signed confession is a signed confession at the end of the day.'

'Is it though?' Paul grimaced. He had something on his mind; something was troubling him.

'What? Is it what?'

'Is it a signed confession, if it doesn't say my name?'

Stark glanced at Steph. He looked puzzled. 'I'm not with you, Paul.'

'Well, I was aware, in like, an out of body experience that I wasn't able to answer questions cogently and the men were bullying me to admit it. Taking advantage. I'm not stupid, and I somehow found enough inside me, God knows where from, not to sign it. I hope I'm not in any trouble.'

'I'm not with you?' Stark picked up the copy of the notes that Carl Davidson took and pointed to the bottom of the page. 'It's there, Paul.

Your signature.'

'That's not my signature.'

'What is it then?'

'Can you read it?' Paul asked.

Stark leaned closer to the piece of paper to scrutinise the scribble. 'Not very well…hang on. Bloody hell, Paul, you signed "I am confused" on every single page, you clever bugger.'

'Someone was guiding my hand that day, I tell you. I didn't know what the hell was going on and then suddenly it popped into my head right at the end. Just to give some indication that things weren't right.'

'Ho!' Stark smacked the table. 'You have played a blinder there, my friend.' Stark looked at Steph who was astonished. 'Unbelievable.' She muttered.

'I've not seen that done before, Paul, it's a stroke of genius.'

'I don't know how it happened. I just wrote what was in my head.'

'That is going to make things a lot easier.'

'So, can I go home now?' Paul asked.

'Very soon, Paul. Very soon. Leave it with me. It will be in days, I promise.'

'Oh, I hoped you meant I could go now. That's something I suppose.'

'It doesn't work like that I'm afraid, Paul. We have to go back to the court; it will be treated as urgent, though I assure you.'

'Thanks.'

' Is there anything else you can tell us that might help?'

'In what way?'

'To help us find the real killer.'

'Oh, crikey, I don't think so. I wish I could. That's all I remember, hang on, no, there was something, it came to me just after lock-up a couple of nights ago. It might be nothing.' Paul flicked ash into the tiny tin ashtray screwed into the table.

'It might be something, what is it?' Stark asked.

'I remember stirring after I dozed off. It could have been a minute later, or an hour later, I've no idea, but I heard a sort of clicking noise.'

'A clicking noise?'

'Yes, about three or four times.'

'Inside the house?'

'No, it was distant, maybe outside the front window.'

Steph nudged Stark's elbow. 'Toby and the gun.' She moved her finger as if pressing a trigger, reminding Stark about the clicking the gun made, and how Toby recalled hearing it outside.

'Who's Toby?'

'Oh, it doesn't matter. Well, I suppose in fairness, it is only right, you know. It's gone out to the press. There's been another attack. We think it is the same man.'

'Oh, my God.' Paul put his hand to his mouth. 'That's terrible.'

'I know. We need to find this guy. He is not going to stop.'

'This is crazy.' Paul said, shaking his head. 'And I'm stuck here, Charged with murder and rape of my own bleeding daughter. This is so bloody wrong.'

'I know. Leave it with me to get this sorted for you as soon as possible. I will make sure the powers that be are informed, and let's get you out and give you the chance to grieve properly.'

'Thank you.'

'No need to thank us, Paul, I am sorry you have been through this ordeal in the first place.'

He sighed. 'Aye. Me too.'

Paul signed the notes, this time with his proper signature, and they all stood. Stark beckoned the guard over. Paul and the detectives shook hands, and the prisoner walked over to the guard as he approached. 'Somebody will come and get you.' The guard said to the detectives.

'Okay, fine, thanks.' Stark said.

Paul stopped and turned. 'Sorry, who are you again? What are your names?'

'DI Dave Stark.'

'Stark. Right, thanks.'

Dave and Steph sat down. 'That's a turn-up.' Stark said.

Steph smiled. 'Mole's going to be shitting his pants.'

'No, he won't. People like him think they are invincible. He's right really, so Paul signed that he was confused, what does it mean? Other than he was confused. Nothing does it?'

'I suppose. It means it isn't a signed confession, though, boss.'

'Yes, it helps Paul, but what I mean for Mole, is it isn't going to finish him off or anything like that. Wagstaff won't be impressed, I wouldn't think, but that is about as much as it is. It doesn't prove Paul Masters has been written up in a false confession.'

A metal door slammed in the distance, but then there was silence.

'Boss?' Steph said.

'What?'

'What if they don't come for us?'

Stark laughed. 'Don't start that.' He stood up and looked through the windows at the connecting rooms. Dusk was approaching outside, and the light had lowered a little in the place. 'Although I can't see anybody coming.'

Stark sat down. 'Better settle in for the night then, Steph.'

She laughed. 'Hang on; I think I can see someone.' A peaked cap, presumably with a person beneath it, moved along the high windows, heading in their direction. 'Thank God for that.'

*

DC Steve Aston carried a tray of drinks towards the large circular table at the back of the police station bar. It was the prime spot. Out of the way, no listening ears, but a regular supply of alcoholic beverages on tap. Steve handed out the drinks, whisky for Jim, Guinness for Nobby, Lager for Ashley and the boss, Bitter for Charlie, G&T for Steph, Bacardi and coke for Cynthia.

'Hold on, who's is the coke?' Steve looked around the table.

'I think you'll find that's yours, Steve.' Ashley said, shaking his head.

'Oh, yes, silly me.' His face reddened, and he smiled along as Ashley tossed a beer mat at him.

'Get a grip, Steve.'

'Maybe that should be his nickname, "Get-a-grip-Steve".' Jim observed.

Ashley joined in. 'That works, "Where's Get-a-grip-Steve? Oh, he's outside with "Low-cut-Steph".'

Charlie laughed, 'Waiting for "Grab-a-granny-Ash".'

Nobby pointed the finger at Ash. 'Oi, watch the mouth.' He meant it.

'It was only a joke, Sarge.' Ash pleaded.

Nobby put his arm around Steph and squeezed her. 'It doesn't matter; we have to look after her at the moment.'

'Oh, yes, sorry, I forgot for a minute.' Ash said.

Steph smacked Nobby on the shoulder with her clenched fist. 'Gerrof!' She wrestled free from his grasp. 'Stop bloody fussing will you! No need to apologise, Ash, I thought it was quite a gentle one when I think what you could have said.' She winked at him. She adjusted her top now wrinkled up by Nobby's over-protective arm. 'Jesus Christ, Nobby.'

'What?'

Stark sipped his pint. 'Alright, guys and gals lets have a bit of decorum, please.'

The chattering and hi-jinx cooled as the focus went on to their detective inspector. 'I want just to make sure everyone is up to speed with the latest developments.'

Charlie and Nobby lit a cigarette. Nobby rubbed at his shoulder, Steph could pack a punch. He gave her a sideways glance; there was a low-light of tension bubbling.

'I can tell you the key elements from my perspective first.' Stark said. 'I will do a briefing sheet update, so there is no need to take notes at the moment. Steph has been doing some work with young Toby, in fact, no, let me work backwards a bit. Steph and I went to see Paul Masters in the clink. The long and the short of it is he hasn't done it, of course. A couple of things of note from the little tete-a-tete we had; one is that the tennis ball is not his, as we suspected. The other more amusing aspect,' he glanced at Steph who smiled, 'is that he didn't sign his name on the notes.'

'What do you mean, boss?' Ashley asked, wearing a confused expression.

'I suppose that isn't strictly true, he did sign them, but instead of his name he wrote in a scribbled signature the words "I am confused", but he made them look like his name if you get what I mean.'

There were groans and laughter. Charlie clapped his hands together. 'Sneaky bugger.'

'Perhaps not as confused as he thought, on reflection.' Stark said.

'That's tricky for Mole, isn't it?' Nobby said.

'It's tricky alright, but it won't finish him, Nobby. What does it mean really? Mole and Davidson's word against Paul Masters. It's a bit of an embarrassment, though. A lesson for us all. Always check the signature is legit.'

'Classic.' Jim said.

'The main thing is we will be able to get him out of prison fairly sharpish, I'm hoping Waggy comes in here for his tipple before he goes home, and I can give him the cheery news. I can't get hold of him on the phone. He must be out of the office.'

Stark had a drink of his beer. 'The other thing Paul Masters said was that he had heard a clicking sound outside his window, he thinks it could be the offender perhaps.'

'A clicking noise?' Cynthia asked.

'I know, you are thinking, "what type of clicking noise", have you tried describing a click?'

'A click is a click, boss.' Charlie said.

'Thanks for that, Charlie. Fucking brilliant.'

'It is, though.' Charlie shrugged.

Stark laughed. 'I know, I'm only winding you up. I need to think about what it might be that has caused it. Why? Because of the kid…'

'Toby.' Steph corrected.

'Thanks, Steph, yes, Toby, he also said that he heard a clicking noise outside, so it could be something the offender is doing.'

'A similar click, or the same?' Charlie asked.

'Smart arse.' Stark said.

'Maybe something on his bike?' Ashley offered.

'Could be, Ash. Toby also said that the man spoke 'funny.' Again, quite what that means I'm not exactly sure. Maybe an accent? A speech impediment? Who knows, but it is worth bearing in mind while you are making your enquiries.'

Nobby put his arm around Steph. 'We click, don't we dearest?'

Steph shrugged him off. 'Nobby! You know in a minute…'

'I'm attentive, aren't I? Supporting you. I'm your boyfriend for God's sake.'

'Well, don't. I'll let you know when I want that kind of support, thank you.'

Nobby shook his head and sighed.

Ashley was biting his tongue. 'It seems funny to hear the Sarge referring to himself as a "boyfriend". Don't you think?'

Nobby produced his pointy finger again. 'I won't tell you again, young Ashley.'

'Alright, can we focus, please?' Stark said, irritated. 'Toby also said that the man had read him a bedtime story.'

'Seriously?' Cynthia spoke up. 'That's not normal, is it?'

'No, it's not, Cynthia, it could imply that he is known to Toby or indeed Sandra Teversall.'

'Does the kid know the bloke's name?' Nobby asked.

'No, he doesn't, unfortunately. To be honest, on reflection, I don't think he is known to them. I just think he's got a pair of brass balls. Bear in mind; he's already done Paul Master's house. They don't know each other, so. Anybody else got anything?'

Charlie piped up. 'We had an exhausting walk, didn't we Jim?'

'Oh, aye.'

'A bloody ten-mile walk in the blazing heat. It played havoc with my, erm, knee. Thanks for that, Nobby.'

Nobby smiled. 'Bloody hell, Charlie, it was a mile, two if that, man.'

'It seemed like ten. Anyway, we came across a cyclist, and he's seen the offender. Just to confirm, he did have a tennis ball with him while standing outside the Teversall's bungalow, so it is his ball he uses, as the boss said. It's some weird shit, but it's a good cover if he gets stopped or owt who's going to think, oh it's a tennis ball he must be using it as a gag?'

'We need to get this out to the troops on the ground. If they stop anyone with a tennis ball, who has a bike and is in his thirties, he is to be nicked.' Stark said.

'The other thing the cyclist said was that the offender's bike was orange, but he said it looked like it was self-sprayed, there were no labels or badges or shit like that on it.'

Cynthia jumped in. 'Aunty Dot said he was about thirty, grey hoody, white tassels on it. If you think about it, he is really quite distinctive.'

Stark agreed. 'He is. I think we need to get Force Intelligence to do a leaflet and we can put this out to the press. Old Waggy was wary because we don't *know* that this is the killer, but sod that, he is a person of interest. Somebody is going to know this bloke, surely?'

There was a nodding of heads and 'good idea' type comments. Stark continued. 'Any news from you, Nobby?'

'I've been writing actions, and I did a quick little run out with Ashley. It was that bloke, Gerald Swan, his name is, who runs the pawnshop on the high street. I don't know if anyone knows him?'

Charlie nodded. 'I know him, Nobby, he's the muscleman shirt-lifter, isn't he?'

'That's him, and he loves a bag of jelly tots.'

Ashley laughed.

'Eh?' Charlie was confused.

'It doesn't matter, anyway, he confirmed Sandra went in to sell a couple of her dead husband's watches. It sounds like she just had Toby with her at the time. There's nothing sinister in it; I guess it's what you have to do when you lose someone.'

'I've got to sort my dad's stuff out.' Steph said to herself.

'Let me give you a hand, then.' Nobby said.

'Nobby, no honestly, I appreciate the concern, but it's all part of it. I need to be on my own when I do it.'

'Why don't you let me help, Steph?'

'Nobby, it's nothing to do…'

'Heads up.' Ashley said.

Wagstaff had walked into the bar with DI Lee Mole.

'Two for the price of one, boss.' Ashley said.

Stark got to his feet. 'This will be fun, not.' He hovered at the table. 'Are we okay with actions for tomorrow, Nobby?'

'Yes, informants and research mainly. I will sort that leaflet out for the press and to circulate the force.'

'And neighbouring forces.'

'Sure.'

'Alright. I'll probably be back in a min. Let me go and give them the good news.'

Stark strode over to the bar.

'Ah, David, can I get you a snifter?' Wagstaff asked. His cheeks were rosy, and as ever, he stood ram-rod stiff, shoulders back.

'I've got one, thanks, sir, we've just been having a de-brief.'

'Excellent.'

'Still struggling, are we?' Mole smirked.

'Investigating, Lee. Still investigating, you want to give it a try someday.'

'Well the CPS wants to press on with the Masters trial.' Mole shrugged.

'They won't when they hear from us tomorrow morning.'

'What have you found, David?' Wagstaff asked.

'The two cases, Masters and Teversall are connected. It is the same bloke, which means it can't be Paul Masters.'

'Connected, by what? Connected how?' Mole asked.

'The tennis ball M.O. for a start and the way he killed them.'

'Why has Masters coughed it then?' Mole sneered.

'I was going to ask you the same question, Lee.'

There you go.' Was all Mole could muster. It made no sense.

'We need to speak to CPS sharpish. He needs to be released from prison, sir.' Stark said.

'Hang on a minute.' Mole interrupted.

'Because of the tennis ball?' Wagstaff asked.

'All of it really, but that confession is worth nothing. It's not worth the paper it's written on.'

'Yes, it is. Why isn't it?' Mole asked, looking a bit twitchy.

'Because he has signed every single page not with his name, but with the words "I am confused." How about that?'

Wagstaff bristled. 'Oh, dear. I need a full report, David. I want all of the reasons that show how it cannot be Masters who killed his wife and daughter, and I will get it sorted.' He looked at Lee. 'I might have to refer it to Complaints, Lee.'

'Why? Because he fucked about when signing. That doesn't mean shit.' Mole was still recalcitrant.

'Perhaps if you had picked up on it at the time, we wouldn't be in this predicament in the first place, would we, now?' Wagstaff downed his single malt and marched out, shouting orders over his shoulder. 'On my desk first thing, David.'

'Will do, sir.'

Mole sneered at the smiling Stark before turning and heading out after Wagstaff. 'Sir, wait a minute…'

*

The killer was calmly looking at passers-by. His tiny flat looked out on to the road, and he would spend hours watching people coming and going throughout the night. He looked out of the window, his elbows on the ledge. The flat stunk of body odour but he was nose-blind to it. Sometimes he would build up ash on the end of his cigarette and try to time it so that if he flicked it down towards those walking below, the trajectory meant it landed on the top of their head. They were oblivious to it, but his success rate was low; the ash would break up, the wind would blow it off course, or he would misjudge it. He liked that he had affected them, yet they knew nothing; he loved the insidiousness of it. It was pathetic really if you think about it; child-like, but that was him. Anything for a small victory. Anything to assert some sort of control on to someone. Even if they knew nothing about it; especially if they knew nothing about it.

He got bored quickly, and when you struggle to sleep, the hours seem like days. His mind was too active to sleep for any significant length. Occasionally he would still have nightmares about his childhood and his mother's aloofness, and her untimely death speared on the railings. His lonely hours stuck in the house, back in the States, with no mother and no stimulation, seeking solace from that dirty second-hand tennis ball. His one real possession. His secret treasure that his mother must never find. His gateway to pleasure.

The killer threw the burning nub end at the head of an old man beneath him and disappeared back inside the window out of view. He lay on the bed and took hold of one of the tennis balls, throwing it up in the air and catching it repeatedly.

After a while, he reached down and grabbed one of the pornographic magazines strewn around his dirty carpet. He tended to focus on one woman at the moment. An older woman, probably fifties. Greying hair and dangling breasts. She was on all fours on the bed and looking back, she was reaching back and separating her labia with her fingers. She was wet, or at least she looked wet. He wasn't to know the photographer had used olive oil to set up the photograph.

He began to play with himself as he lay on his back. The pervert hunched up and lowered his jogging bottoms to his knees, getting erect quickly and he began to masturbate. Quicker and quicker as he stared at the woman's private parts, his mind flickering back to Sandra and Jemma as he began to feel the rush. Bizarrely he put the tennis ball in his mouth and bit down, grunting and snarling as he hammered away at himself. He ejaculated, his hips raised, eyes wild as he struggled to breathe and saliva was growing around his mouth and the ball. He was gasping and straining to finish, nostrils flared, and he thrust one last time, emptying himself wherever it fell.

He grabbed the ball out of his mouth and threw it to the floor, taking in more air, puffing and panting with the exertion of trying to breathe. He lay there for a while and felt his heart pounding and some shouts outside the open window. Semen leaked from his penis on his groin. He reached for a tissue but found none, so he had to use one from the previous day. He dabbed the end of his penis and his thigh. He wiped the wall at the side of the bed where some had landed. There was too much for the hardened tissue, so he just threw it out of the open window.

The psychotic excuse for a human pulled his joggers up and went back to the window. His legs were trembling a little. This was no substitute for the real thing. It satiated him for a while, but there was no power play, no dominance and no terror. This was shit. He needed another victim. Something different, perhaps? Maybe a cuckold. That could work.

9

'True friends are those rare people who come to find you in dark places and lead you back to the light.'

Steven Aitchison.

Jim McIntyre sat in the CID office at the cluster of desks, along with Nobby and Steph, who were in the corner.

Nobby, with Stephanie's help, was sorting through the next wave of action sheets, trying to prioritise the order in which to give them out to the team.

Jim was in full Glaswegian mode. He was a phone shouter; somehow imagining that the louder you spoke, the more people understood. 'D'ya nae ken?' He said.

The man on the other end of the telephone was of Pakistani origin. 'I'm sorry, but I cannot make head nor tail of what it is you are saying.'

'D'ya ken a wen?'

'Ken?'

Jim threw the phone across the desk, and it stretched on the coiled wire before rebounding back towards the base.

Nobby tutted. 'Oi, I'm trying to concentrate here.'

'Bloody foreigners, why employ them if they cannae understand a word you are saying.' Jim huffed.

Steph shrugged out a laugh. 'That's probably what she is thinking, Jim, I can't make out a word of it either.'

'It's a he, not she, and it's a bloody Paki.'

'My tip is to ratchet the Glasgae doon a bit.' She said, laughing.

Jim reeled in the phone by pulling the cord towards him. 'Hello?' Jim wondered if he was still on the line. His tone was tense.

'Hello, sir. I am doing my very best to be helping you, sir.'

Jim tried his best Queen's English. 'Can you get a forensic report on the tennis ball, what make is it, where it is manufactured, where it is distributed to, what shops sell it, that sort of thing.'

'Let me get a pen, sir.'

'Oh, for fuck's sake.'

'Jim, calm down, you know nothing is straight forward.' Steph said.

Jim was grumpier than usual today because he was stuck making office enquiries again while Nobby gave the others more exciting actions. Find a connection for the two murder scenes, what sort of action was that? Where do you start?

'Hello, sir, I am having a pen.'

Jim spoke in broken-down English, pausing over each word. 'Where.'

'Where.' The man repeated.

'Can you.'

'Can you.'

'Buy.'

'Buy.'

'The tennis ball.'

'The tennis ball.'

'Brilliant. Now 'Where.'

'Where.'

Nobby slammed his pen down on the desk. He had finally snapped. 'For Christ's sake!' He reached into his bottom desk drawer and pulled out the office tennis ball and threw it at Jim's head. 'Mail him that fucker!' It bounced off Jim's bonce, onto the table and landed in his coffee cup splashing the dregs onto Jim's notes.

'Oh. Yes, that's really fucking clever, Nobby. Look at this mess now.'

Nobby and Steph were in stitches, laughing at the red-faced Scotsman winding himself up into a frenzy.

'Hello, sir?' The voice on the end of the line crackled.

*

Detective Cynthia Walker was driving, and Charlie Carter sat squirming in the front passenger seat. He had left his sphincter cream at home, and he was suffering big time in the summer heat. He seriously thought about diverting Cynthia to his house to pick it up. Maybe later. They were off to see one of Charlie's top informants.

'Who is it we're going to see? I know you said head for Lenton industrial estate, but who is it precisely?' Cynthia asked.

'If I tell you that I'll have to kill you, I'm afraid.' Charlie said with a glint in his eye.

'Oh.' Cynthia glanced at him.

'Only kidding, young Cynth, we're going to see Cranky Franky.'

'Okay. I'm intrigued.'

'You should be. You're in for a treat. Have you got any informants, Cynthia?' He asked.

'I sort of had one a few months ago.'

'Sort of? What does that mean?' He smiled.

'He just told me something as a favour. I didn't pay him or anything. I wouldn't know where to start, paying informants is all a bit of a mystery to me, I've no idea how that works.'

'There's nothing to it. So what was in it for him then?'

'It was a 'her' actually Delotisse Brown.' Cynthia pulled the indicator lever down and moved into the left-hand lane as she approached the lights.

Charlie laughed. 'Delotisse Brown, she's a barrel of laughs, I do like her.'

'Do you know her then?'

'I've known her since she looked like you, erm, no offence.'

'None taken.' Cynthia looked at Charlie and smiled.

It seemed like everyone in the community knew Charlie, so Cynthia shouldn't have been surprised that he knew Delotisse. There were many hard men, particularly among the black community who would do anything for Charlie. He had done a lot to help them over the years, usually when they had been young, not in a condescending way, but a show of kindness or compassion. It mattered not to Charlie if they were black, brown, pink or yellow, you had to pot all the colours to win a game of snooker, he would say.

'What is the first rule of handling an informant?' Charlie asked her.

'Erm, look after them if you can.'

'Not quite, well sort of I suppose. No, the first rule of having an informant, Cynthia, is don't tell any bugger who it is.'

'Oops.'

'Oops, indeed. Don't worry, Delotisse is safe with me. Bear it in mind though, Cynthia, not everybody is like your Uncle Charlie.'

She giggled.

Charlie liked Cynthia. She was going to become an excellent detective someday. She was keen to learn, and she was mature and down to earth.

'How do you stop anyone else using her then? If no-one knows they are telling you bits?' Cynthia asked.

'You are supposed to register their names at Force Intelligence, give them a codeword.'

'Oh, I get it now.'

'For example, if you had checked with Force Intelligence, you would have seen that Delotisse is a registered informant to me.'

'Oh, crap. You're kidding me?'

'Nope. Don't sweat it, Cynthia, I'm not precious, if she wants to tell you stuff that's fine but you need to keep me in the loop, or anyone else if they are registered to them.'

'Sorry, I wasn't aware.'

'Don't be daft, it's fine, the problem is they can play one off against the other and ideally you want to limit the handlers to two people at most.'

'I've learnt something there, Charlie.'

'Then, my life has not been in vain.' He laughed along with Cynthia.

The car fell silently momentarily with Cynthia inwardly cursing herself about Delotisse.

'So what do you do then, if you want to pay them money?' Cynthia asked. 'This is the problem; really, it is all shrouded in mystery; it seems to me. It's something I need to get into now that I'm on CID, well, trying to be, you know what I mean.'

'The paying bit is straightforward, really, Cynthia. There's no great mystery to it. You have to put in a report through Dave Stark; there is a Pro-forma, you put what info they are offering and what you think that info is worth in cash. Headquarters will disagree, allocate you less than you ask for, and you pick the money up from Force Headquarters. Always ask for more than the informant expects and never promise anything.'

'It sounds a bit dodgy, Charlie, it's a bit open to abuse, isn't it?' She said candidly.

'Maybe, but so long as you have a DI like Dave Stark or a DS like Nobby Clarke to witness the payment, and to sign that it was indeed handed over, you are fine. You're covered.'

'I hate to think what Mole and Davidson get up to.'

'Don't even go there, Cynthia, the mind boggles. You would be surprised at some of the informants. A lot of the gob-shites, supposed hard-men are on the books. They usually get recruited when they are blubbering in the cell, expecting a stiff sentence.'

'Okay. Interesting.'

'Isn't it? People wonder why I'm not afraid of a lot of these bad bastards, in the town, particularly at my age and infirmity...'

'Age and infirmity.' Cynthia repeated as she laughed.

'…but the reason is, they know, that I know, they are a grass. They leave you alone or are overly friendly with you.'

'Wow. I'm amazed.'

'And you thought it was because I was a hard nut, didn't you?'

Cynthia smiled. 'Of course.'

'Their motivation starts when they are facing their first big sentence, usually. Most of them want a letter sending to the judge rather than money. A lot of them can just steal money anyway, know what I mean? So, money isn't always the motivation.'

'I suppose so. How does the Judge's letter work then?'

'If they come up with good information about a case that is more serious than their pending case, and you couldn't have solved it without their info, then you've got a chance. Then you can write the judge a letter asking him to bear their "co-operation" in mind when sentencing the informant. The sentence is reduced accordingly.'

'You're joking.'

'I am not joking.'

'Wow. This is a whole new world.'

'Obviously, the letter is not mentioned in open court.'

'A risky business.'

'It can be Cynthia. Most of the time I don't bother writing to the judge because there is no time, and when I see them when they come out, I make a fuss about what a light sentence they got, even though it was par for the course.'

'Naughty.'

'Yes, but also fuck 'em.'

Cynthia laughed. 'It does go against the grain, investigating a criminal, and then actively helping them get a low sentence for the crime you've nicked them for. It is counter-intuitive.'

'Counter what?'

'Counter-intuitive.'

'I'll take your word for it. It's a bit of a murky world, I know that, but they come in all shapes and sizes. I've got informants I've known all their adult life, and we're kind of friends. They aren't all criminals. One woman had her kitchen done on the strength of the info she gave me about an armed robber.'

Cynthia laughed. 'I like it. How did she know about bloody armed robbers?'

'She was married to one.'

'Ah. I see. Blimey, if only the public knew.'

'Pull down here, Cynthia, just round the back of this warehouse on the left.'

'This looks a bit bleak.'

'Trust me, it is.'

Once out of the car, the two detectives approached the heavy metal door and banged on it. After a few seconds, heavy bolts clanged open, and a large black gentleman in a leather jacket peered around the door.

'We're here to see Franky.'

A female's voice resounded from the back. 'Who is it?'

'Who is it?' The man repeated.

'Tell her it's Charlie Carter.'

'Some old dude called Charlie Carter.' The man shouted.

'Tell him to fuck off.' The mysterious woman was succinct at least. She was playing the game, that is all.

'Fuck off.' The bouncer said, closing the door, but Charlie's foot prevented it. He pushed at the door, and a brief scuffle began which became almost comical when Cynthia reached over Charlie and hit the man-mountain on the head with her writing pad. 'Alright, let him in.' The voice echoed down the corridor, and the guard opened the door wide for the detectives to go through.

The incongruous pair walked along the hardwood floor to the end of the hall and saw a desk with green plants and foliage dotted around and a black woman in her early fifties, sitting in a burgundy studded leather chair. She wore a low cut dress and was dripping with gold.

'It is members only, here, Detective Carter and I would appreciate it if you did not force your way into my establishment. It looks bad for business.'

'Would you prefer I came back with a dozen cops, a sledgehammer and a warrant? I was doing you a favour, Franky.'

'Yadda, yadda, yadda. Please go fuck yourself.' Her nails were long and beautifully manicured. She looked like she was living the high life, but she seemed out of place in such dismal surroundings.

'Do you want him out, Miss Franky.' The heavy asked.

'No. Answer the door; we have a customer.'

There was a bang on the door. Charlie mentally noted the knock, quick, quick, slow; quick, quick, slow.

'It's Tyrone; he's early today.' Franky observed.

'Psychic too.' Cynthia said.

'Who's the chickaboo?' Franky asked.

'Don't be…erm, racist? She's my partner.' It confused Charlie that a black woman might be racist towards another black person. He wasn't quite sure what the rules were.

The heavy door was opened once more, and the bouncer spoke to the visitor. 'Liquor in the front, poker in the rear.'

Charlie shrugged out a laugh. 'Nice strapline.'

When the meat-head returned, Franky instructed him to take a break in the bar.

'Are you sure, Miss Franky?'

'It's just a paperwork check, it's fine. Back in 30 minutes, yeah?'

'Okay. Shout me if you need me.'

He left with a glance at Charlie, who gave Mr Muscles a wide toothy smile. Charlie refused to be intimidated.

When alone, Franky got up from behind the desk and walked around to Charlie. She hugged him warmly, and she kissed him on the lips. 'Lovely to see you, Charlie. How are you keeping?'

'I'm good, thanks Franky, this is Cynthia, she's new to the game.'

Franky extended her slender arms to shake Cynthia's hand. 'Pleased to meet you, sorry for the insult, I have to keep up appearances.'

Cynthia's mouth hung open. She was confused.

'Can we go somewhere out of the way?' Charlie asked.

'No, sorry, Charlie, I have to monitor the CCTV, it's a new thing, you can see people on the screens as they approach, yeah? I'm worried at the moment as I think we are going to get a hit.'

The two detectives leaned over and saw four black and white screens.

'Very impressive, I don't think we have that, do we?'

'I don't think so.' Cynthia grinned.

'I have had to invest in security. The Kelly crew are threatening us again. It's a take-over bid. It's not gonna happen, but I'm expecting a bit of fun from them any time soon.'

'Let's hope it's not in the next ten minutes or so.' Charlie said, only half-joking.

'What are you after, Charlie? It must be something serious if you are coming to see me, yeah.'

'It is Franky. We have a maniac on the loose. Killing, raping.'

'Shit.'

'Yes, it is shit. Grey hoody, grey tracksuit bottoms, about thirty years old. Has an orange bike.'

'Okay. It means nothing at the moment, but I will keep my eyes open.'

'I would doubt anyone like that would come here, would they?' Cynthia asked.

Franky rested her hands on Cynthia's forearm. 'Bless you, darling, yes they might come here, a lot of the gang-bangers use bikes, they earn so much money from drugs and robbery they don't know what to do with it. So they come to give it to me at the Poker table. I'm more going for the Chinese crowd, though, big-time gamblers. Asset light, cash-heavy.'

'It's a growing market, Franky.' Charlie said. 'Give me a call if you see the dude will you?'

'Of course. When are you taking me out for dinner again? I never see you nowadays.'

'It's a busy year; we must have a catch-up, though. Lincoln has a lot of country pubs, out of the way. What do you think?'

'I'm all yours, darling, you know that yeah?'

'Give me some sugar, then Franky.' Charlie said, smiling warmly.

They embraced and bizarrely kissed briefly on the lips again. Cynthia's jaw nearly hit the floor. 'Hey Missy, look after my Charlie, he's not as young as he used to be.'

Cynthia laughed. 'I will don't worry.'

Franky looked Cynthia up and down. She looked pleased and was nodding her head. 'Look at my beautiful black girl being a detective an all. I'm proud of you, girlfriend. Who's black, yo daddy or Mommy?'

'Who…oh, I see, yes, Dad's black, Mum's white. Dad was Windrush, came over in the sixties. Or was it the fifties? It was nearly thirty years ago, I think.'

'That's better. Safer. White dad's don't understand this shit.'

'He's cool. Everyone respects my Dad.'

'These young niggers don't give a fuck about all that, though. Anyway, you know all this. Yeah?'

'Yeah.'

'You be careful, chic, the brethren don't like us niggers talking with the man, yeah?'

'I know. Trust me, I know.'

'If you ever need to talk, just let Charlie know, yeah?'

'Of course, thank you, Franky.'

The boss lady afforded her a hug, and the two made their way out of the iron-clad door. They walked to the CID car in silence. As they got in, Cynthia felt in something of a daze.

'Thank God you parked in the shade, Cynthia.' Charlie said as he wound down the window.

'What just happened?' She said.

Charlie laughed. 'Me and Franky go way back to when she was a foxy young woman.'

'Why all the love?'

'A bit nosey, aren't we?'

'Oh, sorry. I didn't realise it was personal.'

'I'm only kidding. It's not personal. Franky and I have a special bond.'

'She says "yeah" a lot; I know that. I'm intrigued. Want to share, or is it private?'

'It's not private. It's ages ago now, Cynthia.'

'I know, but I'm interested.'

'You don't want me swinging the bloody lantern, Cynthia; you would have been about three years old, I would think.'

'No, go on Charlie, I'm interested in stuff like this.'

'Okay, if you insist. About twenty years ago, Frankie's lad got caught up with some bad dudes, and they were going to take him out.'

'They all say that, though, don't they?'

'No, you misunderstand me, Cynthia. This was a day away from happening. It was on. He would be in the boot of a car and never seen again. These guys don't mess around. 'Yardies' from Jamaica had a hand in it. Proper job.'

'Wow. How come you were involved?'

'I had dealt with Franky for shoplifting a year or so before, and we got on well. She had been stealing food, and she was desperate, anyway I sorted that out for her. So she came to me to see if I could help out. She was terrified, bless her.'

'You would be, wouldn't you? How could you help with that, though?'

'That's what I thought. Anyway, I had a bit of a think about it, and I arranged to have a sit down with Mr Bastard. In a pub, it was a bit hairy, being the only white guy in there.'

'Now you know what it feels like.' She smiled.

'Sure, but this was a hostile environment, Cynthia, all the punters had been initiated into this dudes gang. They owned the place.'

'Who is it? Who was Mr Big? I might know him.'

'I'm not going to say, Cynthia, for your protection and others. No disrespect. I've met this guy a couple of times since and he would not appreciate word going around that we converse in friendly terms, a bit like how Franky was with us.'

'I hope he didn't kiss you.'

Charlie laughed. 'Not quite. Franky's always been like that; there is nothing in it.'

'I believe you.' However, she gave Charlie a quizzical look. 'What did you say to the guy? Mr Bastard as you call him.'

'I was very matter-of-fact, explained a few realities to him.'

'Such as?'

'That I knew he had put a contract out on the boy and that it needed pulling back. And if he didn't, I would make his life fucking hell. I would nick him, his mother and father, his wife, his mistress, and introduce them to each other. I had to make him think it wasn't worth the aggro just because he perceived this kid had disrespected him, that's all. I was careful to explain that it was not a threat. It wasn't, to be honest. I was explaining to him exactly what would happen, and what he didn't expect would be coming his way.'

'I take it, it worked.'

'Thank Christ, it did. In fact, it was Mr Bastard who first set Franky up in business. Hence me and Franky have a bit of a bond. It's lasted all these years.'

'Wow. Charlie, you amaze me sometimes.'

'I amazed myself that night, trust me, it wasn't pleasant. I wore two pairs of underpants, especially.'

Cynthia laughed. 'I bet Mrs Carter worries herself to death, doesn't she?'

'No, she's in blissful ignorance. I don't tell her anything about all this. It's not fair on her, is it? I've got a feeling she thinks I'm a lollypop man helping the kids across zebra crossings.' He laughed.

Cynthia turned on the ignition. 'You're so nice, Charlie.'

'Nice? Me? I thought you were a good judge of character. Come on; I'm getting peckish, swing past the greasy spoon on the way back to the nick, will you? I fancy a quick brekky.'

Cynthia shook her head as she put the gear stick in reverse, and they backed out of the car park.

'You've lived, Charlie. I'll give you that you've lived.' She said.

'So they say. I just hope our killer rocks up at Franky's. If he does, he's toast. I think I'll have toast instead of fried bread today, thinking about it. Be a good boy.'

'I don't know where you put it all, Charlie.'

'I will give you a clue; it goes in my big fat tummy.' He grinned.

*

The door chime heralded DC's Ashley Stevens and Steve Aston as they walked into Fat Doris's chip shop. It wasn't called Fat Doris's, but that was how all the locals referred to it. It was 'Butler's Hill Fish n' Chips,' according to the fading blue paint above the door which had been weathered over the years. Thankfully it was empty when the boys went in.

'Do you want fish?' The teenager asked. 'It'll be five minutes.'

Ashley smiled. 'No, thanks.' He produced his warrant card and showed it to the lad with the wire mesh scoop, as he proceeded to swirl it around the boiling fat. 'We're from the CID. Is Doris in the back?'

'Who's after me?' A voice asked, before showing her chubby, reddened face around the door frame.

'Hi Doris, we're from the CID, can we have a word, please?'

'In here, do you mean? In the back?'

'If you don't mind.'

'No, of course not, let them in Gary. I haven't got long though, I've got five bags of spuds to put through the peeler, it'll be rush hour in twenty minutes, and that goes on for two hours at least.'

'A two hour rush hour? How does that work, Doris?' Ashley grinned.

'You know what I mean.' She laughed.

The two detectives stood on the small step and entered the mysterious back shop of the local chippy. It was full of odds and sods; cardboard boxes both full and empty, sheets of paper for wrapping, pickled onion jars, hundreds of small packets of tartare sauce and tomato sauce, cans of cheap pop, small boxes of hundreds of small wooden forks, a large tub of salt; all of the paraphernalia required to feed the starving hordes of Hucknall. There was also a mop and bucket, which on Ashley's closer inspection, looked like the water needed changing. A couple of uncooked chips floated on the top of the murky contents. The focal point for Doris was a machine that continued to rattle away as she stood observing it. The device was a cross between a small top-fill washing machine and a candyfloss maker. Doris was tipping some spuds out of a sack into the top. It rumbled around noisily, and the abrasive metal sides stripped the potatoes of their skins as they whirled around.

Doris was in her late forties, rosy-cheeked, very overweight and had a white gown-cum-dress and apron, made of thick cotton. The sleeves were rolled up, displaying swollen forearms with lots of scars festooning them, caused by burns over the years. 'You don't mind me working as we talk, do you?'

'No, not at all crack on, Doris.' Ashley said.

'How can I help you, boys?'

Ashley took the lead. 'We are investigating a couple of murders; you may have seen them on the news lately.'

'Oh, I have. Isn't it terrible? He wants bloody castrating. Dirty bastard, and that's swearing.'

'We're doing the rounds, visiting the main focal points in the community to put the word out, and to see if our suspect has visited them.'

'Right. Who is he then? Do you know his name? Does he live around here?'

'Strange, we were going to ask you that.' Ashley grinned. 'We think he's probably fairly local, Doris, but we can't say for certain yet. We don't have a name for him, but there are a couple of distinctive things about him. Things that might help you pick him out if you saw him.'

Doris took her hand off the button, and the barrel stopped spinning. As it ground to a halt, she emptied the now skinned potatoes into a large plastic tub which she carried over to a similar looking machine, somewhat inconveniently placed right across the room from the peeler. Steve and Ashley dutifully followed her and watched as she emptied the tub into the top and were moderately impressed when the potatoes gave birth to chips, zooming out an orifice at the bottom into another container at a vast rate of knots.

'Wouldn't you be better having that next to the peeler, Doris?' Ashley asked.

'Probably, duck, but it was like this when we took the shop over.'

Steve stroked his chin. 'Yeah, but…oh it doesn't matter.'

'What does he look like, this fella? What do I need to look out for?' Doris asked.

'He's about 30-ish, average height and build, but he wears a grey hoody with white drawstrings, and he has an orange bicycle, which he has probably spray-painted himself.'

'They don't bring their bikes in here, lovey.'

Ashley laughed. 'No, I know that, but I bet they lean them against the big window don't they?'

'True enough, they do.'

'I thought so. I've seen customers do it regularly when I've driven past.'

'It does ring a bit of a bell, but we get so many folks in here, they all merge into one. I know the locals, the regulars, and I can tell you their orders, but he certainly isn't one of those. I can keep a lookout, though. I'll tell the others.'

'That would be great.'

'Dirty little bleeder, he is. When you get him, you want to bring him here and feed his dangly bits into this chipper.'

Ashley winced as he laughed. 'Of course, we will.'

'What do you want us to do if we see him then?' Doris asked.

'That's a good question. I think you should try and delay the order and give the police a call and explain what the issue is.' Ashley said.

'I ain't got time to do that, ducky, anyway he will know it's us what's rung.'

'I can only ask. Would you prefer to give me a ring, personally?'

'Eh, cheeky!' She nudged him and let out a cackle.

Ashley laughed, as did Steve and the two detectives exchanged glances. 'I meant to speak through my extension, Doris.'

She cackled again. 'Oh, that's worse!'

'For God's sake, Doris, behave, will you?'

'I'm sorry, you've got to have a giggle ain't ya? Anyway, what good would that do, calling you, he'll be long gone, that's if I can get hold of you.'

'What I was going to say is to keep any money he gives you and put it to one side. Slip it into an envelope. Then give me a call.'

'Keep his money. Why?'

'We can get the note fingerprinted.'

'Ah, got you. Alright, my duck. That's clever. We can do that.'

'That's great, Doris, thank you very much.'

'Did you want anything to eat, lads?'

'Mmm. I haven't had a bag of chips for ages.' Steve said.

'What about a Spam fritter, Steve?'

'It's alright he's taking the Mickey, I don't eat meat.' Steve directed the comment to Doris.

She seemed taken aback. 'Don't eat meat? How come. Have you got something wrong with you? Are you allergic, then?' Doris asked with all sincerity.

'No, I'm a vegan.'

'A what? A virgin?'

Ashley laughed. 'That as well.'

Steve ignored the comment. 'A vegan. Trying to be, more vegetarian I suppose most of the time. We don't eat anything that comes from animals.'

'Eh? Why? I don't get it.'

'We don't like harming animals.'

Ashley added, 'He eats rabbit food, vegetables and salads, all that sort of thing.'

'If you like animals so much, how come you're nicking all their food. Ooh.' She threw her head back and burst into uproarious laughter, which Ashley did too. He was laughing more at Doris than the joke. Steve coloured up.

'Very funny. Go on then; I'll have a chip and pea mix if I can.' Steve said.

'I'll have the same, please, Doris.' Ashley said.

'Do you want batter bits?'

'Oh, yes please.' Ash said, rubbing his hands together.

'Not for me, thanks.' Steve said.

Suddenly the loudest shout came from her chubby face. *'Gary! Two mixes, one with batter bits and one without - on the house.'*

She heard him grunt a reply and the tapping of the metal mesh scoop as he bounced off the residue oil.

'I'm ever so sorry, but I'm going to have to kick you out lads. It's peak time. Sorry to be rude.'

'No, that's fine, Doris. We've done anyway. Thanks for your help.'

'Anytime you're passing, call in. Always on the house for the boys in blue, here.'

'Great, thanks. I might just take you up on that.' Ashley smiled.

The two detectives strolled out of the back shop, through the service side of the counter and through the now open drop-down shelf, to the customer side. Gary lowered the shelf behind them and handed them a tray each with the steaming hot food inside. He pressed a wooden fork into the pea summit. Both detectives were now salivating and gave their thanks as they stepped outside pausing only to add salt and vinegar.

Nothing much was said as they were stuffing their faces while sauntering along the pavement towards the small car park where Steve had left the CID car.

'This is heaven.' Steve said.

'I shall be going there again.' Ashley said as he chewed.

Steve was oblivious to the small chunk of cigarette ash that landed on his head.

*

Dave Stark stared out of the window of his office on the first floor of Nottingham Police Station, as he sat at his desk. It was just blue sky, with an occasional wisp of cloud seeking company - Stark was seeking inspiration. The windows were open to try to get some air in the room, but it seemed to make little difference. It was baking. As usual, his door was wide open. He only closed it for private or confidential confabulations.

He had begun a list in his jotter of things that might make a clicking noise. It was not as easy as he had thought it might be.

Toy gun

Bicycle wheel

Gears on a bike

Broken bicycle bell

Bike spoke clicker

Camera

He was struggling to concentrate and became distracted by a Robin that had landed on his window frame outside. He wondered if it might hop into the office. Stark glimpsed Nobby Clarke walking past.

'Hey, Nobby.' He said in a whispered tone.

The DS stopped just past Stark's doorway and backed up before walking in. 'Yes, boss.'

'Look out there at that Robin.'

'Robin? We don't get them in summer, do we?'

'That's what I thought, but it's there look.'

'Oh, Christ, yes.' Nobby walked over towards the window, and the Robin flew away.

'Well done, Nobby.'

'What have I done now?'

'Your bloody great bulk walking towards it will have caused a vibration.'

'I was only trying to get a closer look. Any joy on the list? Have you started yet?'

'That's what I'm doing now. Have a seat. You might be able to help.' Nobby duly obliged.

'Why are you still whispering?' Nobby asked.

'I don't know.' Stark whispered, he continued, this time with a normal tone of voice, 'I've had a brain freeze thinking what might cause a clicking sound, like the one Paul Masters and young Toby heard.'

'There will be loads.'

'Go on then, like what?'

'Erm, there would be…erm…actually. I suppose it depends on the type of click.'

'Bloody hell, Nobby don't get started on all that again. A click is a click.'

'I'm not sure it is, you know.'

'Nobby forget all that, let's say it is any type of click in the world, choose from the vast pallet on offer. Give me anything that remotely sounds like a bloody click.'

'Sixty Six?'

'Haha. It's trickier than I thought.'

'Erm. Let's see; I take your point. It's not that easy, is it?'

'Do you want a cuppa, boss? It might help the old brain start whirring.'

'I doubt that very much. But, go on then, I'll have one with you.'

Nobby left, and Stark returned to his list.

A gun.

A pen.

A light switch.

A flick knife.

In the corner of his eye, Stark noticed the Robin had returned to the window sill.

Nobby returned with two steaming mugs of tea, and the Robin flew away yet again. Stark shook his head.

'I'm on a roll here, Nobby.'

'Great, what have you got?' He placed the mugs on Starks desk. 'Do you want a ciggy?'

'Go on then; I'll join you, I'm smoking too many cigars, they're giving me a sore throat.' Nobby offered the pack to Stark, and the DS lit the cigarette for him with his lighter which sent Stark a bit boss-eyed as he tried to line the end with the flame. Nobby returned to his chair.

'I've got, a toy gun, bike wheel, bike gears, spoke clicker, broken bicycle bell, a camera, a gun…'

'Jesus, boss, that is the bottom of the barrel.'

'A pen, a flick knife.'

'That's better. Possible, but is it loud enough to be heard through a window?'

'Not sure. Sound travels at night, I guess.'

Nobby took a sip of his tea. 'What else?'

'A light switch. That's a possibility, isn't it?'

'It's a good one, but outside?'

Stark drew on his cigarette and looked at the end. There was no smoke emanating from it. 'I'm not sure I'm fully in here, Nobby.'

Nobby returned to re-light the cigarette.

'Bloody hell. What an idiot I am. It's just come to me.' Stark said.

'What is it, boss? You've got that look on your face again. You're having one of those moments of inspiration, aren't you?'

'I bloody am, Nobby, get your coat.'

'I've just made a cuppa.'

'Never mind the cuppa. We need to go back to Sandra's bungalow. I've had a thought.'

10

'To have a "light-bulb moment", the power has to be on.'

Jennifer L. Feuerstein

Stark walked in front of Nobby over the uneven ground around Sandra Teversall's bungalow.

'Are we going inside, boss?' Nobby asked, still unsure of the nature of their business at the deserted bungalow.

'No need.'

'Where are we headed?'

'Outside the point of entry, and exit; the kitchen window.'

Stark paused at the window and had a look around at the surroundings. What would be the best way to walk down the drive, starting from this position? He pondered to himself.

'If you were going to commit a murder in the dead of night, Nobby, and you had a bike, would you bring it right up to the house, if you had a choice to leave it out of the way?'

'Mmm, not sure. They're a bit noisy, and a bit clunky aren't they?'

'I think so. I reckon there is a big difference between riding around a house and doing the actual murder, don't you?'

'Sure. What is it you are getting at?'

'Just bear with me. If you were going to sneak up to the house without a bike, you would choose to leave it well out of the way, on the drive, wouldn't you? Out of sight from the road, mind.'

'That's the only way in unless you went down to Wighay Farm, but that is miles down the wrong way and pitch black. I can't see that as the best option.' Nobby offered.

'Unless the bike was up here from the get-go and because you know you are going to kill Sandra what does it matter if there is noise after she is dead?'

'Aunty Dot left around 6 pm when the killer was still hanging around, apparently casing the joint. Assuming Sandra went to bed at 10 pm, which is pretty early, and say he broke in at midnight or even one o'clock, that is a 6 or 7-hour wait. Surely he would piss off and come back later?' Nobby suggested.

'In which case, he would more likely leave his bike on the drive to quieten his approach in the stillness of the early hours. And we know Sandra was in bed when she was attacked, so it was some hours later that he paid a visit.'

'What is this all about, boss?'

'Taking the assumption that he would not bring his bike up and wanted to use stealth so as not to alert the occupants, the best place to leave the bike would be on the drive. It just would be.' Stark seemed to be trying to convince himself of the premise.

'Yes, it would have to be some way down in case she had the windows open and she heard the approach.' Nobby looked puzzled. What was Stark getting at? He scratched his head and lit a cigarette. He didn't offer

Stark another one; it would be an expensive business at nearly £1.50 a packet.

'Let's have a walk, Nobby.' Stark said.

'Where are we going now?'

Stark didn't answer but led the way. He walked at a moderate to fast pace and headed around the house to the drive, which was more of a dirt-track road, 300 yards long. Nobby drew level and started to increase the pace. 'Hang on a bit, not too fast.' Stark said. 'We'll be running at this rate.'

'Why? What are we doing?' He chuffed on his cigarette.

'It is a little experiment, just humour me.'

'If I'd known we were going walkabout I would have locked the car up.'

'It'll be fine; no-one would want to nick that pile of bloody junk. You still have to use a cranking handle to start it, don't you?'

Nobby laughed. 'Just about.'

'Be fair though, Nobby, it usually starts on the third turn of the key.'

'Sometimes, on the second.'

'There you go then, bloody luxury.'

'What are we doing, back-tracking his route in?'

'Sort of, but doing it this way may give us more of a chance.'

'A chance of what exactly?'

Stark didn't reply, and they continued their meandering.

'Christ it's hot.' Nobby said and paused to stub his cigarette out.

'Okay, let's stop here.'

'Why here exactly?'

'Because this is the place where you finished your cigarette.'

'Erm. Okay.'

'Get your lighter out.'

Nobby did just that.

'Give it a go.' Stark said.

It clicked into life.

'And again, Nobby.'

He did it again.

'Keep doing it.'

Nobby complied. 'Hang on boss, I don't want to knacker my lighter up.'

'Anything?'

Nobby stopped clicking. 'Shit. The clicking noise. Young Toby said he heard a clicking noise, and the bloke had a funny voice, whatever that means.'

'Yep. We are bloody idiots. It was when you gave me a light in the office that it dawned on me, belatedly I admit.'

'That's going to be the clicking noise, isn't it? Most likely.'

'I think it probably is. You are an experienced killer. You are aware that you leave clues at the scene. So you are wary all afternoon and collect any of your nub-ends from around the scene. Later, in the dead of night, and the middle of nowhere, you've just done a murder and the first thing you want as you get outside…'

'Is a fag.' Nobby said.

'A fag. It sounds like his lighter is a bit dodgy or he needs a fill-up.'

'Okay, fine, but why are we here?'

'Because this is how far we got with you smoking a cigarette to the end. Is our killer going to worry about his cigarette end after he is so far down the drive? I'm not convinced he would. Let's start looking—any sort of cigarette butt. Say ten yards either side of where we have stopped.

The two scoured the ground for a minute or so. 'I'm not getting anything.' Nobby grunted.

'Keep looking.'

'Hang on. Over here boss, in the hedge.'

Stark walked over and looked at the nub end. 'It needs preserving for fingerprints.'

Nobby moved his face closer to it.

'What type is it?'

'That's weird.'

'What?'

'The brand, near the filter.'

'What about it?'

'I've never heard of it.'

'What does it say?'

'Lucky Strike, what the fuck is that?' Nobby asked.

'Lucky Strike? They're American.' Stark said.

The two detectives blurted out in unison. 'He spoke with a funny voice!'

'He's a yank.' Stark said.

*

Stark and Nobby had returned to the office. It was a hive of activity with detectives researching their tasks ahead of carrying them out. They all sat in close proximity apart from Steve Aston who had beaten Cynthia to the kettle to make the boss and Sarge a cup of tea. Stark had been explaining to Jim McIntyre the issue around the cigarette stub they had found, and how it might be of interest to the inquiry and the conversation had broadened out to the wider team.

'This might sound a silly question, sir,' Cynthia said, 'but we don't *know* that this is the offender's cigarette butt do we?'

'No, of course not, we're making a minestrone.'

'Eh?'

'We have developed a hypothesis using the clicking sound that has been described by Paul Masters and young Toby. We have certain ingredients; the distance walked with a lit cigarette, and a sprinkling of knowledge that, according to Toby, the offender "talks funny", plus the cigarette butt is an American brand which brings it to the boil.'

'He thinks he's bloody Fanny Craddock.' Jim said, laughing.

Stark smiled. 'We are piecing this information together to try to make it work in our favour. It is active thinking, critical thinking if you like.'

Jim looked heavenwards.

'I think it is brilliant, sir.' Cynthia said.

'I don't know about brilliant, it is conjecture if anything, but oak trees from acorns grow.'

'How does this become anything, though? How will it play out?' Cynthia asked.

'Jim will take the nub end to the lab for forensics to examine. They will unravel it and make it a small flat piece of paper, and they will check it for fingerprints, and if he is known, we will be paying him a visit.'

'But he wore gloves, according to SOCO.'

Stark smiled. 'He did, but…'

Nobby interrupted. 'Have you ever tried smoking a cigarette with gloves on?'

'No, I guess it would be difficult to hold.'

'Exactly, and also, Cynthia, remember that the mind-set for the criminal is that the further away from the scene they are, the more lax they become with their habits. That is why when you have a blank scene, you have to try to widen it out a bit. Put yourself in the offender's frame of mind. Put yourself in his shoes and use the highest likelihood as a scenario, if you can.'

'That needs experience, I suppose.' Cynthia said.

Stark shrugged. 'Not necessarily. Think of it as a salute.'

'Eh?'

Stark backed his observations up by saluting. 'Long way up, short way down. Tentative and around the houses before the crime, shortest way out of there afterwards.'

'Ah, I get it.' She smiled. 'I was just trying to understand where we go with it, that's all. I still think it's brilliant.'

She rested her chin on her hand as she listened to Stark, her eyes wide, and her long eyelashes flapping. She had more of a crush on him every day.

Steph mocked her. 'Ooh, sir, I think you're brilliant. Can I get you anything, sir? Yes sir, no sir, three bags full, sir.'

They all laughed.

'Bog off, Steph. Leave me alone. I wanted to know where it will lead, that's all.' Cynthia played along. She wanted Stark to know how she felt in any case if the truth were told.

Stark ignored Steph's gibe. 'Having said all of that. Where will it lead? Possibly nowhere, possibly somewhere. There are some big assumptions here. But they are valid ones. Ones not to be ignored; you have to play the percentages. Always play the percentages where life and death are concerned, Cynthia.'

Jim interrupted. 'If we've finished having the basic lesson in being a detective, can we finish off?'

Cynthia looked chastened.

Stark wasn't having it. 'Hang on, Jim, Cynthia is right to ask questions; it is the sign of a good detective. Maybe you could learn from her?'

Jim sneered. 'I doubt it. It's fucking basics, man, Christ.'

'Only it is not basics, is it? Because if it were, I would be batting off all of your suggestions to go and do what Nobby and I have just done. Yet, funnily enough, I don't remember you mentioning this is what we should be doing, Jim?'

'You know what I mean.' Jim said.

'Not really,' Stark winked at Cynthia, but was terse in his response to Jim, 'do as Sergeant Clarke asks and take the nub end over to headquarters. I want it done straight away. Any problems come back to me. Is that basic enough for you?'

'Jeez, It's getting like you can't say anything nowadays.'

Cynthia felt chills and tried to hide the shiver that ran down her spine as Stark protected her from Jim's barbs. DC McIntyre gathered his gear together, along with the exhibit, and slunk out of the office.

'What are you on with, Ash?' Stark asked.

'Just thinking about how and why the killer has chosen these particular victims.'

'I've asked Jim to do a bit of work on that. Let'snot duplicate work. Anything come up?'

'Not anything solid, but I was thinking about the open window aspect. Is the killer picking houses with open windows?'

'Okay, and what are you doing?'

'I'm just looking at M.O's in the locale where there was an open window burglary, and someone was disturbed, or there is any forensic evidence found.'

'Sounds good. Have you found anything of note?'

'I've just seen this one; I will look at it later; man disturbed trying to break in through an open kitchen window on Portland Road. It was a few weeks ago, but it might be worth checking out.'

Charlie piped up. 'I bet there will be a few of them, Ash. It's a bit hit and miss, mate.'

'Yes, but if there is forensic evidence, it might throw something up.' Ashley insisted.

Charlie shrugged. 'If we had some bacon, we could have bacon and eggs; if we had any eggs.'

'What?'

Nobby laughed.

Stark didn't. 'Don't leave it, Ash. We need more dynamism in this bloody office. Some positive thinking. Looking at how we *can* do something, not trying to find ways why we can't.'

'Bearing that in mind, Charlie, do you mind looking at this action, while I carry on researching?' Ashley read out the details. '86 Portland Road, Charlie, someone called Kim Shaw.' Ashley gave him a piece of paper with the details on it.

'Off you go, Charlie, chop-chop.' Stark said.

'Yes, sure, boss. I was only…'

'I know, just crack on will you?' Stark seemed more testy than usual.

'Get your coat, Cynthia, we're on the road again, kiddo.' Charlie said.

'Great. Only I'll leave the coat if you don't mind, it's thirty degrees outside.'

Cynthia smiled as she squeezed past Stark, resting her hand on his shoulder as she did.

Charlie laughed. 'It's just a turn of phrase.' He stood up. 'Ouch, ya bugger!' His piles had not improved.

*

Stark decided he would count it as his lunch break, but if he didn't do it now, he never would. He arrived at the large house in only fifteen minutes, and before he knew it, he was sitting opposite the therapist for the second time. Linda was quiet, looking at him, smiling. She hadn't said much since he said 'this isn't working.'

Eventually, she spoke. 'Explain to me what happened.'

Stark shifted in his seat and a dull ache re-surfaced in his stomach. 'It's annoying because it makes no sense to me why I would feel like this, it's craziness.'

'I know it seems that way. You've mentioned that to me, David, so just tell me what happened exactly.'

'I was doing a press conference, I mean they aren't always particularly comfortable to do, granted, but within a couple of minutes, I was bathed in sweat, and I mean drenched. It was awful. The worrying thing was that my boss noticed, I'm sure of it.'

'Did you try the tapping?'

Stark shrugged out a laugh. 'I was tapping more than a morse code telegrapher on D Day – it made no difference I'm afraid.'

Linda laughed. 'I love your turn of phrase. Okay. Why do you think it didn't work?'

'I was hoping you were going to tell me, Linda.'

'We will get to that, this is quite normal, David, but I just want your take on it.'

'I think the problem is, I am aware that all eyes are on me, and at the same time I am trying to formulate answers while thinking about what I can and cannot divulge. So the tapping and breathing are behind all of this, I never get there. They are ancillary to it. It is like patting your head with one hand and rubbing your tummy with the other at the same time. Do you understand what I mean?'

'Of course I do.'

'The tapping and focus are not there; the real focus is on me dealing with the situation. Does that make sense?'

'Yes, it does.'

'If I could sit in a quiet room before or after then I can see some benefit in it because there would be no distractions. I just don't have the luxury of being able to do that, not always anyway. It isn't that sort of an environment.'

'Alright, I get it. We need to think about how to combat it, don't we?'

'Yes, please, that would be good.'

'You know you can go to your GP and get some medication that will help if it is endangering your work. What we do here will work too, and without getting addicted to happy pills, but it can take longer. It isn't an overnight thing, David.'

Stark grimaced, 'It is tempting to go on the pills, to be honest, particularly with my boss letting me know he has clocked it, but I don't want to see my GP, they record everything and anyway pills are a last resort, as far as I can see. I'm not a quitter lets give it a chance.'

Linda smiled encouragingly and then sipped at a glass of orange juice. She stood up and walked to the window, which gave a beautiful view of her back garden and the fields beyond.

'I love this place.' Linda said.

'I bet you do. It is very nice.'

'Five years before I bought the house, I was a dysfunctional mess. I had been working in the local council admin offices for several years, and I was desperately unhappy. I was effectively being bullied, abused and was generally everybody's punch bag. I was not "in" with the in-crowd, shall we say. I have a willing nature, and of course, they love to flog a willing horse until it is time for the knackers yard. I wasn't sleeping; I was tormented and desperately unhappy, heading for a nervous breakdown I would say. Then one day I stood up…' She laughed. '…and I just said "Fuck you, fuck you, oh, and particularly fuck you, you sad bastards," and I walked out of the office.'

Stark laughed too. 'I like it.'

'It is spoken of to this day apparently.' Linda giggled. 'I don't know where it came from; I was so timid in those days.'

'Perhaps that's what I need to do. Will it work at the next press conference do you think?'

'Mmm, it is probably better if you don't.'

'Oh, alright, then.' He smiled.

'That's how I got into all of this. A friend recommended someone, and I took the counselling. I was the patient, yet after a while, my outlook improved. I blossomed and decided to get qualified myself. It turned my whole life around—best thing I ever did. I still see some of the sad, grey, people who I worked with, shuffling into the council offices, zombie-like. Thank God I got out when I did.'

Stark glanced at his watch. 'Sounds like it was meant to be, Linda.'

'Have you heard of the 5,4,3,2,1 method, David?'

'You will be unsurprised to know I have not heard of the 5,4,3,2,1 method.'

'It's just another tool.'

'Okay.

'The first step is to look around at your surroundings and identify five things you can see at the moment. Next, identify four things you can hear, three things you can feel, which could be your feet in your shoes, a wedding ring, or something like that.'

'Okay.'

'Then two things you can smell and one thing you can taste, which could just be your tongue or a sweet, or a drink.'

'Let me write this down, or I will get it arse-about-face.' Stark muttered to himself as he wrote down.

5 see.

4 hear.

3 feel.

2 *smell.*

1 *taste.*

As he finished, he looked up from his pad. 'What is that all about then, Linda?'

She walked back to her chair and sat down. 'It will help you to stay in the moment and not get carried away into catastrophic thinking.'

'Catastrophic thinking. I like it. We always have to anticipate the worst-case scenario, so it comes as second nature to us, I suppose.'

'*That* is the worst-case scenario, constant negative thinking, that many of us do. We go straight to the most horrendous consequence there could be, and it dominates our horizon. Of course, it never happens. What's yours, David? Fainting or vomiting?'

'Fainting, I guess, but hang on how did you know that?'

'It is a regular theme, and we need to find out why. What has triggered this? Is it something you have experienced or seen perhaps? My tip is that when you prepare for these events that trouble you, stop yourself from imagining and living through some imaginary scenario that in all probability will never happen.'

'Easier said than done, Linda. How do I do that?'

'The hardest bit is to catch yourself doing it. If you can master that, just shout it out in your head 'CATASTROPHIC THINKING.' Then use the techniques I've said 5,4,3,2,1. It is worth a go to bring you back into what is real, not imagined. It will get you back into the moment. Away from the "what ifs".'

Stark glanced at his watch again. 'I'm so sorry, but I have got to go, Linda.'

'I understand. I'm glad you came to sort this out, David.'

'Am I a fruitloop?'

She laughed. 'We try to avoid those sort of terms. What do you mean exactly?'

'I don't know, am I mentally challenged or whatever the new buzz word is?'

'You have a mental health disorder called anxiety.'

He looked to the floor. He seemed deflated. 'Oh.'

'But, don't forget, Mr Ego that, probably eighty per cent of us have some sort of mental health issue to a greater or lesser extent. It's just that people don't think to get themselves checked out. They will have a medical check-up, but they don't check up on what is between their ears.'

'Eighty per cent?'

'I would say so.' She smiled reassuringly. 'Including me. If you think about it, it is far more normal to acknowledge this and work with it than not. Most people are oblivious to their levels; they are moody or mardy or sensitive. These hide other issues. It is the extent of the other issues that matter, I suppose, and how it affects people's quality of life.'

He seemed more elevated after receiving this news. 'And those around us, of course.'

'Of course.'

'I'm afraid I have to go, but thanks again, Linda.'

'No problem. We need to talk some stuff through with you to get to the bottom of it.'

'It's difficult at the moment. I feel guilty stealing half an hour with you now.'

Linda stood as Stark prepared to leave, and they meandered towards the door. 'I understand, David, but you should put this as a priority. What else is more important for *you* at this precise moment? Your mind is telling you through your body and your responses to situations, that things need sorting out.'

'I know. I will. It just might be a bit erratic, that's all.'

'Hug?'

'Eh?'

She opened her arms wide. 'Come on give me a hug.'

'I don't do hugs.' Stark blurted out.

'You do now. Come on.'

They embraced, and Stark felt better because of it. He was conscious of how hard her breasts felt; he knew that.

'Wow, you're firm.' Linda said. She ran her hands down his arms. 'You must work out.'

Stark grinned. 'I used to.'

'Impressive.' They released their embrace. 'Try the techniques out, even when nothing is happening, yes?'

'Will do.'

As the door closed behind him, Linda returned to the window and looked out at the fields.

*

Janet Thraves used tweezers to slowly dismantle the cigarette butt with the manual dexterity of a heart surgeon. She had done it many times. It was quite dry and brittle, and this was of concern as it was necessary to use the chemical ninhydrin on the cigarette filter paper, and there was a danger it could fragment. The process entailed the paper being soaked in the purple ninhydrin solution and photographic paper used to imprint the chemically enhanced sweat particles forming the fingerprint. The residual print can then be examined much like any other fingerprint taken from dusting with aluminium powder which is the recognised process.

All that is required is an image of a fingerprint sufficient to identify so many loops and whorls to compare with records and obtain a name and then to directly correspond with the person's fingerprints once they were in custody. It was a two-part quest, to identify a person whose fingerprints they were, and then to connect that person with a crime scene or object of interest to obtain evidence for a court.

The paper had been separated from the filter, and its brown speckled appearance looked totally clean until it was flattened and put through the chemical process giving it the purple tint. The fingerprint was clear. After checking through the fingerprint records, Janet rang DC Jim McIntyre and told him she had good and bad news.

'What d'ya mean by that?' Jim said.

'The good news is that we have managed to garner a fingerprint which is sufficient to identify an offender.'

'Brilliant!'

'Yes, isn't it? The snag is...'

'There's always a bloody snag.'

'There is, and this one is that we have no trace of this person on file.'

'No trace? A bloody experienced burglar and serial killer and he's never been nicked?'

'Not in this country he hasn't, could he be foreign, do you think?'

'Possibly American.'

'They do sell Lucky Strike cigarettes in this country, Jim. I wouldn't say he was American just by the brand.'

'No, of course, he might not be, but we have other reasons to think he could be.'

'Okay well, it looks like Interpol need to be notified in that case, he may be a visitor to the country. I don't know; it's not for me to say, I suppose. I'm not privy to all the information.'

'Customs might be able to help as well, perhaps?'

'Perhaps, Jim, but that is more your bag than mine. I'm just the lab rat.'

'Overall it is good news Janet, and I owe you one for doing it so quickly, wish me luck.'

'Good luck, Jim.'

As Jim put the phone down, he looked at the clock on the wall. He was hoping to get an early pint in the bar, and he could see that getting away from him. He opened his little rollerdex and found the general phone number for Interpol.

'Got to start somewhere.'

'Sorry, Jim?' Nobby asked.

'Och, it's okay I'm talking to mysel'.'

It took a while to get through, but a man with a French accent eventually answered the phone. 'Metropolitan Police Interpol.' That sounded weird for a start. Jim wanted to give the impression he knew what he was doing, but Interpol requests were few and far between. He ended up writing down a list of 'must-haves,' for the formal request for a fingerprint to be compared in multiple countries. It was quite a long list.

Stark walked into the main CID office. There was just Nobby and Jim McIntyre. Stark could hear Jim talking exasperatedly down the phone, 'Yes, I will…triplicate…I know, that's why I need to know from you so that the application isn't refused, why dy'ae think I'm ringing you, man?

Allocation number, yes. Twenty-four hours, why so long? Yes. No. Of course. If I can. I know. Okay, yes, bye.' Jim slammed the phone down.

'Alright, Jim?' Stark perched his backside on the corner of an empty desk.

'Alright, boss. It's bloody Interpol; they want everything in triplicate, copies of the blown-up image of the print, a full report on the case, the urgency level, the importance of the task, blah blah blah.'

Stark nodded. 'I know it is a nightmare, have I missed something? Interpol?'

'There's a print on the cigarette-end we sent in. I've only just found oot.'

'Excellent. So not known in the UK, I assume?'

'No trace here.'

'I'm telling you he's going to be a yank.' Stark said, energised by the news.

'My concern is that Interpol will refuse the task, to be honest, boss.' Jim said.

'Why?'

'Because the cigarette end was found in a bush three hundred yards from the scene of the murder. There is nothing to connect it to the murderer now is there. Not really.'

Stark wiped his hand over his mouth and chin and grimaced. 'I take your point. That is the reason for the request. It's one of those where you have to tell them who has done it so they can search their records to see who has bloody done it.'

Jim laughed. 'You're right there, gaffer.'

'I don't think we need to be too explicit with the distances though, do we?'

'Sir?'

'Well, you have to use a bit of ringcraft now and then, don't you? "The hedge of the property attacked" is a fair description of where it was found, is it not?'

'I suppose you could say that.'

'Alright, I will leave it with you, Jim, but let me see it before you fax it over, will you?'

'Aye, it's going to take a while.'

'I know, use the briefing log for the details. Steer it to the USA as the priority, but include Canada and Europe.'

'I will don't worry. By the time I get all this together, he will have done another three more bloody murders, don't worry aboot that.'

'Don't say that Jim, he is due another, and I just pray we get a breakthrough on this print and that it is our offender.'

'Think positive, boss, that's what you keep telling me.'

'Christ, have we got to the pitch that Jim McIntyre has to tell me to think positive? Are things really that bad?'

'Fraid so boss.' It was rare to see Jim laugh, and it was phlegmy and turned into a coughing fit. It was born as a laugh but sadly died within a couple of seconds.

*

The killer's name was the rather exotic-sounding Orlando Welles; he had never been there, Orlando that is. It was the inspiration to do so, that had prompted his mother, in a moment of lucidity, to give it to him as a name a few days after he was born. It was one of those moments where the new mother suddenly develops a fantasy that their child will become someone exotic, or somehow different to the ten generations that had preceded her, who were all alcoholics or abusers of some sort or another. Orlando, perhaps inevitably, became known as 'Lando' to his street friends, just out of laziness.

The serial killer, 'Lando Welles,' bounced his tennis ball repeatedly on the floor and caught it each time with aplomb. He was skilled with the ball, that was something he had developed over the years. That and killing. Not much of a CV but it was all he had.

As he sat on the bench at Broomhill cemetery, he could smell the freshly cut grass around the graves. Adjacent was a football pitch where shouts of excitement could be heard. It was a stark contrast; the vitality of youth and the sombre finality of death, butting against each other.

The previous burial was a non-starter. It was a single woman in her eighties, some old bastard burying her husband. She might as well have jumped into the hole herself, to save a bit of time and money, he thought. There were half a dozen mourners at most. It depended on your point of view as to whether this was a good thing or not; had he no friends? Or had he merely outlived them all? Anyway, she was unfuckable and too easy to kill. No sport. No challenge.

Out of the corner of his eye, he could see the mourners carrying the coffin towards the freshly dug grave. Some of these were wailers, real shrieks and heavy sobbing were piercing the heavy summer air. Welles began laughing. This was hilarious. What was wrong with them? He took a more lingering look. It seemed promising. She was in her early forties, and she had a partner, a big guy, husband, no doubt.

This fitted his thoughts about the cuckold element. And now he was that bit older he felt up to it. A few years ago, he would have avoided it like the plague. Sure, it might be a bigger challenge than usual, but it was new and exciting and a fucking risk. What was the worst-case scenario? Death. Who gives a fuck? Prison, Nah, fuck that shit, he could slit his own throat if required, but the chances were, it would go as he surmised. The big brave man would be a walkover, not a deterrent. He would be a pussy cat. He wouldn't have the guts to do anything. It needed to be the right venue, though. Marshalling two people is difficult, and he needed to be able to dominate the only exit to the room and secure it, then he could move around more freely. He needed to see the layout of the house before making his final decision.

There was a boy opposite the man and woman, seemingly aloof from the adults. He didn't want to be there, and the kid gradually moved himself to the back of the group and began undoing a sweetie of some description. It had fiddly paper and was taking a little time to get it open.

Welles moved around to the other side of the funeral party, slowly, with guile, feigning indifference, encircling, like a lion spotting a baby antelope dropping back from the herd. He was confident he could reach the boy, and he knelt. The kneeling obscured him from those facing him, and he then lay down. The loose grass was sticky, and the ground hard. He rested on his elbow and waited - now he threw the ball. Perfect. The boy picked it up and turned around. Welles beckoned him over.

11

'I was a devil in other countries, and I was a little devil in America too.'

Josephine Baker.

Charlie had driven due to the unspoken rule of alternate driving when in pairs and it took a couple of heaves to get himself out of the sunken seat once he had applied the handbrake. It qualified for two 'Ouch ya bugger's' as he unravelled himself from the small car.

'It's the house in the corner, Charlie.' Cynthia said across the roof of the vehicle.

'Right.' Charlie arched his back to give it a stretch and squinted in the bright sunlight.

Cynthia looked thoughtful, 'I was thinking that if this burglary was our offender, this Kim Shaw could have been sexually assaulted when she was burgled, and just not said anything to the police at the time. You never know. It does happen, doesn't it?'

'It's possible, Cynthia, you'd better take the lead with the questions and if you think it is better that I go outside for a cig so that you can have a heart-to-heart, just give me the nod.'

'Okay, great.'

Cynthia slowed her pace to allow Charlie to catch up, and he tapped on the glass-panelled door with his car key. There was no sign of life, but then the distorted view given by the glass revealed the shifting shape of a man ambling down the hall towards them. He seemed in no hurry. His gait was that of an elderly man; his legs were bowed.

'He couldn't stop a pig in an alley. By the looks of it.'

'Charlie!' Cynthia playfully slapped his arm. 'Behave. He can't help it. You will be like that one day.'

'I am now, I reckon.'

The door opened slowly. The man seemed out of breath. 'How-do.' His shoulders were a little hunched, and this made his head bow down slightly. He was only small in stature. He wore trousers with braces and a white shirt, collar undone, revealing grey whiskers at the base of his neck, where he had missed with the razor.

'Hello there. I think we have the right address - we wanted to speak to a Kim Shaw?' Charlie said.

'Pardon? I'm a bit hard of hearing.'

Cynthia raised her voice. 'We need to speak to Kim Shaw, is she in?'

'Yes, that's me, how can I help you?'

The detectives had made the mistake of forgetting that Kim is a unisex name.

'We're from the CID, from the police, is it okay to have a brief chat? Nothing to worry about.' Charlie said.

'I'm sorry lad; you'll have to speak up.' He cupped his trembly hand behind his ear. Mr Shaw was hard of hearing, but sometimes 'cocking a deaf 'un' gave him a bit of time to formulate a response to a sentence. His 'cogs' didn't go around as quickly as they used to, he would say.

Charlie repeated the introduction. 'I said, We're from the CID, is it okay to have a brief chat? Nothing to worry about.'

'Alright, no need to shout. Aye, wipe your feet on the way in, lad.' Charlie hadn't been called 'lad' for some considerable time.

They strolled down the hall behind the unsteady gate of Mr Shaw; the house had an older person's smell to it. A sort of disinfectant come urine, type of fragrance.

Mr Shaw's tartan slippers scraped along the carpet in a shuffle. With the slow progress he was making, the hallway became congested, as was Mr Shaw's lungs by the looks of things because he had to stop halfway along due to an impromptu coughing fit. He began hacking the phlegm up as he leaned on the wall with his arm outstretched. He reached into his pocket for a tissue and deposited the mucus into it and returned the tissue from whence it came. Cynthia grimaced as he did so.

'That's what thirty years down the pit does for you.' He said over his shoulder, before continuing at a snail's pace.

'I think your sexual assault theory is down the swanny, Cynthia.' Charlie whispered.

'Just a bit.' She replied.

Mr Shaw continued on his way, and in time they managed to get into the living room. Charlie and Cynthia then starburst towards the vacant armchairs. The elderly gentleman lowered himself onto the settee so far before falling into it and letting out a gasp. Charlie did the same, 'Ouch, ya bugger.'

'Eh?'

'Nothing it's fine.' Charlie rubbed at his knee. 'Just a bit of grief.'

'What?'

Charlie shook his head and glanced at Cynthia, who was stifling a giggle.

The living room was a classic octagenarian's: settee and chairs with frills on the bottom – check. Antimacassars on the backs of the furniture – check. A wooden clock on the mantlepiece – check. Floral carpet – check. Painting of horse (or African wildlife) on the wall – check. Numerous pottery figures on a shelf – check. Brass ornaments around the fire – check.

'How can I help you?' Kim asked once he'd got his breath back. His voice was a bit croaky, perhaps from the exertion of answering the door or a precursor for further handkerchief use.

Charlie offered a hand as if introducing Cynthia on stage, to indicate she would do the talking, as they had previously agreed. 'We are here about the attempted burglary you had a few weeks ago.' She said.

'Oh, aye.'

'What can you tell us about it, Mr Shaw?'

'Blimey, there's not much to tell really, lass. I was asleep in this chair, and I couldn't bring myself to go to bed.'

'Why was that? Is it because the bed is upstairs?'

'No, well, partly I suppose, but my wife had just passed away...' He sighed. '...and it took me a while to face getting into bed without her there. We'd been married fifty-two years, so...' His voice trailed off.

'I'm sorry to hear that, Mr Shaw.'

'Aye, me too, gal. I used to cry a lot then and tended to nod off in the early hours. I had the radio on. Folks ring in and chat, so it was a bit of company for me, you know.'

'So, you were asleep in the chair and what happened then? Did someone come in?'

'I don't think I was quite with it, and it was that hot spell we had, and like a daft bugger, I left the window wide open in the scullery, next thing I know someone was climbing through it.'

'Did he get in then?'

'No, I'm not that quick on my pins as you've noticed, but I thought I'd heard summat outside just before. I'm a light sleeper, and so I got the poker and went to see what was up.'

'How come you've got a poker, Mr Shaw?' Charlie asked.

'Say again.' He did the cupping behind the ear again.

'The poker, how come you've got it, when you don't have an open fire.'

'It's from the old house, we were there for nearly forty years, and it had seen us through that. I didn't have the heart to throw it away.'

'What did you see in the kitchen?' Cynthia leaned forward.

'It was that youth trying to get in. It startled me at first, so I shouted 'ehup!' at the top of my voice.'

'Okay.'

'Then I started at him with the poker. I'm not very strong, but I'm persistent.'

'Cynthia's the same, aren't you?' Charlie said.

'Eh?'

'It doesn't matter.'

'What? Hitting him?' Cynthia asked.

'I bloody did, I caught his hand as well, that made him yell, I can tell you. Then I threw the milk jug at him. It went all o'er him.'

Charlie laughed. 'Good for you.'

'What did he do then?' Cynthia asked.

'It went all o'er him as I said. He was getting fed up by this time, and he said something, but it's swearing.'

'It's okay; we've heard it all before.'

'Are you sure?'

'It's no problem. What did he say?' Charlie said.

'Eh?'

'Bless you, it's fine, Mr Shaw, honestly.' Cynthia said.

'"F off grandad" and "silly old C", I've not heard that language since I was down Linby pit. He was annoyed, mind you.' Mr Shaw began coughing again, and he continued with a wheeze in his voice.

'He got back down eventually and took hold of the yard brush. Daft bugger smashed my window. In a temper, it was. Then he was off, like lightning.' He coughed again.

'Too much trouble for him probably.' Charlie said.

'Say again?'

'Are you taking the…' He paused and noticed Cynthia giggling at the side of him. Charlie raised his voice, 'Too much bother for him.'

'Aye, lad, probably.'

'Can you remember what he was wearing?' Cynthia resumed.

'Not much, my eyesight's not too good, I thought he had an anorak on, but it had been nice weather, so I don't know.'

'Anorak?'

'Yes, with a hood thing over his head. I think it was an anorak. I couldn't see his fisog it was too dark in the scullery, any road up.'

'Ah. Got you.' She nodded at Charlie, realising it could well be a hoody top, to which the old guy was referring. 'So you rang the police.' She said.

'Aye, they were ever so good, they were here in five minutes. The kettle hadn't even boiled. It took a while to light the gas; my hands were shaking, and I was coughing like a good un. It was all the excitement; I shouldn't wonder.'

Cynthia smiled. 'I bet they were glad of a cuppa.'

'They were an all, and I was glad to see them. They got my window boarded up and arranged everything for me. You won't hear me say a bad word against the police, they've got a job to do.'

'I don't think they found anything forensically, did they?'

'What's that?'

'Fingerprints, or anything like that.'

'No, nowt like that. Nobody else came after them bobbies called in. Why? Should they have done?'

'It depends, on the list for the day, but anyway, it doesn't matter, at least you weren't hurt.'

'No, but *he* was. I heard his finger crack when I caught him a good un. I'm not as weak as I look in a scrap.'

'You heard that then.' Charlie said.

'Eh?' Charlie shook his head disbelievingly.

Cynthia smiled at Mr Shaw before she spoke to Charlie. 'I wonder if we should check the hospital?'

'What do *you* think we should do, Cynthia?'

'Yes.'

'There you go, yes. Of course.' Charlie said.

Kim spoke again. 'I'm ever so rude; I haven't offered you a drink, Hilda used to do all that, you know. I forget half the time. I don't get many visitors. I'm out of practice.' He smiled.

Cynthia thought the old fellow was sweet. 'We're fine, thank you, anyway. How old are you Mr Shaw, if you don't mind me asking?'

'As old as the year, dear.'

'87? Wow, that's a good age.'

'It doesn't seem it in these slippers sometimes; I can tell you that, lass.'

Cynthia laughed, smiling warmly at the old gentleman. 'Are you alright, Mr Shaw, being on your own, I mean. Does anyone help you at all, from the council?'

'Oh aye, yes, they are ever so good to me. A woman comes in and does for me, and I have meals on wheels. They're lovely as well. I'm lucky I tell you. I thank my lucky stars every night.'

'Bless you. Okay, Mr Shaw, thank you so much for your help.'

'I don't think I've been able to help much have I?'

'You have actually. Do you know if the police said anything about checking the hospital?'

'They wouldn't have done that, lass.'

'They might have. It's okay, we can check.'

'No, they won't have, because I never mentioned the bit about the poker, I just said I shouted. I didn't want to end up in the clink. Sorry about that.'

Cynthia laughed. 'You wouldn't have been arrested, Mr Shaw.'

'You say that, but I've read about it in the paper.'

'Don't believe everything you read in the paper.' She smiled. 'There's no need to get up; we can see ourselves out.'

'Okay, well, thank you again. Will you make sure it's properly on the latch, the door, I mean.'

'We will don't worry. Thank you for your time.' Cynthia took hold of his hand and rubbed it with both of hers. She knew the power of the human touch. 'Goodbye, Mr Shaw.'

'Goodbye, lass.'

'Goodbye, Mr Shaw.' Charlie said.

'Eh?'

*

Detective Superintendent Wagstaff looked as though he had the world on his shoulders. He was hunched forward on the chair, his forearms resting along the length of his thighs. His hair was, unusually, slightly unkempt and his waxed moustache marginally unsymmetrical.

'The Chief's incandescent.' He told Stark as they discussed the murder case in the DI's office.

'Ah, well, if he's that heated up, he's only got one way to go. He will cool down.' Stark leaned back in his leather chair behind the desk and put his hands behind his head.

'David, he's on the bloody warpath.'

'I don't mean to be glib, but what else can we do, sir? They make me laugh, they always stamp their feet and have a bloody tantrum, but I notice there's never any suggestion what else to damn well do.'

'I know, but getting Paul Masters out of prison because of unsafe evidence, has gone down like a lead balloon with the CPS, and they are going to write to the Chief. I daren't tell him that a letter is winging his way to him.'

'When is Masters being released?'

'Tomorrow, hopefully.'

'That's good. I did tell you it was dodgy from the start, sir.'

'I know, bloody Lee Mole is not on my Christmas card list at the moment.'

'You know my views on him; he was always going to catch a cold with the way he carries on. We have to be positive, though, and work our socks off before there is another murder. I think the killer is an American, by the way.'

'Yes, I saw the update, thank you for sending it through so promptly. America is a big country though, David, it might be handy to have a name.'

'Funny you should say that.' He glanced at his watch. 'I'm confident we will know who he is very shortly, any minute now in fact. I've arranged a call from the FBI which should land in the next few minutes. I will be amazed if they don't know this guy. He will have a record as long as your arm in the States, you watch.'

'I hope you're right, I really do.' Wagstaff seemed to perk up a little at the optimistic tone that Stark was taking.

'The M.O. at the home of the Master's family was that of someone who has done this before, taking on two women in a house when you know a man is asleep....'

'We *think* he knows a man is asleep.'

'Okay, taking on two women when we *think* he knows a man is snoozing downstairs, takes balls and a recklessness to be admired.'

'Not admired, surely.'

'No, I misspoke, not admired, but you know what I mean; it's not his first rodeo, is the point I'm making.'

'No. I doubt it is. Especially if he's from Texas.'

Stark laughed. It was quite funny to say it was from old Waggy.

The Superintendent continued, 'Surely some of the locals would be aware of an American suddenly in the locale? Have your lads got their ears to the ground?'

'We keep speaking to informants, and nothing has come up yet. He might travel in to us from elsewhere, for all we know.'

'What on a bloody pushbike?'

'You could go a few miles on one. He could get on a bus with it.' Stark said.

Wagstaff laughed. 'It's hardly the Boston strangler, is it? Next, you will be telling me he carries a bloody push along shopping trolley and wears a cloth cap.'

'He might do sir, you never know. We're getting closer, that's the main…'

Stark's phone rang 'Here we go.' He grabbed the handset. 'This could be it. - DI Stark.'

Wagstaff could only hear the strident tone of the voice on the other end and not the content discussed. Thirty seconds into the call, Stark smiled and gave Wagstaff the thumbs up. Once the phone call finished, Wagstaff was keen to know what was said.

'Come on then, let's have it.'

'That was Special Agent Pelkola, they've identified the killer's prints.'

'Excellent. Well done, David.'

'As I thought, he is known, well, he is more than known, he is a suspected serial killer and has been for years. They were close to nicking him when he disappeared.'

'They might have told us he was heading our way, for Christ's sake.'

'Sir, they cannot communicate from one County to the next in the States, never mind talk to other countries, they're all individual entities, it's crazy.'

'It sounds it.'

'To be honest, I'm not sure they knew where he had fled to, although Agent Pelkola didn't quite say as much. We have to be a bit careful because apparently, they sent out his details on Interpol to European countries when he disappeared off the radar, and we haven't picked it up this end.'

'We get scores of those every day at Force Intelligence, from all around the world. I get piles of the stuff on my desk and if it's non-specific about location, who the hell is even going to see it?'

'Apparently, someone called Superintendent Wagstaff has seen it and signed it off. According to this Special Agent.'

'That's me.'

'I know.'

Wagstaff coughed and blustered, 'Yes, but in fairness, David, as I said…'

'I doubt there will be any shit about it, sir, it was over six months ago, and as you say non-specific, he could have been anywhere in the world, for heaven's sake.'

'Exactly. Still, no need to advertise it is there.'

'Oh, God, no, of course not.'

'Anyway, carry on.' Wagstaff cleared his throat, more out of embarrassment than the need to do so.

'The fingerprint belongs to suspected serial killer Orlando Welles. He left a few fingerprints at "home invasions" during his early burgling career. Just before he fled there was a burglary at some Hick town, and a passport belonging to a Chuck or Charlie Peston was stolen. They think he has used that to travel here. The FBI didn't know this until they've backtracked. It wasn't filed properly at the Sheriff's office. This is what I'm saying, nobody talks to each other once you get past the County lines.'

'They are not immune to criticism themselves then.'

'No, not by a long chalk. Anyway, they have done a bit of digging, and Peston aka Welles booked a flight just over six months ago to Heathrow Airport.'

'Finally, something tangible.'

'I know, good isn't it? It's going to be him, sir, no doubt. He is faxing me all the stuff over, and I will go through it. We've finally got a name, and we will see what he looks like when I get the documents through. His mug shot will be amongst it all.'

'Get Force Intelligence to put a bulletin together once we get all of his details and photographs will you?'

'Of course.'

'It's looking good, David.'

'Looking good, sir.'

*

Cynthia was on the telephone in the main office. She looked so elegant as she sat with a rigid back and crossed legs, sideways on to the desk.

Her long, beautifully painted nails were wrapped around the handset. She had been waiting for the person on the other end to return with the records she had requested. It must be nearly five minutes ago, maybe more. She sighed.

'Who are yae on the phone to?' Jim McIntyre asked.

'QMC hospital admin. That burglary me, and Charlie went to; the offender might have had a broken finger.'

'Jeez Hen, what's that got to do wi this bloody murder case?'

'It could be our man. I want to see if he's an American.'

'Dyae know how many burglars there are in this country?'

'I know. It's just a hunch.'

'I think you've been watching too many Starsky and Hutch programmes, young lady.'

'Oh, Jim, that was years ago. It's not even on telly anymore, is it?'

Jim returned to his paperwork and didn't see Cynthia stick two fingers up at him behind his back.

The woman's voice came back on to the line. 'Hello?'

'Yes, hello.'

'I have some details for the date you quoted, you were right, after all, there was a report in Casualty of a man presenting with a suspected broken finger.'

'Great, what can you tell me about him?'

'Not a lot, I'm afraid we have to consider patient confidentiality. I cannot give you his details. Maybe your senior officers can apply through a court.'

'You're joking? Look I am investigating a series of murders here, you may have seen them on the news, this is important.'

'I know, and yes I have seen them, but it's more than my job is worth.'

'Can you just tell me if he was treated?'

'I can tell you he was treated for severe bruising, and he wasn't X-rayed...'

'Hang on, does that mean he must be a British Citizen?' Cynthia asked before the woman had time to finish.

'What do you mean?'

'To get free NHS treatment, he has to be confirmed as British, am I right?'

'Yes, but.'

'Did he show ID?'

'Yes.'

'Oh.' Cynthia seemed deflated. 'So, it isn't our man. Never mind. Thank you anyway. I don't suppose you can give us his name just for completeness?'

The woman was squirming. She wanted to help but felt hamstrung. 'I want to help I do, but erm, hang on. Stay on the phone, please.'

Cynthia could hear rustling in the background and then the woman's voice speaking to a colleague. 'Terry, can you take this file back for Barry Manners?'

She heard the mans voice reply to the admin clerk. 'Who?'

'Barry Manners. Thanks.' She returned to the phone. 'Okay? So. I cannot tell you his name officially, I'm afraid.'

'I understand. I've got you. Thank you so much.'

'I have a daughter. Good luck.'

'Thank you; you're a star.' She put the phone down.

Cynthia wrote the name 'Barry Manners,' on her pad.

'Barry Manners? British. It's not him.' She sounded deflated.

'Told yae it was a waste o' time.' Jim sneered.

'I know, but at least we know it isn't him.'

'Just file it, Cynthia, and get on wi some real police work will you?' Jim spoke to her so rudely far too often, unless Charlie or Nobby was about then he kept his mouth shut.

Instead of two fingers, she chose to put her tongue out at him this time.

Steve Aston was sitting at the table near the door as Cynthia walked out of the office. He smiled at her. 'Don't worry, Cynth, I've had the same problem with the tennis ball enquiries, there are millions of them it's a non-starter.'

'I'm glad I'm not on my own.' She said.

'Bin it!' Jim shouted again.

Cynthia walked out of the office, shaking her head. She bit her tongue. She didn't need an enemy like Jim McIntyre when she was trying to win a permanent place on CID. It was late, and she was ready for a drink. She decided to look for Nobby. It had been a long day, and they had earnt some small respite, surely?

*

Phillipa Jones and Grant Robinson kissed as they lay in bed. Grant didn't officially live with her, but he might as well have, as he stayed over most nights. As always, his hands were all over her, and she arched her back as he reached lower. She took hold of him and began to rub. He kicked the quilt down to the foot of the bed. She was voluptuous, not slim by any stretch of the imagination, but Grant liked 'a bit of meat on the bones,' which is what he said to her on their first date, two years ago and it did not go down overly well. It turned out to be true, however, and he was always after her attention and groping her, every chance he got. She joked she couldn't wash the pots without him coming at her from behind and caressing her breasts. It was getting to decision time, though. Two years is a long time, and though she was very fond of him, he was quick to temper sometimes, and she wondered if there was something or someone else for her out there, in the big bad world. She liked the fact that Grant was a bit of a tough guy, he was a powerful man, and everyone seemed to respect him and his physical presence. Phillipa felt protected when she was with him. She found that machismo quite attractive; it wasn't for everyone, but it was for her.

She had a lot on her mind, and she was tired. Quite frankly she could just do with getting her head on the pillow and getting to sleep, but he wanted it, so she would give him extra attention first and then hopefully it wouldn't be too long once they did the deed. He never quite hit the spot, unfortunately, and she had only ever faked her enjoyment, and sometimes she couldn't be bothered to do that. Tonight would be one of those nights.

She reached a second hand under the quilt. She felt Grant starting to thrust his hips. That was good. He was so big; big chest and arms, muscular build, not so big downstairs though, but he was strong and fit. She could feel it in his handling of her. Sometimes he would be a bit too rough with her when they had a play fight. She didn't like that. It was a sign of insecurity in her mind as if he had something to prove.

'What was that?' Phillipa said.

'Mmm.' Was all Grant could muster. 'What?'

She stopped what she was doing. She sat bolt upright. 'Grant, what was that? Did you hear it?'

'What? Don't stop now, for God's sake.'

'Someone is outside the house. I can hear them moving around. I'm sure I can.'

'Don't be daft. Come on, Philly.' He put her hand back on his penis, hutching up the bed so she could reach it. She didn't respond. Her head was tilted, her muscles taut, as she listened.

'There. Listen.'

'I can't hear anything.'

'I'm not joking, Grant, I can hear something. I'm serious.' Her face bore an expression of alarm, and her heart was beating fast.

'Jesus, Philly.' He lay on his front and put his head over his arms. 'I'm going to lose it in a minute.'

'No need to get angry about it.'

'I don't mean lose it, in that way, I mean this.' He raised himself on his side and his penis, like Philly, looked deflated.

'Listen. It's a clicking sound, right outside the window. Put your pants on.'

Grant sighed. 'It's somebody walking past; it's what happens when you live in a bungalow. Come on, Phil, don't stop now.'

'There again, did you hear it? Listen.'

'What? No, Philly, there is no clicking. I'm listening. What do you mean clicking, anyway?'

She pushed at his bulk, and it scarcely moved; she was annoyed at his lacklustre response and swung her legs over the side of the bed. 'I will have a look then if you won't. Thanks a bunch. I thought you were supposed to protect me?'

Grant laughed. 'Don't show your tits to the bloody world.'

Phillipa got to the curtain and tentatively drew it back to get a view. She gasped. There was a man at the end of the open-plan garden, in the street, under a lampost. He was looking straight at her, smoking a cigarette. He didn't move an inch. She quickly dropped the curtain and ran back to the bed. She was breathing rapidly. 'I told you. He's there; he's out there.'

'Who is? What are you on about?'

She smacked his shoulder. 'Get off your arse and go and have a look.' She was out of breath; the man was sinister-looking; it spooked her.

'Bloody hell. Christ. Don't get your knickers in a twist.' Grant rolled over and went to the window, as he looked out, he saw nothing. 'Phillipa, there is nobody out there.'

'There is, under the lamppost.'

'I'm telling you there is nobody there, come and have a look if you don't believe me.'

Phillipa slowly walked to the window.

'See.'

There was no one there. 'He *was* there, standing under the lamppost, in a grey hoody and smoking a damned cigarette. You think I am imagining it, don't you? I'm telling you, Grant, he was there. It's freaking me out. I'm scared.'

Steve took her in her arms. 'Come on, Phillipa. Nobody is going to hurt you. I'm here. No one in their right mind is going to set foot in here. I'd break his fucking neck.'

'What if he isn't in his right mind? He looked a right nutter. Don't forget there is that bloke on the loose.'

'What bloke?'

'The killer, that bloody maniac, Grant, on the news, killing everyone.'

'Everyone?' He laughed.

'You know what I mean.'

'I'd still break his neck. Come on, let's get back to bed.'

'I'm going to read for a bit.'

'Hold on what about this?' He flapped his semi-erect penis at her.

She laughed. 'You can put that away. I'm not in the mood now.'

'Fucking hell, Phillipa.' He was not happy.

'I'm sorry, Grant, I'm serious, just let me read for a bit, maybe in the morning.'

Grant pushed her, making her stumble, and pointed his finger at her. 'You are bang out of order. I didn't have you down as a prick teaser.'

'Really? You're doing this?'

'It's different for a bloke.'

'Is it? Well, tough titty. If you'd got off your arse quicker, you would have seen him, yourself.'

Grant flounced into bed. He was agitated now. He pulled the quilt over him in a fit of pique. 'There are some things you just don't do to a bloke, Philly.'

'I'm sorry, Grant, but you can't just turn me on and off like a tap.'

'Forget it.' He was sulking now.

Phillipa sighed and got into bed. Grant could hear the pages turning as he simmered next to her. Neither would get to sleep for the best part of half an hour.

*

Nobby stuck his head around the Inspector's office door. 'Are you having a bevvy, boss? Last orders.'

'Maybe in a bit.'

'Sure, what's up?'

Stark lifted the shiny, floppy wad of papers off his desk. 'This.'

'What's that?'

'It's the stuff from the FBI in the States, we've got a name.'

'Fucking ace! Who is he?'

'You won't be surprised to learn he is a suspected serial killer on the hoof.'

'Shit!' Nobby sat down on the chair and leaned forward. He clapped his hands together and then rubbed them as if it were a chilly night and not 26 degrees. 'This will be fun.'

'That's what I thought. It's some geezer called Orlando Welles using the alias Chuck Peston. He's come over on a nicked passport.'

'That puts a whole different complexion on things, doesn't it?'

'It sure does. We need to be careful with this dude, Nobby. He's managed to evade capture from the FBI, so he isn't some common or garden numpty. I need you to be on your mettle. We need to profile him. Understand him. It might not be as straightforward as we think.'

'Do the lads know?'

'Not yet.'

'Is there enough to nick him, do you reckon?' Nobby asked excitedly.

'Fuck that; he's coming anyway. We will work out the details later, even if it's for the American stuff in the first instance. We will be able to hold him for weeks.'

'Nice. Have we got an address for him yet?'

'Not yet, but we will. Orlando Welles, or Chuck Peston, or whatever the hell he calls himself will be getting the big knock soon, don't you worry about that Detective Sergeant Clarke.'

'Okay, you know while I'm in the process of not worrying about it, do you think we could perhaps have a little drinkypoo? The team have been hard at it today, and the local council won't be able to give us an address on this youth yet anyway. We can sort it all out bright and early in the morning. Nothing is spoiling.'

Stark thought about it for a couple of seconds. 'Come on, then. Rally the troops. They've earned a pint.'

12

'Demons are like obedient dogs; they come when they are called.'

Remy de Gourmont

Grant lay on his back snoring. His mind had been whirring, and he'd had difficulty getting to sleep what with a scrotum full of semen, but now he was in the land of the fairies. In his slumber, far away in the recesses of his mind, he could hear a distant call.

'Grant.'

He turned over, but the voice was still there.

'Graaaaaant.' It was quite a high pitched tone, almost as though it was mocking him.

'Graaaaaant.'

He could hear sobbing as his brain tried to work out whether this was a dream or real. He opened one eye to see Orlando Welles standing next to Phillipa who was crying and had a tennis ball rammed in her mouth. Welles held Phillipa's hair in his left hand and with the other held a large kitchen knife with the point pressed underneath her chin. She was naked and shaking uncontrollably.

'Grant.' The high pitched mocking voice said again.

Grant jumped to his knees on the mattress and Welles drew the knife down, ready to strike. He was a big guy, but Welles would kill him outright, no messing.

'What the fuck? Who the fuck are you?' Grant was trying to make sense of what was happening.

'I'm here to kill ya'll.' He grinned. Welles was very matter-of-fact in his reply.

'Come on then, drop the knife.' Grant said, raising his fists.

The killer laughed. 'Drop the knife? I don't think so.'

Grant stepped off the mattress, keeping his fists raised. 'A fair fight, come on I'll take your fucking head off.'

The man spoke softly and showed no emotion. 'I'm going to kill you both. I can do that now, or later. I don't give a fuck.'

Grant suddenly took in the seriousness of the situation. It registered that this was him; the killer; the psychopath, and he was not going to mess around. A cold shiver ran down his muscular back, and his initial rush of blood dropped like a stone, and he lowered his fists. His courage shattered into a thousand fragments onto the floor, and he went pale with fear. 'Okay, look, let me go. You can have her, man. You can have her. Just let me go, yeah?'

Phillipa made a noise through the tennis ball as he said it.

Welles began laughing. 'Jeez dude, you don't give a shit, huh? If you try to leave, I will kill her. It's your call.'

'Fine, just let me go. Kill her, if you want. Wait, I'll go out the window, it's all good.' Grant started to back towards the window; Welles was blocking the door.

Welles thought this hilarious as Phillipa's one chance of survival turned out to be apathetic, a cowardly piece of excrement, intent only on saving himself. The crazy man was laughing maniacally as Grant went all trembly and backed towards his only chance of escape.

As Grant moved ever closer to the window both arms extended in a conciliatory fashion, Welles slowly edged himself and Phillipa towards the same destination.

Grant began to let out a sob. 'Please. Don't kill me. Just let me go. Stay cool, yeah?' He was sniffling; a sort of a half-cry. He turned to the window, with Welles mocking laughter ringing in his ears. Grant opened the handle and pushed the window ajar at the same time as he put his hand onto the wooden ledge to vault through the gap to freedom. Grant cried out in agony. The knife blade seared through his hand and into the wooden ledge with incredible force pinning him in situ.

Welles pushed Phillipa to the floor, down the side of the bed, and Welles quickly retrieved old faithful, his own trusted knife from his pocket. He closed the window that Grant had opened.

'Isn't he muscular?' Welles said to Phillipa. She stared straight ahead.

Grant continued sobbing. 'That fucking hurts, man, It hurts! Please, I'm sorry.'

Welles began rubbing at Grant's bare buttocks. 'Why would I let you go, Mr Hunky?'

'Please!' Grant sobbed like a child hearing his puppy had died.

Welles lowered his tracksuit bottoms and moved his body against Grant's. 'A hairy Mary, I like.'

Grant was just sobbing. He was trying to stop the blood in the pierced hand and to see if he could remove the blade without pain. He couldn't. 'Not that, please.' He sobbed.

'You don't fancy me, big buck? Mmm?'

'Yes, but no, It's just not my thing.'

'Are you insulting me, young Grant?'

'No. I fancy you; I do, I promise.'

'You want to please me with your mouth, don't you big guy?'

Phillipa couldn't believe what she was seeing, and her heart sank, with any chance of escape seemingly lost. So much for all Grant's big talk earlier.

'Yes.' Grant's shoulders heaved as waves of terror flooded over him. 'I need to pee.'

'Off you go. She's right there. Piss on her, she's a piece of shit, right?'

'I'll wait.'

'Tell her; she's a piece of shit, Grant.'

'You're a piece of shit.' Phillipa's head lowered as he said it.

'Off you go. Piss on that piece of shit.'

Grant hesitated.

'Do it!'

Grant turned his hips and relaxed his bladder. He urinated on Phillipa who did not move as his warm urine spattered over her. Welles chuckled.

'You soppy bastard. You are going to do everything I say, aren't you.' He cuffed Grant around the head.

'Yes.'

Welles rubbed at Grant's hair. 'That's a good boy.' He then batted him across the head again.

Grant cried out. 'Ouch.'

Welles couldn't believe him. 'Ouch? You fucking pussy. Where did you find this fucking cuck from, huh?'

Phillipa stared down at the carpet and didn't say anything. Some of Grant's urine had gone into her mouth, and it tasted foul. She felt like she was going to be sick but was frightened this would anger the madman.

'Ready to go? Mr Muscles?'

Grant was still crying and nodded. 'Hey, Phillipa, Grant wants to suck my dick, wanna watch?'

As tears fell onto the carpet, she nodded.

*

Stark's team were in good spirits in the police station drinks club. The gang crowded around the bar, chatting away, thrilled at the news that there was a name for the killer. It had been a long day, but they were making real progress now. All things being equal they could get this bastard caught tomorrow before he struck again. It was a real buzz of excitement. Everyone was in high spirits.

'Don't let this turn into a boozy bender, guys and gals; we have a big day tomorrow.' Stark announced.

Steph looked worried and whispered into Nobby's ear. He seemed to realise what she was saying, and then he turned towards Stark. 'Can I have a word, boss?' Nobby asked.

'Yes, what's up?'

Nobby walked away from the crowd and Stark followed him, clutching his pint of lager.

''What's up, mate?'

'Nothing, it's Steph. You know it's her Dad's funeral tomorrow?'

'I didn't, but I do now.'

'She's worried that you are going to need her for the raid tomorrow and it is the one day she can't get involved.'

Stark laughed and beckoned Steph over.

'Steph, you should know me better than this. What did I tell you?'

'I know, but...'

'No buts, of course, you don't come in tomorrow. You shouldn't be here now, for heaven's sake.'

She looked relieved. 'Thanks, boss.' She hugged him.

'Alright, not too much.' Nobby said.

Stark was grinning. 'What are you going to do with him, Steph?'

'Who Nobby? God knows.' She said.

'What about me, though boss...' His DS asked sheepishly.

'Why do you want a hug as well?'

Nobby laughed. 'Well, if you're offering...no, but seriously, I want to be at the funeral to support Steph, and to pay my respects.' Nobby said.

Steph interjected before Stark could reply. 'Nobby, it's fine. I've got my sister there and all of Dad's friends.'

'Come on, Steph, I should be there with you.' Nobby put his arm around her waist.

Stark puffed out his cheeks. 'You are a little bit trickier, Nobby.'

'There you go, Nobby it's fine.' Steph said.

'I'd like to be there, boss, but I know you need me also. It's awkward.'

'I could try to get Carl Davidson off Lee Mole and use him for the day.' Stark said, thinking aloud.

Both Steph and Nobby said 'No!' in unison.

'I need a DS, Nobby; things could get complicated. Maybe if there is a lull we can sort something out?'

Steph spoke again. 'Look, the lads would never forgive me if we had Davidson over, I would never forgive myself either. Please, Nobby, just this once. Do as I ask?'

'You're not going to throw this in my face in a year's time, are you?'

'Who said it is going to last another year?' She laughed, Stark joined her.

It was Nobby's turn to get a hug from Steph. 'You sure, Mrs?'

'I'm sure I promise. You need to be where the killer is, not with me at a funeral.'

*

Welles had moved on to Phillipa, and he was positioned behind her. He had dragged her up on to the bed.

'Look at this, Grant. I'm fucking your woman.' He glanced behind him at Grant, who was staring at the carpet. 'I hope you're watching this.'

Welles suddenly quickened his action, grabbing her hair and pulling it back before he ejaculated into her, and both he and she let out a groan.

Welles rolled over on to his side, knife in hand.

'Did you enjoy watching that, Grant?'

'Yes.'

Welles shook his head and chuckled to himself. This guy was a complete jerk. Welles dismissively pushed Phillipa off the bed onto the floor. She landed in a heap and curled into a ball, sobbing and wailing.

Welles was still out of breath from his exertions with Phillipa, and he sat on the bed for a few seconds, to recover. His mind was racing with the possibilities that Grant's total emasculation now gave him.

'Just how far would you go to survive? Little baby, Grant?' Welles was intrigued by this guy. Blood was pooling and dripping off the captive's hand, on to the window sill and then the carpet. The knife was secure in the wood, and his hand was now totally numb. 'Well?' The killer demanded an answer.

'To survive? Anything. I want to live. Can't you see that? I've done everything you asked me to do.' Grant began to sniffle and struggled to hold back the tears.

'I can, Grant, I can see that. Would you do *anything* though? I wonder. I guess you just might.' He beckoned Phillipa over towards him. 'Come here, you fucking slut.'

She was sobbing.

'Get here, bitch!' He growled. She slowly and trepidatiously moved towards the two men on her hands and knees.

'Stand there.' Welles instructed.

She struggled to her feet and tried to cover her nakedness with her arms and hands. She staggered over and stood opposite Grant but could not bring herself to look him in the eye. He repulsed her so much. Phillipa shuffled backwards until her back was flush against the cold wall; her limbs were floppy, and her spirit was all but gone.

Welles was playing this curious situation for all it was worth. The deviant squeezed the tennis ball and wrenched it from her mouth, putting it in his pocket. It was wet with saliva and tears. 'Scream, or try to move, and you're dead. Is that clear?'

Phillipa nodded. She rubbed her forearm across her mouth to clear away the saliva. It felt good to be able to breathe normally again, but this momentary blessing was quickly overwhelmed by the desperation of her predicament. She was frozen to the spot; nobody had ever told her that beyond immediate fight or flight responses lay complete and utter compliance.

Phillipa could finally speak with the bastard. She whispered as she spoke. 'You've had your way. Can't you just leave us alone now, please?'

'It sure as hell don't work like that, Missy.'

'Please, we won't say anything, we promise.'

'Now, here's the deal, Grant.' Welles stepped behind him and held his knife at his jugular vein. 'In half a second I can stick this knife in your jugular, sever it, and no matter what you do, you will be as good as dead, understand?'

Grant nodded and made a squeaking sound as tears rolled down his reddened face. He had become childlike and felt such a terror in the pit of the stomach that he could barely function.

'I am going to pull that knife out of your hand and give it to you.'

Phillipa's eyes widened, and for the first time, she looked at Grant, who returned her gaze. This could be the chance for which she had been silently praying.

'One of you guys is going to die, and you Grant, because you've been such a good kid, can decide who.'

'No. I can't do that.'

'Yes, you can, you just need to decide: Shall I kill you? Or will *you* kill Phillipa? What do you think, Phillipa?'

'Grant, he will kill us both, don't do this. It's him we saw on the news, he's killed everyone, he will kill us. You know what to do right?'

Welles laughed. 'That's cute, Phillipa, a little secret message that he should turn the knife on me, that's real cute, good job. The problem is that Grant, here, knows that he will be dead if he does that. He can't react quicker than I can stick this blade in his vein. Will he sacrifice his life for you? What do you think? Look at him.' Grant wiped at his tears, his mind racing. Welles continued. 'So we are back around to who is going to die. What's it to be, Grant?'

'He didn't kill the kid, Phillipa.' Grant said.

'What kid?' She said.

'There was a kid at one of the houses, and he let him live, didn't you?'

'I truly did, Grant, I truly did. Just like I will let you live.'

'Grant. Accept it; he will kill us both. Don't do this.'

'Who do you trust, Grant? Me with a knife at your throat, or the beautiful Phillipa who is trying to get *you* killed. She doesn't give a damn if you die. That's a crock of shit right there, Grant. Who do you believe? Mmm?'

'You.'

Phillipa's heart sunk. Grant was lost, he had succumbed to a sort of insanity of total compliance even in the face of his own death, he was going to do this. How could she shock him out of this subservience?

'Thank you, Grant.' Welles kissed him on the cheek. 'That's sweet. Why thank you.'

'Grant, don't do this, please.' Phillipa pleaded. 'Come on, man-up; you're stronger than him, you can do this.'

Welles put his right hand over the handle of the butcher's knife, and pulled it out of the sill, causing Grant to yell. 'Shush, little puppy.' Welles whispered. The blade was still piercing Grant's hand. 'Hold your hand so that I can pull it out.'

Grant grimaced as the maniac freed the blade. Welles moved Grant towards Phillipa, and he placed the point of the blade to her chest. He used the point to find the right place on her torso. 'Here's the thing, Grant, you have to get the blade between the ribs, like so, and it needs to just be at a slight angle to rupture the heart, see?' Grant's blood from the blade dripped down her body. A slow trickle which Welles seemed to like. 'Beautiful.' He said.

Grant nodded. 'Okay. I will definitely live, if I do this, yes?'

'I am a man of my word, Grant. Trust me, if I say something, I mean it. Are you calling me a liar?'

'No, no, not at all. I was just checking, that's all. I didn't mean anything by it.'

Phillipa began to sob and closed her eyes. She shook her head and started saying the Lord's prayer. 'Our father who art in heaven…'

Welles joined in. '…hallowed be thy name…' He whispered to Grant. 'Now, Grant. Now!'

Grant took hold of the handle of the knife with his good hand, with Welles still loosely holding it. An expulsion of air came from Phillipa as Grant rammed the knife into her chest, piercing the lung and heart. She collapsed to the floor. And Welles grasped the large knife out of Grant's control.

Welles began whooping, breying, and laughing. 'You fucking jerk, Grant. You fucking moron.'

'Why?'

'Why? Because I lied, Grant. I lied, my friend.' Welles rammed his knife into Grant's jugular to the hilt and the spray of blood splattered onto the wall. Grant fell to his knees and then forwards on to Phillipa's lap. He died before she did.

Welles sat on the edge of the bed to watch the pair of them twitch and go through the final death throes. It was a high he had never known. Welles was overly excited. Grant was so perfect he had to die. Welles had accidentally learned a new trick; the knife through the hand; it was like a crucifixion. He was already planning his next little adventure. He needed to take a few minutes to calm down; so he studied the bodies for a while. Like an art-critic might study a sculpture. That was what they were to Orlando Welles, a beautiful piece of art, arranged in an embrace of death that he had orchestrated. It was wonderful.

After a few minutes, he was gone. He disappeared away into the shadows of the night, yet leaving behind him greater darkness—the infinite black chasm of death.

13

'But being confident you are right is not the same as being right.'

Steven D. Levitt.

Stark was at work early and found DC Cynthia Walker hard at it.

'Morning, Cynthia, I thought I would be first in the office today.'

'No sir, I couldn't sleep. Something's been niggling me.'

Stark put the kettle on. 'Do you want a drink?'

'Yes, please. Do you want me to make it?'

'No, it's fine, thanks. So what's been niggling you? You should be sleeping the sleep of the innocent at your age.'

'This psycho dude. He's had the FBI on his tail all this time and never been caught.'

'Yes, I know, he's going to be no fool, I get that.'

'Yes, but is he really going to hang on to the name, Chuck Peston?'

'Fair question, Cynthia. I like the way you are thinking.'

'Jim gave me a hard time about ringing the hospital yesterday, and I discounted the bloke because he was English, not American.'

'Remind me who this is again?'

'This was the bloke who Kim Shaw hit with a poker and damaged his hand.'

Stark laughed. 'Oh, yes, good old Mr Shaw.'

'I checked the hospital, and they were cagey about telling me who it was. But there was someone who presented with a hand injury the next day.'

'Interesting.'

'That's what I thought, but I let Jim put me off.'

Stark walked over with two mugs and sat down next to Cynthia.

'Don't ever let anyone put you off, Cynthia, I want different thought processes in this office, I don't want you all to be clones of each other. Nobody has a monopoly on being right, not even me.' He smiled.

'That's what was niggling me. Why discount him because he has an English ID? He could just as easily steal another passport or any identity documents, and as I say, I can't see him keeping the name that he knows the FBI will eventually trace.'

'No, I think you're right, that is something we should follow up. Have you pursued this train of thought any further?'

'I have. The woman on the phone sort of hinted at the name of the patient, somebody called, Barry Manners.'

'Good for her. And?'

'I think I've found something. There was a burglary in Brixton a few days after our psycho landed at Heathrow and nothing was taken apart from cash, birth certificate and a passport. The thing is…'

'The thing is, what?'

'The name on the passport is Barry Manners.'

'Goodness me, Miss Walker.'

'There is a copy of the passport on the crime report, and the photo of Barry Manners looks pretty similar to the FBI photo of Orlando Welles.'

'Okay, interesting, but I would imagine…'

'Hang on, boss, I've dug into it a bit more, and he has changed the address on the passport from Brixton to one in Nottingham. Passport office didn't get notification of the theft, so they just sent it out. The victim never bothered renewing. He's been claiming benefits under the name Barry Manners too.'

'Cynthia Walker, you little beauty.'

She blushed. 'Thank you, sir.'

'Let's get this right; the serial killer is this maniac called Orlando Welles. He knows the FBI wants him and so he steals a passport in the name Chuck Peston and uses it to fly to England.'

'He does.'

'Then pretty sharpish he does a burglary in Brixton and steals a passport in the name Barry Manners which he is now using as an alias.'

'It looks that way.' Cynthia said.

'Unless he has changed again.'

'He could have, but it was only a few weeks ago he was at the hospital, and he is still claiming welfare under that name.'

'What's the address?'

'Flat 2, 16 Lancaster Road, Ruffs Estate, Hucknall.'

Stark grinned and put his hand out to shake Cynthia's, she took it and then managed to steal a hug. Nobby walked into the office.

'Sorry, am I interrupting something?'

'No, you daft bogger, Cynthia has just done some great detective work. We've got an address and a new alias for our killer; we think he's now using the name, Barry Manners.'

'Nice one, well done, Cynthia.'

'Thanks, Sarge.' She smiled modestly.

'Let's get moving.' Nobby shrugged.

'A quick briefing and we can get out there.' Stark grinned. 'Where is everyone?'

'They're in the canteen, grabbing a bacon butty. I've told them to come straight up.'

'Great, start formulating the arrest plan, I don't want any hiccups with this bastard, make sure we have a dog man, and some SOU if they are around. He's a nutter with nothing to lose.'

'Do you think that's on his CV, sir? A nutter with nothing to lose.' Cynthia said, feeling buoyed by her success.

Stark laughed. 'It probably is. I know it's on mine.' Cynthia laughed in return.

'It's likely to take a couple of hours to get the extra resource, boss.' Nobby said.

'That's shit. I've got to think about safety first, though, Nobby.' Stark said.

'Do we need all these people? We can just down the fucker.' Nobby said.

'I'm sure we can, but think about the aggro if someone gets hurt or worse when we know how dangerous he is.'

Nobby seemed disappointed. 'You're right as always. I just want to get my hands on him.'

'Don't we all, Nobby? Don't we all.'

*

Stephanie Dawson and her sister Margaret had opted for an early burial for their father. Steph knew she wouldn't sleep much the night before, and the last thing she wanted was to be waiting all day to bury him. They wanted it to be a lovely, quiet, private affair and toast his memory with a pre-lunchtime glass. There was no need for a big wake. There wouldn't be many mourners, so Margaret had asked Steph if it was okay just to do some sandwiches at the Horse and Groom, in Linby.

The burial had finished, and they had bid their goodbyes to most of the guests. The two sisters sat on the bench, while the residue of those attending was chatting in the car park. They were both in a black two-piece – jacket and skirt. Steph lit up a cigarette. There was a slight tremble in her hands as she lit it. She was struggling to hold the tidal wave of sadness inside. It felt like it could burst out at any moment. It was painful, and she ached with the subconscious effort her body was making to restrain all this pent-up emotion.

'This reminds me of Weston Super-Mare. Sitting here like this.' Margaret said.

'Crikey, you're going back a bit, aren't you? How old were we, nine, ten?' Steph asked.

'Probably around that age. Remember, we decided that the bench on the prom was a dolls hospital. What a lovely holiday that was, the sun was always shining, and Dad was, well just being Dad—being silly. He was a good Dad, wasn't he? We were lucky.' Margaret took hold of Steph's hand.

'You're right, sis, we were lucky. We just didn't know it at the time. You think everyone has a childhood like us, but when you get older you realise, sadly that is not always the case.'

'Good old Dad.' Margaret said.

'Good old Dad.' Steph repeated with a sigh.

'Thanks, Dad.' Margaret shouted to the sky.

'Thanks, Dad.' Steph shouted even louder to the heavens. Some of the mourners craned their necks to see what was happening.

'Are we losing it, sis?' Margaret shrugged out a laugh.

'Probably. Dad would be laughing, though if he could see us.' Steph smiled.

'He would too. He would love to see us like this. We should meet up more often, shouldn't we?'

'We should. We should make time in our busy lives before it's too late.'

'It's a deal.'

They both knew it was unlikely, but the thought and the intent behind it were nice. Steph sucked at her cigarette and blew a cloud of smoke out with a sigh.

'It's about time you packed that habit in, Steph. I don't want to lose a sister as well.'

'You've got a nerve, haven't you, Margaret Dawson, as was.'

'As was.' She smiled. 'What do you mean. Anyway?'

'You started me on the bleeders. If you hadn't told me how great they were, I would never have started in the first bloody place.'

'Oh, yes.'

'"Oh, yes," indeed. In any case, life is too stressful for me to stop; the smoke keeps the demons away.'

'Can you remember when Dad caught you and bought you a packet of cigarettes and told you, you had to smoke them all.'

'I know, and then he got bored after two cigarettes, so I ended up with a free packet of cigarettes.'

'Crazy.'

'Good old, Dad.' Steph said again under her breath.

'Watch out, sis, the next funeral is here.' Margaret turned to look over her shoulder as she spoke.

'Already?' Steph threw the cigarette onto the path and stubbed it out with the sole of her shoe.

'We'd better shift ourselves.' Margaret said.

'I know, but I don't want to.'

'I don't. Isn't that strange? I've been dreading it for days, and now I don't want to go.'

'It's probably because it is the final goodbye.'

Margaret began to cry, and Steph held her hand, rubbing it and smiling sympathetically.

'You're setting me off now.'

Stephanie stood up, and Margaret joined her. They embraced. 'See you at the pub, sis.'

'See you there.

Steph walked to the car park as Margaret veered off towards her husband, chatting to one of the stragglers.

Steph sat in her car for a few minutes and cried. It all came out. Her stomach was twisted into knots, and she was overwhelmed with the last goodbye of someone she had loved and respected all her life. She was used to death, but when it is someone you care for, it is different, and no amount of training or experience could help restrain her sorrow. Nor did she want to, in truth. She caught her breath enough to start the engine.

Margaret and her husband, James, walked down to the car park after standing respectfully to allow the other mourners to come past them. They waved to Steph as she drove off.

'Poor Steph.' Margaret said.

'Poor you.' James said.

'I know James, but at least I've got you and Matthew. Incidentally, where is he?'

Right on cue, their son came running up to them from the grass bank, and they got into the car together. James was driving and looked in the mirror to reverse out. 'What's that?'

'A tennis ball, Dad.'

'Where the hell have you got that from?'

'A man said I could keep it.'

'What man?'

'Someone from the funeral, I think.'

'Oh, okay. That's good.'

'I think he gave it to me, anyway.'

'What do you mean, you *think* he gave it to you?'

'We were talking, and great uncle Ted came over, and the man cycled off. I suppose I can ask the man if I can keep it when we get to Aunty Steph's.'

'We aren't going to Aunty Steph's; we are going to the pub first.'

'Oh, I thought it was at Aunty Steph's we were going to.'

'No, never mind I'm sure whoever it was will figure it out.' James reversed out and turned the wheel to get the car moving. 'Cycled off?'

'Don't worry about it, James, did you draw enough money out to buy drinks?' Margaret asked.

'I hope so; we're not buying everyone a drink are we?'

'Yes, we are, for Dad.'

'Bloody hell, Maggie.'

'There's only going to be twenty or thirty people turn up; I should think if that?'

'Twenty or thirty people? It adds up, you know.'

'Do you think a hundred pounds is enough?' Margaret asked.

'It should be, what is it 85 pence a pint? It is those that suddenly drink spirits when the round is free. We can draw more out if we need it.' James said, shaking his head slightly.

Margaret sighed. 'I'm looking forward to getting home, to be honest. I'm getting one of my heads.'

James held her hand. 'Sorry to go on about prices and beer and all of that nonsense. The main thing is it has gone without a hitch, and you've done your dad proud. You've done great. I'm proud of you.'

Young Matthew threw the tennis ball into the air and caught it.

Margaret smiled and covered his hand with hers. 'Thanks. Thanks for everything, James.'

'That's why I'm here; it's in the contract.' He smiled. 'Right, let's go and get that drink.'

*

Orlando Welles was on a roll. He lay on his bed, his mind whirling with the excitement of killing Phillipa and Grant, but this just seemed to fuel his instincts to go again. He was hungry for more. More killing. More devastation. He was drunk on the enormous high that events with Grant had given him. He felt indestructible. Invincible.

It had only been by chance that he saw the funeral arrive as he cycled to the paper shop, hoping that the news would have hit. It hadn't. He didn't realise the undertakers started shoving them in the ground so early in the day. It was worth taking a look, just out of curiosity. He was glad he did. He had another address; another one lined up. The boy had pointed out the busty blond who lived at the address, and she looked pretty hot to him. There was something about her that appeared slightly off. She looked different to other women, but he couldn't quite put his finger on what it was. It was her walk or bearing, something that gave her an air of importance. Maybe she was just a pompous prick. Whatever it was, she needed bringing down a peg or two, and he was just the man to do it.

As usual, he bounced one of his tennis balls against the wall and caught it repeatedly as he planned his next move. It helped him think, and the neighbours had long since given up complaining.

His own filth surrounded him; tissues, food wrappers and residue meals scattered around on a couple of plates, now green and furry with mould. He had weird posters peeling off the walls, some satanic quotes and some morbid battle pictures of dismembered and rotting corpses. There were hundreds of tiny words and little notes he had written on the walls, random thoughts, perversions, plans and warped desires. It wasn't a place that you would take someone back to on a first date.

His mind was whirring. He would have a scout around first and see what the lay of the land was. There was no rush. It looked like this next one would be straight forward, and his previous attack with the loving couple was so glorious it gave him an idea for the follow-up. Spearing Grant's hand in the window sill had triggered an excellent thought. It was worth trying his new plan at this next one. It would ratchet the viciousness up even more, and give this murder a unique flair to complement his trademark tennis ball technique.

*

Stark and the team had arranged a rendezvous in a pub car close to Orlando Welles address. Some of the officers had inevitably got caught in traffic in the convoy over. Once together, Stark re-iterated everyone's roles and checked they were clear how it was to go. It only took a couple of minutes and then they drove around the corner to the address.

The plan was for Stark and Nobby to make the arrest with a dog man, so they would go up the stairs to the door of the flat. Two Special

Operations officers would remain at the foot of the stairs for back up if required—one at the door with a sledgehammer.

Ashley, Cynthia and Steve Aston were to go to the rear of the premises with two Special Ops guys. They wanted no mistakes. Welles had to be taken without any prospect of escape, or indeed injury to any of the officers.

Stark intended that once Welles was arrested, the rest of the Special Ops guys, assisted by Cynthia and Steve would do the search of the premises, organising and bagging and tagging exhibits. Ashley would travel back with Nobby and Stark and sit in the back with laughing boy.

Stark and Nobby had their wooden truncheons up their jacket sleeves, adjacent to their forearms, so they could quickly drop them down into their hand in a split second. It seemed unlikely that this nutter would come without a fight. He had nothing to lose, and they needed to be swift and go in hard.

As the officers settled into place, a quiet fell ahead of the storm. Stark could hear noises behind the door. A rhythmic banging of some description. Stark looked puzzled at Nobby who shrugged. Someone was inside, of that there was no doubt. They waited a few seconds to give the back garden team a chance to get into place, and then Stark beckoned the man with a sledgehammer to the forefront. It took two whacks to get it open and the door almost split in two as they charged in. Sledgehammer man stayed at the doorway, and the two cops from the stairs couldn't resist coming up to join him.

Stark and Nobby were met with a bare backside in between a pair of legs and two shocked faces as they entered the first room on the right. The young couple were making love in the bedroom, and this was clearly the source of the rhythmic banging that had puzzled DI Stark. All was now revealed; literally.

'Morning.' Nobby said with a stupid grin on his face, his gaze automatically falling on her bare breasts.

The woman pulled the blanket over them hastily.

'We're the police.' Stark said a little sheepishly. 'Where's Orlando Welles.'

A head appeared above the top of the quilt; it was the young guy. 'He's not here. He doesn't live here. I think he had the flat before us.'

'Oh, poo.' Nobby said.

*

Welles continued to bounce the ball against the wall as his mind wondered. Periodically he would have a thought, and he would then stop and use a stubby pencil to write notes on the wall of his bedroom. It showed up quite well on the magnolia paintwork. There was quite a lot of these little notes festooned around the walls often accompanied by crude drawings. His handwriting was tiny and spidery; spikey, like the hatefulness of the content, it imbued. Most of it was fantasy stuff or fetishist and more often than not, didn't actually happen when he made his attacks, but it helped him have an aim when he was in full flow. It was no good trying to dream up what he wanted to do in the moment; that could end up being embarrassing; he had to be definite, in control. Show no weakness or indecisiveness.

He wrote on the wall, 'Stigmata.'

He tried to light a cigarette, but his lighter had been playing up and was on his last legs. He needed to get a new one. After several clicks, it failed to work, so he threw it across the room. He would settle for matches for the time being.

He resumed his ball throwing and then paused after three or four catches. He had been trying to think of the name the boy had said, but it was just before the old guy walked over to him and he scarpered on his bicycle. It was on the tip of his tongue. He threw the ball again for a few rounds and then it came to him. He stopped the ball throwing and got his stubby pencil out again. He wrote on the wall: 'Steph - kinda rhymes with death.'

14

'Nothing that you plan is going to work out. Everything is going to be totally different than the way you expected. And things will constantly challenge you. Wherever you look, the world is not as solid as it seems to be.'

Eckhart Tolle.

Nobby stood in the hallway, scratching his head while the young couple got themselves dressed in their bedroom. He could hear them whispering to each other excitedly and giggling.

'DS Clarke to control.' He spoke on his radio.

'Go ahead, over.'

'Border-upper required at Flat 2, 16 Lancaster Road, Hucknall, please. It will need a replacement door.'

'Ten-Four, stand-by. From the duty Inspector, any arrests, over?'

'No, none, over.'

'Ten-Four.'

Stark was whispering to Cynthia in the hallway. 'What's gone wrong, Cynthia? I thought this was his place?'

Cynthia was shocked and worried that she had messed everything up. 'So did I. This is the address on the passport and his benefit claims, honestly.'

'He's not been here for ages apparently.' Stark said in hushed tones, clearly disappointed.

'Could they be lying?' She asked.

'Who, the couple? No, it's legit.'

'How is he getting his benefits information, then?' Cynthia asked.

Stark clicked his fingers. 'I bet he's having his mail forwarded on via the Post office. Sneaky bleeder.'

'Shit, yes. He could be, but why do that?'

'The police are after him, didn't you know?' Stark said with not just a hint of sarcasm.

'Yes, but…'

'Cynthia, this is a guy who has been avoiding the FBI for God knows how many years, so it will come as second nature to him to cover his tracks. I knew it wouldn't be straight forward. I bloody knew it.'

'I'm sorry, sir, I honestly thought…'

'No need to apologise, Cynthia, it was a good piece of detective work, everything points to him living here, we are just one space removed. I'll get Jim McIntyre to speak to Post Office Investigations. As soon as we get the address he is having his mail forwarded to; then we will be quids in. Don't worry; we are getting closer because of your work, don't forget.'

'I just feel bad, that's all.'

'Well, don't. Trust me if you messed up you would know about it. If it had been left to anyone else we wouldn't have even known about this place, now would we?'

Cynthia grabbed Stark's hand. 'Thank you, sir. That's nice of you to say. I'm lucky to have someone like you as a boss. That much, I do know.'

'That is why I like you, Cynthia, you're such a good judge of character.' Stark gently pulled his hand away.

'Hey, boss.' Nobby shouted. 'They want you on the radio.'

'Who is it?'

'Control shouting you up.' The DS handed the radio to Stark.

'DI Stark to control, are you calling me, over?'

The operator sounded a little flustered, short of breath; 'Sir, report of a double murder has just come in. It sounds like it is our man again.'

'Damn it!' Stark cursed. 'Ten-Four, pass the address, we will travel straight there.'

Stark seemed agitated in the car. He kept shaking his head and was tight-lipped. 'We go from putting the door in to nick the bastard, to travelling to another killing, for Christ's sake.'

'That's the way the cookie crumbles, boss.'

'It's a ball-ache, I know that.'

'Have you got Jim researching the postal address thing as I asked, Nobby?'

'I did. It's all in hand.'

'Wagstaff's going to love this.'

'It can't be helped, boss. It's not our fault, is it?'

'Great, I'll tell him that shall I? I will just shrug my shoulders and tell him it can't be helped.'

'Alright, boss, just saying, that's all. Don't take it out on me.'

As Nobby drew the car up at the address, Stark muttered to himself. 'Another bungalow.'

A uniformed police officer was standing at the door. Stark was still raw with the devastation of the loss of more lives. They got out and walked over to the young officer, who saluted Stark.

'How long you been in the job, son?' Stark asked.

'I've just got my probation in, sir, two years.' He was a little flushed and self-conscious, as he rarely got a chance to speak with CID.

'And you still don't fucking know that you do not salute a senior officer who isn't in uniform.'

'Ah, yes, sorry, sir. I didn't think.'

'Well, get off the door and put somebody on it who *can* think.'

'Yes, sir.' The young officer's head dropped as Stark pushed the door open.

Nobby was keeping quiet and followed Stark into the house. This wasn't like his boss, but the growing pressure was immense.

They could see the bodies from the living room and sauntered towards them, mindful not to mess any evidence up. Stark sighed as they stood in the bedroom doorway; it was carnage; both bodies were on the floor entwined. It was vile beyond belief. The dead man was on his knees, his face buried into the lap of the deceased female, who was in a seated position. Her back was against the wall, and she had slumped to one side. Both were naked, and the lividity of settling blood could be seen as a patina on the skin; the pitting of purple staining on the man's face legs and chest. The same was evident in the woman's legs and posterior. The injuries to the male victim's neck, and the female's chest was visible, and a large amount of blood had pooled on the carpet around them. It had sprayed up the wall to the side of the male, and some blood appeared to be on the window sill.

'No tennis ball?' Nobby said.

'Doesn't look like it.' Stark said. 'It's him, though, isn't it? It's him, alright.'

'No doubt. He is one evil bastard.'

'He sure is, Nobby.' Stark moved around to see around the floor of the two bodies. 'Nope, no tennis ball?'

'I can't see one, either.'

'Maybe it's gone under the bed. As I say, it's him, though. What a fucking mess he's made of this pair. Poor sods.'

Nobby agreed. 'He's not messing about is he?'

'He isn't. He's got some bollocks taking on this dude, look at the size of him.'

'He is one formidable killer. You've got to give him that.'

'The only thing I want to give him is a set of handcuffs, Nobby.'

The two detectives took a couple of steps towards the bodies at which point the kitchen knife on the floor became evident; the pooled, congealed blood had concealed it. 'That big knife looks like it has done the chest wound. I'm not sure about this guys neck though. It looks a much smaller wound.'

'It could be that it wasn't inserted as far in, maybe?' Nobby observed.

'Could be.'

Stark looked behind him, as he heard shouting outside. There was a hell of a ruckus disturbing the quiet of a death scene. 'Where is he?' It was Wagstaff, in a complete fluster, who came marching in.

'Hang on, sir, watch out for the evidence.' Stark said raising a hand.

'Evidence! You've you got a bloody nerve, haven't you? It's a disaster! There I am briefing the Chief Constable that you are arresting the offender today, and the next thing we know is that there has been a double murder and no bloody killer. I've never been so embarrassed in all my life! It's a fucking disaster, man!'

'We're not thrilled about it either, for that matter.' Stark said.

'What the hell is going on, Inspector?' Wagstaff was red-faced and breathing heavily.

'The flat we went to is being used as a forwarding address for the killer, we think.'

'You *think*. Think! Any chance we can get to *know* something for once, instead of this mammoth bloody guessing game? How many more are going to die while we stand about with our hands in our pockets *thinking* things?'

'Just hold your horses, sir...' Stark was getting annoyed now.

Nobby interjected. 'Shall we go outside, it looks like Scenes of Crime have arrived.'

The three senior detectives walked outside in silence and moved away from prying ears as Nobby and Stark lit tobacco.

'Is it our man?' Wagstaff asked.

'It looks like it to me.' Stark said.

'This is bloody serious, David, the Chief's going to have my arse in a hammock for this bastard.'

'I feel sure that in the next couple of hours we will have him in custody, and then the Chief might be calmed a little.'

'Right, go and get the little shit, now! Not soon, not in ten minutes, or next bloody week, get him nicked! Get whoever and whatever you need, and go and get him or we will both be in a big hat by Monday.'

'That's exactly what we are going to do.' Stark said as he and Nobby headed back to the car.

'I've not seen the Superintendent so wound up before.' Nobby said.

'He's under a lot of pressure from the Ivory Towers. To be honest, I'm as pissed off as he is, but it must have been embarrassing for him sitting there giving the Chief the good news when this came in.'

'It's a nightmare.' Nobby said, stating the bleeding obvious.

Stark took hold of Nobby's arm. 'Hang on, let me try and get hold of Jim from here.' Stark went over to a woman in a dressing gown standing at the door of her house. 'Have you got a phone I can use, my love?'

'Yes, of course. It's just awful, isn't it? She's lovely, Phillipa is, but him, I knew he was trouble from day one. I reckon he was knocking her about. Have you got him yet?'

'Erm, sort of. Where's the phone?'

Stark was ushered into the woman's hallway and dialled the police station number. He was put through to Jim.

'What have we got, address wise, Jim?'

'That's good timing, sir, the Post Office Investigation department have just called me back. Have yae got a pen handy?'

Stark did the pen mime with his hand to Nobby, who responded by pocket tapping and eventually pulling out a piece of folded A4 and a biro. 'Go for it, Jim.' Stark said.

Stark repeated the information out loud. '23 Green Close, Butlers Hill, Hucknall. Thanks, Jim, see you later.' Stark put the phone down. 'Thanks love, much appreciated.'

'What's happened then? I heard she was dead—what a thing to wake up to. This is going to set me right back, this is. I'm already on pills for my nerves. You never think it's going to happen to you, do you? It must be serious if the CID is here. Is that right, then, she's been killed?'

'Thanks again, love.' Nobby said dismissively, but with a close-lipped smile.

The two detectives headed towards the car. 'Do you know the address,

Nobby?' Stark asked.

'Yes, it's a shit hole.'

'Get on the radio and tell the team to meet us there, they are probably still at the previous address. Tell them to drop everything. Let's get this fucking idiot in custody.'

*

Fat Sandra eyed the man suspiciously as she battered the sausages at Butlers Hill Fish 'n' Chip Shop. She could see the orange mountain bike propped against the large window, albeit obscured by condensation and an array of handprints. The man who had caught her attention was third in the queue. She hurried as quickly as she could to the telephone in the back and dialled the number and extension that DC Ashley Stevens had given her. It rang without an answer. She waited but was worried the man would be served before she got through. She waited some more. She couldn't know the CID office was deserted apart from 'Happy' Jim McIntyre. Jim was too busy with his paperwork to answer his own phone, never mind running errands for young Ashley and answering his. It would wait, whatever it was.

Sandra put the phone down and waddled back into the shop area and gave the man sneaky glances as she busied herself behind the counter. From what she could make out, he looked dishevelled and was wearing the grey hoody that Ashley had mentioned. His hands were dirty, and he had his hood up, despite the warm day. The man didn't engage with anyone and tended to keep his back to her, looking out the window. She felt sure it was him. Sandra moved in front of Gary and continued serving. It was a big order, and the weird guy looked impatient.

'Just waiting for chips.' Sandra said to those queuing. 'Two minutes, that's all.'

The man looked out the window, searching out clear patches that weren't smeared condensation so that he could see outside. After a minute or so, he stepped back from the glass when he saw the cars arrive at speed, and men run up the stairs to the house a few doors down. That was his house. Or at least the house where his room was. They were detectives. No doubt. Who else wore suits in the summer heat? What else was it - a raid by Real Estate sellers, keen to make a sale?

Orlando Welles was used to this. He had been on the move his whole life. He'd had much closer shaves than this, and would be resourceful enough to find a new place fairly quickly. In truth, he had been thinking about moving back to London in any case; he was more anonymous there. It was too close-knit around this area; everyone seemed to know everybody else's business. This environment was not best for a serial killer.

'Two minutes, ya say?' Welles asked the portly owner.

'They're ready now love.' Sanda said with a smile.

'Okay, I'll wait in line, if they're ready.'

'No problem, sorry for the wait.'

Sandra hadn't seen the detectives run into the house as she used the big scoop to move the chips around in the vat of hot fat. Nor had Ashley seen the orange coloured bike propped up against the chip shop, just along the way. If he did, it didn't register. His focus was elsewhere – to get to the back of the premises as soon as he possibly could, to prevent Welles from doing a bunk.

The line moved along pretty quickly. Welles paid with a five-pound note, which Sandra rang into the till, but placed at the side of the drawer. She gave him his change, and he thanked her politely. 'Thanks, Ma'am.'

He was American. As the door slowed to a close behind him, Sandra returned to the back shop and dialled the number yet again.

Welles left the shop with his bag of chips, and quietly wheeled his bike down the back streets and away. It was time to move on. Just one more visit tonight, and he would be gone. It would be a memorable farewell, and he had it all figured out.

*

Nobby sat on the edge of the bed in Welles' room. 'I can't believe this.' He had his head in his hands.

'I wouldn't sit there, Nobby, you don't know what devils glue might be on it.' Stark said.

Nobby laughed. 'Fair point.' He stood up. 'What a hole this is. The place stinks to high heaven.'

'The décor's a bit…shall we say, individual?' Stark observed. 'At least we know this is his place. We just need to wait for him to return.' Stark wasn't wholly convinced that it was that simple and was peeved that he would have to update Wagstaff, once again, that they had not caught their man.

Nobby took in the surroundings. 'How the other half live, eh, boss? I think he could do with a bit of a spring clean?'

'I doubt the one season would be enough, somehow.' Stark smiled.

The occult posters and the strange scribblings and drawings that covered much of the wall caught Nobby's eye. 'This is one fucked up kid.'

'Have you just figured that one out, Nobby?' Stark said.

'No, but what is all this graffiti about?' The two of them began reading some of it.

'Death and glory.'

'Funeral Blues.'

'Pip squeaked.'

'Graaaant.'

'It's just nonsense, isn't it?' Nobby said, not realising how close he was to seeing the name 'Steph,' daubed on the wall.

'It's evidence, Nobby, that's what it is. We need to get it photographed, but the priority has to be to catch him. It means nothing until we have him in custody. If he goes on the run, how many more are going to die?'

Ashley appeared in the doorway with Cynthia. 'Nice pad,' was all he said.

Cynthia shivered. 'This is creepy.'

Nobby saw through the window a liveried police transit van pull up outside, with the Special Operations officers. 'Here come the cavalry.'

'They took their time. They left when we did.' Ashley said.

Stark rubbed at his chin, already sprouting five o'clock shadow. 'How many of them is there?' Stark asked.

'They were leaving one guy at the old house to tidy things up. It looks like we're going to get a complaint, by the way. The kid's Dad turned up and started kicking off after you'd gone.' Ashley said.

'Fuck that, how many are here, uniformed bobbies, I mean.'

Nobby interrupted as he watched them decant from the van. 'Three, by the looks of things, they'll be here any second.'

Sure enough, the pounding of footsteps on carpetless stairs heralded the boys in blue.

'Not here, then?' The balding sergeant said.

'No, but he should be coming back. It's his place.' Stark said. 'You guys will have to wait here in case he does. Are you okay with that – is three of you enough?'

'Yes, it suits us. No worries. Paddy Watson will come over shortly when he's done at the last place. Christ, four of us should be plenty.'

'Don't forget he's an armed killer.'

'It's fine.'

'Brilliant, thanks, gents. We are going to have a run around the town centre; he can't be miles away, surely? It's better if we do it in plain cars.'

'Yes, sure. We might have to introduce him to Mister Wood.' The moustachioed sergeant tapped at the hilt of his truncheon tucked down the side of his trousers in its special elongated pocket.

'Don't take any risks, just down the bastard. Ask questions later.' Nobby said.

'Sounds like a plan.' The PS said.

'You've got photo's, and you know what he is to be nicked for don't you?'

'Yes, we've got the briefing pack, it's all fine. Leave it with us. We'll have him, no problem.'

Stark and the detectives shuffled out of the confined space and away down the stairs to begin their tour of local streets. Once again, this was not how it was supposed to go.

As soon as the Special Ops officers heard the door slam downstairs, they mooched around the flat and began reading the pencil work adorning the walls: 'This is some fucked up shit. Look at this "Stigmata", what is he a religious nut? And this one, "*Steph- kinda rhymes with death*". What the fuck is that supposed to mean?'

'God knows.'

15

'Is the gift of life not also accompanied by the gift of pain?

For without the latter, we could not fully appreciate the former, and therefore both would be squandered.'

Craig D.Lounsbrough

DC Steph Dawson had seen things in her career that no-one should see; mangled children, terrified rape victims, the subjects of paedophilia, murder victims with their brains seeping into the carpet and yet she had never been so upset as she was now. This was something from which it was impossible to distance oneself. And it hurt. It hurt like flaming hell.

The crying came in waves, real sobbing, none of this tear trickling stuff; she probably shouldn't be driving, but she was. She had to get home. Steph had been holding it in for so long, it was all flooding out of her, and she was powerless to resist it. When she tried it hurt, even more, it was too strong, too powerful. Steph had refused her sister, Margaret's, offer for her to stay at her house for a night or two. Steph needed space, some peace, and her own bed. There was no way she could go into work tomorrow, not after this. Nobby said he would ring her later and so she could sort it out then. Two or three days on her own should be enough for her to get her bearings, although she felt a little guilty doing so in the middle of a murder enquiry. In fairness, she would understand if it was anybody else needing to take time off, so she felt that the team would be sympathetic, given the circumstances.

It was rare for Steph to feel so vulnerable. The death of her father was all-encompassing. Her eyes were sore, her head was thumping, she was dry-mouthed, and she physically ached. The pain of such a loss had impaired Steph's whole essence. The image of her dad's coffin being lowered into his lonely grave kept forcing its way into her thoughts. It had throughout the day; at the wake and beyond, and yet again, now, as she drove home. In life, she and dad had gone about their day-to-day business and sometimes, over the years, scarcely seen each other for large periods of time, yet somehow his death had made her DNA ache. He was old, and she knew he wouldn't be around forever, but it still slammed into her like a wave in a hurricane. The order of things had changed on an immense scale, and it was irreversible. It was that finality which shook her more than anything else.

The heat didn't help. She had the car window down for most of the journey, but when in the more congested traffic in town she wound it up, to hide her pain from pedestrians at zebra crossings and traffic lights. She had an old Vauxhall Viva car, and sometimes the window would get dislodged and stuck when she opened or closed it. She would have to wiggle the glass at the same time as winding the handle on the door while lodging the steering wheel in between her knees. All of this merely to prevent others from seeing her distress. It is a strange side effect that crying and heartache bring with them a feeling of embarrassment to put the cherry on top of our misery cake.

Steph couldn't stand the window being up for too long, it was so damned hot, and she used some of the tissues piling up on the passenger seat to wipe sweat from her forehead and cleavage. She also tried to repair the leaking mascara to prevent panda eyes. It was a lost cause.

Steph turned the corner close to her block, and the gravel cracked under her tyres; she did not see the cyclist until the very last second, and she stood on the brakes. Inside the car, it juddered and scraped to a halt and then stalled. Outside there was a squeal of tyres causing heads to turn. She had managed to avoid hitting the buffoon.

Steph, being Steph, shouted out of the window as he manoeuvred past, explaining to him that he should pay more attention when crossing a road; well, sort of: 'Watch what you are doing you fucking dozy prick! I could have killed you, you fucking moronic bastard.' She let it all out; her emotions were on a knife-edge.

The cyclist seemed taken aback. 'Pardon me, ma'am,' was all he could say and in a second he was off like a shot.

Steph was breathing heavily from the near-miss, and her heart was thumping harder than Rocky Balboa going for the knockout. She sat for a couple of moments to get herself together. All she could see was her dad's coffin being lowered into that cold dark hole, again and again. A shiver went down her spine, and her eyes began to fill up with tears once more. How could she get rid of that raw image?

At least she was almost home now. It was a modest apartment, but it was hers, and it was home, and as we know, home is where the heart is, and now, unfortunately for poor Steph, home is where a serial killer is. She was oblivious to what the guy on the bike looked like, or even sounded like. Steph was focussed on her outburst, born from demons that had swirled around her fuzzy head all day. She was in family mode, not police mode.

Steph re-started the stalled car and trundled carefully into her car parking space. She couldn't even be bothered to wind the window fully up as she got out, that was how deflated she felt. For two pins, she would have put her fist through the fucking thing. Nothing mattered right now. She sauntered to her front door, shoulders hunched, carrying an invisible coal sack of grief which seemed to weigh more oppressively with every step she took.

It was at times like this she was grateful for being on the ground floor rather than have to pound the stairs. Once inside the apartment, she quickly opened all of the windows, trying to get air into the place. It was baking hot, and the heat was accompanied by stale air. She could smell her Dad. Steph stopped in her tracks in the living room; she wasn't expecting to see her father's slippers behind the chair. She had no crying left, and she just sighed. 'Oh, Dad. How many times have I told you?' Self-conversation was perhaps more prevalent in a person living alone and emerged the moment she entered the door. Steph assumed everyone did it.

Her father had only been living at Steph's for a few months, it wasn't ideal, and they had often clashed. Both were strong-minded. She struggled to adapt to his habits when she was so entrenched in her own. Maybe she should not have been so hard on the poor old guy in his twilight moments.

Steph hadn't the heart before now to move his newspaper from the arm of his chair, and as she did, she looked at the half-finished crossword. His writing had become a scrawl, and on closer inspection she realised that the answers were just random words, merely to give the pretence that he was perhaps not as affected by his fading brainpower as he was. She shook her head; it was typical Dad. Steph found herself kissing the newspaper before throwing it in the bin.

The open windows were not bringing much relief from the heat. Steph headed into the bedroom to open the one in there. After she had opened it, she noticed a parcel on her bedside table. A present? 'Nobby.' She said. 'You daft bugger.'

She put her handbag down at the side of the crudely wrapped parcel. It brought a smile to her face. It appeared to have more layers of Sellotape wrapped around it than wrapping paper. A three-year-old would probably have done a better job. Maybe he was in a rush, she thought. Perhaps it was just Nobby. She read the label. *'Thinking about you. Sorry for being a pain lately. Love Nobby Xx'* It was a nice thought, particularly when she knew how busy he was, to take the trouble to buy it, wrap it, and drop it around. It was very kind of him. He was so protective of her. He meant well, and he was a genuinely decent bloke. She shouldn't be so hard on him.

In truth, she just wanted to collapse on the bed, but she was intrigued. Steph went to get scissors from the kitchen and returned into her bedroom, sitting on the side of the bed to open up the present with some difficulty. It needed several precise cuts of the Sellotape to finally released the small box inside. She hastily dropped the scissors down and finished the job with her fingers, being careful not to crack a nail. Gold earrings. 'Thanks, Nobby, you big soft sod.' She said to herself.

She turned to the mirror on the bedside table and peered into it while holding the earings against her lobes. 'Holy shit.' She could see a bedraggled, weathered face staring back at her. It was a reversible mirror, and the magnified side was facing her. She shook her head in disdain, her mascara was smudged, her blonde hair greasy from sweat, and way too many wrinkles for her liking. She was a beautiful, voluptuous, older woman in truth, but she never really believed that. Men had always been attracted to her, she wasn't blind to that, of course, but she still felt that if you had good boobs, blokes never saw anything else. She didn't give herself enough credit. Steph once tested a new guy, whom she had never met when she had a low cut top on and after they had spoken for a few minutes, she sent Ashley to go and ask what colour hair Steph had. He couldn't remember. 'I rest my case.' She said.

Suddenly her 'spider-sense' began to tingle—the window behind her. Many cops talked of this 'spider-sense', a line stolen from the Spiderman comics, meaning you could sense when something was slightly awry. It wasn't peculiar to cops, of course, everyone gets it sometimes, but maybe it was heightened. Or perhaps they were more prone to trust it? More likely to act upon it. She turned quickly to the bedroom window behind her, but nothing was there—just the curtain's slight movement from a tiny gust of wind that had emerged from somewhere. The feeling niggled her enough for her to walk over, a little tentatively, but again she saw nothing. Close the window? 'Screw that, it's too hot,' she answered her own question aloud.

She started to undress. 'Steph, your chuff stinks, have a shower, you smelly bitch.' She said to herself. She grabbed hold of some pyjamas out of the wardrobe, threw them on to the bed, and continued to remove items of clothing. She suddenly felt a chill down her spine, and she shivered.

*

Stark had insisted they go to the pub next door, for their 'de-brief,' after what had been a very long day. For several days now, the team had been working 8 am until 10 pm, or thereabouts, and he had to make sure they did not burn out. They were all different, of course, but an hour or two in the pub at the end of the shift gave them a chance to talk, and a chance to iron out any niggles between the different personalities should they arise. Tomorrow could be an even longer one. D Day perhaps?

The pub next door had an outside patio-cum-beer garden, and Stark's crew could sit in relative comfort, now that dusk had set in and the air was beginning to cool just a little. The darkening skies thankfully introduced the slightest of breezes, lightening the atmosphere. There was a sense that a thunderstorm may be in the offing.

They were all there, minus Steph, of course. Cynthia had somehow managed to sit next to David Stark, and most of them were puffing at cigarettes. Only Steve Aston and Cynthia abstained; the 'new breed...of boring fuckers,' as Nobby called them.

Steve Aston brought a clinking tray of drinks over and placed it gingerly on the table. He handed Stark the change.

'Finally. Did you have to wait for it to ferment?' Charlie asked. 'I've got a throat like a camel's sphincter, here.'

'It's chock-a-block at the bar.' Steve replied, sweat beading on his forehead.

'Any news from Steph, Nobby?' Stark asked as he put the change in his pocket and reached for the cold lager which he gulped and gave the obligatory gasp of release.

'No, not yet, sir, I'm going to give her a ring in a minute. There's a phone box across the road. Losing her Dad has affected her more than she lets on, you know.'

'Of course, it has, she amazes me.' Stark said. 'You might as well nip next door and ring from the nick for nothing, hadn't you?'

'I might, but you never know who's listening, do you? There is no privacy.'

'I think it would do your image some good if people saw your softer side.' Stark grinned.

Nobby burped out a reply 'Bollocks.'

'Nice.'

'Aren't you going over to her place to see her, Sarge?' Cynthia asked.

'No, I've been given my orders.'

'To stay away?'

'Pretty much. I understand, though, it's not very nice. Sometimes people need time on their own, and she doesn't want me fussing over her. Anyway, I left her a little present just to let her know I'm thinking about her.'

'Ah, that's sweet.' Cynthia said. 'Isn't that sweet, sir?'

'Yes, he is the sweetest detective sergeant I know.' Stark leaned over and pulled at Nobby's cheek.

'Gerrof! It's just to let her know I am thinking about her; it's quite normal. I read about it in a magazine at the dentist's once.'

'She will appreciate it.' Cynthia said, smiling at Nobby.

'Still no news at Welles shit-hole flat, boss?' Ashley asked Stark.

'No. I'm starting to wonder if our friend has clocked the coppers there.

At some stage, we need SOCO to go through the place as well. I hope those cops are keeping their hands in their pockets and not rummaging around everywhere. The priority has to be to get him nicked, though, without creating some sort of hostage situation.'

'The worse thing about this is the knowledge he will strike again, yet we don't know where, or who is next on his list.' Ashley said.

'I've asked Jim to look at the issue around deaths in the family. It's a theme with the families that have been attacked.'

'Only one of them was in the paper, boss, in the obituaries, so I cannae see it being that.' Jim said.

Stark winced. 'I don't believe in coincidences, though. Does he work somewhere to do with these deaths, maybe? I don't know. I doubt he is choosing them randomly? But then again, maybe he is just picking the easiest houses to enter. Let's face it we don't know. The reality is, we know who he is. We just need him in custody, and if those cops at his bedsit keep out of the way, he is bound to come back at some stage. He should be waiting for us in the cells in the morning.'

'I'm assuming they have moved their van off the street, you know, the one with "Police" written all over the bastard.' Nobby asked.

'Surely they aren't that thick.' Stark said.

'It is Special Ops, don't forget, they aren't known to be the brightest stars in the sky, now are they?' Nobby observed.

Ashley had a thought. 'I might drive past on the way home and just check it is not obvious to all and sundry that there are cops in the flat.'

'It's probably worth doing, Ash. Has the circulation gone out, Nobby?' Stark asked.

'Yes, it's gone to all forces, all the local bobbies are searching for the bloke, in between calls. The circulation has got a picture of him on it, and a mock-up of his bike, and clothing. They can't miss him if they happen to see him. I've asked the duty Inspector to keep two on overtime to search for him on top of the regular patrol.'

'And we don't know of any associates or contacts he might have here in good old Blighty.' Stark asked Jim.

'Och, Blighty.' He laughed. 'No, he's a loner, you'll nae be surprised to hear.'

'He'll come.' Stark said, sipping at his pint of Heineken.

'That reminds me I must ring Steph when I've had this pint.'

Cynthia smiled. 'Don't leave it too late, Sarge, she will be tired. She might even be in bed by now, for all you know.'

'Alright, let me finish my pint. Christ, don't you start, Cynthia. You can't win here, one minute I'm *too* attentive, the next minute I'm supposed to be ringing her every verse end. It is like Steph is nagging me by bloody proxy.'

'Always glad to help, Sarge.' Cynthia smiled.

*

Steph had put the radio/alarm on in her bedroom, as she took a shower. It was playing 'You Sexy Thing' by Hot Chocolate.

Orlando Welles padded towards the window from the outside, having seen his chance from the shadows. He pulled the open window further ajar, put his leg through, and within a second he was inside Steph's apartment. Welles had his knife in his hand, just in case, but he wanted to delay interaction for now; he wanted to experience this little adventure for longer. He was sick of just going in all guns blazing; it was like wolfing down a good meal. The killer wanted this to touch the sides; to draw out the experience and savour it for once. He now knew he would be on the run again after this one, and the next opportunity might be some way off. Maybe he could stay the night there, once he had finished with her? The prospect of sleeping with a corpse or indeed just the head, or better yet, a headless body, was something he had pondered many times. It was part of his fantasising ritual over the years. These fantasies seeped into reality; a sick and twisted mind knows no boundaries and his constant thirst for gratification and to some extent notoriety, expanded his repertoire. The realm of humanity which most of us live in does not begin to comprehend a brain malfunctioning to such an extent that no empathy is possible. Where depravity fuels repeated savagery, just to feel something, anything. In reality, after the deed, Welles was often spent, and on an adrenalin low, so he would leave and slink back to his flat. Now, he had nowhere to go.

He paused at the en-suite door and caught a glimpse of the woman's bare backside with soap suds arching over the curve. Nice. Might he take her now? No. Be disciplined—time to hide, to listen, to watch.

Welles quietly moved across the carpeted floor and slowly twisted the door handle to the adjacent spare room. It had a small bed in it, but there were also quite a few boxes and random clothes thrown on top of the mattress. It smelt of an old man.

Steph turned off the shower and bent over, using a small towel to rub at her long hair which she then wrapped around her head. She then got the larger sheet towel and dried her body. She walked into the bedroom. This alerted Welles who had a view as she lay on the bed, the towel underneath her. The monster could see that the woman had shapely hips and a full bosom with big nipples. Her legs were open and her knees raised - she was letting it all hang out - he was getting triggered. Steph sang along to 'Living On A Prayer' by Jon Bon Jovi. She felt much better after her shower, if not a little drained. She swung her legs over the bed and balancing the head towel with one hand, walked naked into the living room. She bent over and picked something up off the floor.

Welles backed away from the door as she approached the spare bedroom. Steph paused momentarily. Wasn't that door closed earlier? It can't have been. She pushed it open, and Welles stood behind it, knife raised, as she threw a pair of old slippers on to the bed and then backed away. He was a fraction of a second from striking. He remained motionless and didn't see Steph falter, pause outside the door once more. She shook her head, muttering to herself, 'Don't be silly.' And Steph returned to her position on the bed after disposing of the head towel on the bedroom floor.

She had left the door ajar, and this enabled Welles to continue his voyeurism. His original plan was to let her drift off, take a bit of cash for his journey, before waking her up to violate her. What he had planned was going to be so shocking, it would surely surpass anything else. It was hard to resist; she looked beautiful lying there, a 'real' woman. There was still something about her that resonated, something different. It was something that while he couldn't identify it, made him feel just a little wary. Suddenly the telephone rang at the side of her bed. It made both her and her killer jump, and she put her hand on her heart before answering it. 'Jesus Christ!' She said.

Welles moved back from the crack in the door and listened intently to the one-sided conversation.

'Hello?'

16

'You really have to let me fight my own battles. You can't constantly second-guess me and try to protect me. It's stifling.'

E. L. James.

'Hows the head?' Nobby asked.

'Much better, thanks, I'm just completely exhausted.'

He could hear the tiredness in Steph's voice. 'I've always said, for the best head in Nottingham, go and see Steph.'

'Stop being a tramp.'

'I'm only kidding.'

'I know…Just Nottingham?'

'Probably the world.'

She laughed. 'Joking aside, Nobby, I could do with having a couple of days off. I know it is awkward with the murder inquiry but…'

'Steph, it's not awkward, you should be off work in any case. Its called bereavement leave. I will put you down for a couple of days and if you need more, just let me know.'

'Thanks, Nobby.'

Steph could hear the traffic rushing past the red telephone kiosk that Nobby filled with his bulky frame. 'How come you've used, the phone box and not the phones in the nick?' She asked.

'Just privacy, I don't want half the nick knowing my business.'

'I suppose so, where are the others, in the bar?'

'In the pub next door, I'm just across the road.' Nobby could smell urine in the phone box; it doubled as a toilet for late-night revellers miscalculating their bladder levels. 'It stinks of piss in here.'

'They all do, don't they?'

'I remember now why I try to avoid using them. I might call around to see you later if you like.'

'Nobby, there is no need, honestly, just give me tomorrow on my own, and I'm sure I will be back to my perky self.'

'I like you when you are perky.'

'For God's sake, Nobby, do you never think of anything else?'

'Just you, my angel.' He was smiling. He glanced outside the kiosk to see a woman staring in at him. 'You will have to wait, Mrs.'

'Who are you talking to?'

''Some woman is waiting outside giving me the dead eye.'

'Let her wait a minute. Anyway, Angel? Christ, you don't know me very well do you?'

'I'm not interested in your past; it's the future, our future that matters.'

It was all a bit heavy for her when all she wanted to do was close her eyes. 'Thank you for the present, by the way; it was a lovely thing to do, especially the note. Its been a tough day.'

'How did it go?'

'Awful, of course. I've been breaking my heart here.'

'Ah, Steph I'm sorry, love.'

'I know. I will be okay, just treat me gently for a little while. The note helped.'

'I spend all that money, and you thank me for the bloody note?'

'Don't be tight, Nobby.'

'Jesus, women. Anyway, I meant what I said, huh.'

'I know.'

'Know what?'

'I know you're a dick.' She laughed.

'Piss off. Get bent.'

'Oh, I forgot I nearly bent a bloke on a bike near the flat.'

'How come? What do you mean?'

'I was coming around Acacia, and he suddenly appeared, I had to slam the brakes on. A right scruffy little bastard he was.' Steph said.

'Fucking prick should have watched where he was going. It will be some low-life day-dreaming about his next DSS payment.'

'You should never judge someone by their appearance, Sergeant

Clarke.'

'Yes, you should.' He peered out at the woman who was now looking at her watch.

'I went ballistic at him as well, poor sod.' Steph grinned and bit at her bottom lip.

'Did you give him a mouthful then?'

'Just a bit.'

'Hang on she's knocking on the fucking glass now.' The telephone box was made up of a red frame with small window panes all around. There was just enough room for one person inside. Nobby raised his voice. 'You'll have to wait a minute. Jesus, what is wrong with people. I bet you got a round of fucks in return, didn't you?'

'No, I felt a bit guilty really, all he said was…'

'Hang on; the pips are going, let me put another ten pence in.' The pips indicated that your time was up unless you replenished the cash box with another coin.

'All he said was, "Pardon me, Ma'am." Soft as shit he was.'

Steph waited.

'Hello.'

'Nobby, no need to put another ten pence in, I'm dropping to sleep, here. No offence. Let the woman use it. I'm knackered.'

'Are you sure I couldn't just come around and give you a dose of Doctor Clarke's magic wand?'

'Nobby, don't, my heads niggling. You aren't giving me a dose of anything, thank you very much.' Steph's eyelids were drooping. 'No chance of anything tonight. Like I say, I'm cream crackered, Nobby, I'm falling to sleep, love.'

'Alright, I'll let you go to the land of nod, goodnight sweetheart.'

'Goodnight, Nobby, thanks for ringing, love.'

'Love you.' He said.

'I know you do.'

'Hey!'

Steph hung up and closed her eyes. Mulling through the conversation and then the image jumped into her mind. Her father's coffin being lowered. She sighed. But within a couple of minutes, she drifted into slumber.

*

Nobby returned to the table to a chorus of 'How is she?' and 'How did it go?'

He sat down on the metal chair, which had trouble accommodating his bulk. 'She's okay, thanks, but she's not herself, of course. She sounded exhausted, to be honest.'

'She's bound to be.' Ashley commented.

'She said she needed some time alone again, which I understand. It's just difficult when you want to be there for someone, you know.'

'It is hard.' Cynthia said. 'Did she like her pressie?'

'Yes, she did bless her. Although she said, she liked the note more than the present. Strange creatures, you women are, aren't you.'

'We have our idiosyncrasies.' Cynthia smiled.

'Idio-what?'

'It doesn't matter, yes, we are strange creatures, we have to be to have anything to do with bloody men.'

There were some 'Oooh's' and 'Leave it out's.'

The conversation lulled. 'Where's Stark? He's not gone, has he?' Nobby asked.

'No, he is very nobly, helping Charlie with the drinks.' Steve said. 'I did offer.'

'It's about time he went.' Nobby laughed. 'Does he even know where the bar is?'

There were a few giggles and a further lull. It wasn't just Steph who was feeling tired, the gang had been hard at it, and when you stop is when you can get a little overwhelmed. Nobby filled the gap by lighting a cigarette and blowing out smoke exaggeratedly.

'What else did Steph have to say, anything?' Ashley asked, trying to keep the conversation alive.

'Nothing, really. I've given her a couple more days off, it's only right, Steph needs to get herself sorted before coming back into all this bollocks. I could tell by her voice that she wasn't right.'

'Definitely.' They all agreed. 'Tell her to take her time.'

'She did make me laugh. She nearly wiped up some youth on a bike and gave him a round of fucks. I would have loved to have seen his face.'

'That's our Steph. Did they have a little exchange of views?' Ashley asked.

'No, apparently he was really polite.'

'He wouldn't have known what had hit him, with a tongue lashing from Steph.' Ashley said.

Nobby looked at him sideways. 'Alright Ashley, she's not here to defend herself you know…' He could hold it no longer and broke into a smile, 'Although, It might have been less painful if she had collided with the poor sod. Physical pain is often easier to recover from than mental scars.'

They all laughed as Stark and Charlie returned with drinks.

'I see what you mean, Steve, it's every man for himself at the bar.' Stark said.

'I did tell you, sir, glad it's not just me. Well, I'm not happy you were stuck a while, sir, but,'

'Steve, It's fine. I know what you mean. It is heaving. It must be the hot weather.' Stark regained his seat and took a drink of the cold beer.

'It brings them all out, does this hot weather, look over there, boss. Nice bit of crumpet, a lovely bit of grumble and grunt.'

Ashley's 'crumpet' radar, as he called it, had alerted him to a couple of young ladies who were beautifully tanned and wearing matching crocheted style mini-skirts in white and pink.

Stark craned his neck. 'Christ. One less knit-one-pearl-one and you would see their landing gear.'

'Sir!' Cynthia was shocked. 'I didn't think you were like that.'

'Like what?' Stark said grinning.

'He's a red-blooded bloke like the rest of us, aren't you boss?' Nobby said.

'I was the last time I looked. Although it was a while ago.'

Cynthia took hold of his hand. 'There's hope for us all then, is there?'

The comment took Stark a little by surprise. 'Erm, I guess so. Are you sure you've not had too many sherberts, Cynthia?' He cast a glance at Nobby who gave him a raised eyebrow and knowing look.

Ashley broke the momentary awkwardness. 'Anybody fancy a stroll over for a little chat with the lovely ladies? In for a penny, and all that.' He glanced at Nobby who grimaced, and he looked like he was mulling the proposition over. Cynthia hit the Sarge on the arm.

'Eh, you! Sergeant! You've just been on the love-phone, you shouldn't be eyeing up other women.'

'I'm not, only at an artistic level.'

'Haha. Yes, like anyone is going to believe that.'

'It's true.' Nobby was laughing and took a drag from his cigarette.

'Poor old Steph.' Cynthia said.

'Aye. I might nip around and see her.' Nobby pondered.

'Nobby, stop it. You've just said she needs her own space. You're smothering her.'

'Why am I?'

'Because you are. Give her some space. She is still mourning the loss of her father.'

'That's why I need to be with her.' Nobby was struggling without his other half. For such a big, brutish, confident ex Para, at times he was like a little lost schoolboy without his woman close-by.

Cynthia was on a roll, with her female advice. She was relishing being the only woman at the table for once. 'Nobby. Listen to me; you got her a lovely surprise; you've rung her. Just give her a chance to get herself together. Give her time. Have another pint.'

'Okay, if you insist. Mine's a Guinness. It's last orders in ten minutes.'

'Trust me, Steph will thank you tomorrow.'

'You're right Cynthia. More like if I go around to see her tonight, she will murder me tomorrow.'

*

Steph was lying on the bed with the towel still underneath her. She was fast asleep, and she would wheeze when she drew in breath and horse neigh when she blew out. It was probably all the cigarettes she had smoked that day at the funeral. She liked a smoke, but she must have been through two packs.

Orlando Welles had waited patiently, just to give her a chance to get fully off to sleep. He had never heard a woman snore like her, and he found it amusing. Eventually, he slowly tip-toed into the kitchen and almost immediately saw the beauty of a kitchen knife in a wooden block. He slowly slid it out and admired it. His new weapon had a solid blade and more importantly a rivetted wooden handle. It was a quality item. He could probably take her head off with it, but he might need a hammer to whack the blade through the spine. With this in mind, he opened a couple of more drawers looking for something like a hammer. He was taking too long, getting distracted, and Stephs erratic breathing had him freeze a couple of times, thinking she had woken up. For now, at least, he abandoned the hammer idea and put his 'old faithful' knife back into his hoody pocket, now that he had the large kitchen knife to do his work. He grinned as he fingered the quality of the knife, smooth dark wood, varnished and a brass rivet which he stroked, it was perfectly flush to the handle. He walked slowly towards the bedroom; his heartbeat was quickening in anticipation with each slow, methodical step.

He took in the view of the naked woman on the bed. He wanted her head in a bucket. He took a deep breath and slammed his hand over her mouth and showed the blade to the startled eyes of Detective Constable Stephanie Dawson which shot wide open in panic. She tried to scream but she was stifled by his smelly hand.

'Shut the fuck up bitch!'

Steph immediately reached down to the side of the bed and grabbed the long metal night torch she'd kept from her uniform days. She kept it there for a reason, and that reason just happened. She brought it down on Welles's head with great force, and he fell to one side, dazed. He saw stars and the pain of the blow raged on the top of his skull. He was moaning and whingeing. She had hurt him.

Steph was up off the bed and instinctively headed for the door. Her keys were in her bag on the bedside table! Fuck! She should have gone out of the bedroom window. She began to shout for assistance at the top of her voice.

'Help! Police! Help!'

She banged frantically on the door with her fists.

The blade went into her shoulder with incredible force and banged her face into the door.

'I don't fuck about bitch.'

Steph dropped to one knee but was determined not to go down. Never go down. She had been in many 'no-hope' situations in the police, and if it had taught her one thing, it was to never go to the floor, if at all possible. She got to her feet despite the searing pain forging like hot steel into her right shoulder. She was scared and in survival mode. Welles pulled out the knife, which had cracked and pierced her shoulder blade, before grabbing his tennis ball from his hoody pocket. He squeezed it sufficiently to force it into her mouth as she cried out and then released it, allowing it to fill her mouth cavity. The killer used his left hand to force her back against the door. He held her by the throat and had the knife raised in front of her left eyeball.

Their eyes met, and both were breathing heavily.

'Clever fucker, eh?'

Steph made a noise through the tennis ball. It was incoherent, but the expression on her face and the flash of her eyes wrote out 'fuck you' clearly enough to Welles. He had noticed she was either heavy or strong because she was not easy to manhandle. He touched at his head. It was bleeding.

'You fucking bitch!' He raised the kitchen knife but stopped himself before releasing the blow.

'I'm going to take your motherfucking head off, doll.' He grabbed at her naked breast harshly squeezing and twisting it like the sadistic bastard that he was, adding further to her pain and Steph grimaced.

She started to resist again, kicking out, and Welles punched her across her face. Steph used her left hand to gouge at his eyes, nearly ripping his eyeball out.

'Fuck off!' He stepped back, and Steph went to kick him in the balls, but he knocked her leg away. Her shoulder was badly injured, and her right arm failed to rise to continue the attack.

'Right, fuck this.' Welles barked, and grabbed her left arm, leaning into her with his body and forcing her forearm flat against the door. She was wriggling and managed to grab a handful of his hair which she pulled with all her might, jarring his head back. He groaned and with great venom pinched some skin on her forearm and thrust the large knife into it, pinning it against the door. He could feel her kneeing him in the thigh as he did until the knife pierced, and then she abated with a cry. Her scream diluted by the gag.

He then retrieved old faithful, his 'go-to' knife, out of his pocket and callously took hold of her right arm, causing her to again squeal in pain albeit muffled by the tennis ball.

'You fucking dare touch me, you whore!' He did the same. Loose skin, whack, pierced into the door. Steph cried out in pain as her arms were now both pierced by the knives stuck into the wood. It was a searing agony that stretched across the length of her arms and met the agony of her smashed shoulder blade.

Welles squealed with delight. He put his face to hers, contorted with mania and high excitement. His spittle went into her eyes as he cried. 'You don't know who you are dealing with. I'm going to crucify your ass.'

Steph was terrified, and she knew she was as good as dead. She also knew exactly who this was and that her only chance of surviving was to fight with all her might, to put him off, to hurt him, to escape, anything but acquiesce. He had got her in his clutches, and she was frightened. She was in agonising pain and completely stuck, now at the mercy of this crazed psychopathic killer.

Welles took hold of each knife handle with both hands, and using all the strength he could muster; he forced the blades into the wood even more.

'Stigmata, bitch. You're like little baby Jesus.' He giggled to himself. 'This is what happens when you fuck about.'

The callousness of his actions caused more shouts of pain from Steph. She was helpless and thought she might lose consciousness. Her vision was getting blurry, and her body wanted to close down, but she was determined not to let it.

Welles stepped back to admire his handiwork and rub his head now sore from the torch blow and Steph ripping his hair. His victim was standing, both feet on the floor, but crucified none the less - he loved it. What a pretty picture that made. Steph couldn't bear his eyes focussing on her nakedness. She tried to cross her legs somehow, but any movement was agony as it pulled on her wounds to her arms and shoulder.

Welles roughly grabbed at her breasts and began to massage them, before slobbering all over them with his mouth licking and sucking at her nipples. Steph closed her eyes and wanted to vomit.

'You should not have hit me you fucking whore. You think you can beat my ass? You're gonna pay, Missy Hissy-fit.'

Steph opened her eyes and just stared at him, grimacing with the waves of pain and the shame of the violation he was putting upon her.

'I'm gonna cut your head right off, and you're gonna watch me do it.'

Steph grunted through the tennis ball her eyes wide with fear.

'But first, we're gonna party.'

Welles moved his hand towards her vagina and tried to get his fingers inside. Again she twisted and turned, despite the incredible pain this caused her.

'You really are a piece of work? What is wrong with you? Give it up. I'll just slit your throat right now; I don't give a motherfucking shit.' Welles couldn't believe the resistance he was facing. This was not how he had imagined it. For a fleeting moment, he thought about leaving, just take her head off and go, but no, she deserved to suffer, the evil bitch. She was spoiling it for him. She had no right to do that.

The psycho ran into the bedroom and returned within a couple of seconds with the large black metal torch. It was the one Steph had used to clonk him on the head. Welles began tapping the hard metal on her head with the heavy metal torch, gently at first and then increasing the strength of the blows until she began to make noises with pain.

'Now, behave, Missy Hissy. You move again, and I am going to bust those brains out your pretty little skull, understand?'

Steph looked away. Her hatred for this monster was contorted on her face.

'Understand!' He raised the torch to strike her.

Steph nodded slowly. She was running out of ideas.

'This torch has a long shaft. I bet you luuuurve a long shaft, huh?'

Welles held the torch by the bulb end and moved the length of it down her body towards her genitalia.

Steph closed her eyes; she was petrified and she knew what was coming next.

17

'Do not allow yourself to be blinded by fear and anger. Everything is only as it is.'

Yuki Urishibara.

Stark and his crew were saying their goodbyes, now standing around the table at the back of the pub. The detritus had quickly accumulated; squashed cigarette packets, full ashtrays, empty glasses, empty packets of salted peanuts, Frazzles and Scampi Fries, spillages trickling over the edge of the table with a moist frazzle boat seeking the shore. It looked like the remnants of a chimps tea-party.

Nobby took the last sip of his whiskey, announcing 'Sip ahoy.' The others groaned and repeated it. 'Sip ahoy, Nobby.' It was usually around this time of night that he started to use this phrase, by now a long exhausted joke. They always played along, to humour him, if nothing else.

'You are having a drive past Welles flat, Ash, aren't you?' Stark said.

'Yes, just to check there are no signs of cops when he comes home. Mainly to see if they have shifted that bloody great police van they drove up in.'

'That's great. It needs to be well out the way, several streets away. Are you going to take a radio?'

'I wasn't going to, boss, there shouldn't be any need, there are three or four cops there, and the chances of me seeing the offender are remote, I would say.'

'Okay, fair enough, just drive past, then, don't get involved.'

'Sure. It's no problem; it's more or less on the way home for me anyway. I'll see you in the morning. See you, folks. Goodnight.' He gave a wave and headed off to the car park next door; it was just a quick step over the small boundary fence of the pub.

The remainder of the group waved and started to trickle away to various 'goodnight' exchanges.

'Hang on a minute, Nobby.' Stark said on the QT.

'Okay, what's up, boss?'

'Nothing. Just hang fire a minute.'

Once the others had gone, Stark lit a cigar and sat back down at the chimps table, with Nobby joining him, who in turn was triggered into lighting a cigarette, as company for his governor.

'Do me a favour tomorrow, Nobby, will you?'

'Yes, sure, what's that?'

'Just check what the fucking hell Jim McIntyre has done with this research into ancillary deaths in the victims household.'

'Ancillary what?'

Stark shook his head. 'We've now had three attacks, and we've learnt that all the victims have one common theme; the death of a relative. I find it too coincidental, yet Jim is saying he cannot see any connection.'

'There must be. You would have thought so, anyway.' Nobby agreed.

'Exactly. It's too coincidental.'

'Hopefully, the bastard will be locked up in the morning, anyway. SOU will have him when he polls up at the flat.'

'Hopefully. If not, get a plan together to think what the hell, or how the hell he could be identifying his victims. Jim's had the action a long time now, and the best he can do is report back that they are not in the obituaries column, but as I said earlier, does our killer work at a cemetery? Is he, I don't know, an undertaker perhaps or a gravedigger. I've no idea, but whatever we need to explore, we need to…'

'Dig deeper?' Nobby laughed.

Stark laughed too. 'Very good, Nobby, for this time of night. But yes, I'm not comfortable with just leaving it.'

'No problem, boss, leave it with me. Am I doing the interview with him, if he's locked up?'

'Yes, we will do it together.'

Nobby smiled. 'Great.' He stood. 'Right, if that is all, Herr Obermeister, I will see you bright-eyed and bushy-tailed in the morning.'

'8 am sharp, Sergeant.'

'Very good, sir.' Nobby did a mock salute, and Stark returned it. Nobby turned to go.

'Oh, Nobby.'

'Yes?'

'What was so funny earlier, when I brought the drinks back? Everyone was laughing.'

'When you brought the drinks back? Oh, it wasn't about you, boss…'

'No, I never thought it was, until now.'

'I was telling them about Steph bollocking some cyclist who she nearly knocked over coming back from the funeral.'

Stark had had a couple of pint's, but that sentence pinged into his brain. Cyclist, funeral.

'Was it a kid?'

'No, a bloke.'

'Did he give her aggro then?'

'No, he just said "Pardon me ma'am," apparently, soft as shit. I just made a joke about what Steph would have said, that's all. She would have chewed him up and spat him out.'

"Pardon me, ma'am?" Stark said.

'Yes, very polite. Poor sod.'

Stark suddenly had a rising feeling of discomfort. 'That's what yanks say isn't it? "Pardon me, Ma'am."'

The two looked at each other for a second and then both began running. 'We'll take your car Nobby; it's closest!'

Stark jumped into the passenger side with the door still open as Nobby roared away clipping his seat belt and pressing down the accelerator all in one movement. Stark almost fell out.

'Let me get in, Nobby, Christ!' Stark clawed to pull the door shut.

'Seat belt.' Nobby said through gritted teeth.

*

'You liked that didn't you, Missy Hissy?' Welles' eyes were wild and his expression sneering, filled with hate and disdain.

Steph nodded. She had gone to another place in her mind and tried to suppress the revulsion, desperately trying to shift her mindset to a more structured place. The tennis ball was restricting her breathing, and she was slavering out each side of her mouth. It was nigh on impossible to think clearly, but in her tortured thoughts, she remembered Stark once saying that "survival is the other side of fear". That's where she needed to get. Steph had to get out of this powerless position and somehow free herself. She wasn't sure how much more she could stand being nailed to the door like this. Her legs were trembling, and she was losing what little strength she had left. The moment she relaxed her arms, and the blades cut into her flesh, it was agonising. Her mind had been flashing through all the rape victims she had dealt with over the years. She was searching for those that survived the ordeal.

What did they do? What was it that might be able to give her a chance? Just for a second. How could she mitigate against his strength and the knives? What weapons were there? How should she behave? Her police training was starting to re-emerge. She had to fight her emotions, suck up the pain and try to stay calm to stay alive. She had to try to out-think this warped bastard. There was no firm answer, no rule book to follow, but her experience enabled her to form the origins of a plan. If nothing else to somehow try to put him off raping her, to buy some time, otherwise he would decapitate her right there at the door while she was helpless. Remaining nailed there was not an option, she had to get herself free somehow.

The killer moved towards her and opened her legs apart. He tried to manoeuvre himself into position.

She tried to talk through the tennis ball. Welles knew he had her beat, and he squeezed the tennis ball enabling him to remove it, and Steph gasped for air.

'Do me on the bed if you have to.' She croaked.

He grinned, exhibiting his green teeth. 'I knew you were a hot-tempered be-atch.' He threw the tennis ball down to the floor and pulled his jogging bottoms down, displaying his erect penis.

Welles, fuelled by this unravelling fantasy was masturbating, and his eyes widened. He was getting too excited. 'You really are a piece of work, you fucking slut.'

'Not here. On the bed.' Was he going to buy it?

Welles loved it. 'If you try any more moves, you know I will kill you, slut. I will cut off that pretty head and fuck your neck. I ain't playing.'

She didn't doubt the threat to be anything but real. 'I know. I know that. You win.'

Her vision was going blurry again, and she was trying to take in as much oxygen as she could now that the tennis ball had been removed. She couldn't pass out now.

Welles pulled the big knife out of the door first, and her left arm flopped to her side blood pouring down her arm and merging with her numb fingers. He held the knife to her throat as he pulled the smaller knife out; old faithful. Steph collapsed to the floor. Maybe she should just let him kill her. She had nothing left with which to resist. Something in her brain triggered. *No. You have to kill him before he kills you.* It was her only chance. It was a considerable risk, it was high-stakes, but desperate times call for desperate measures. What choice did she have?

*

Stark and Nobby could not begin to imagine the hell that Steph was being put through. It was unthinkable and probably a good thing that they did not know. Steph was indestructible; she was tough as nails. Wasn't she? But they knew Welles, and they knew what a depraved psychopath he was, and how he liked to torture and command a scene as he killed. It was all about the power, and the need to feel something, even if that feeling was merely dominance.

Nobby's car was a Ford Granada motor vehicle; it was a big old tank, but he needed the space, and it could go at some speed. Stark was being thrown around inside it and clung on to the door handle with one hand, and he grasped the dashboard with the other.

'Got to get there.' Nobby snarled.

'Nobby, this is crazy, get us there in one piece, man, will you?'

'Fuck that; she needs me. I'm going to kill that bastard if he's touched one hair on her fucking head.'

'Nobby, we don't know it's him.'

'It's fucking him, alright. Why didn't I clock it? For fucks sake.' His anger at himself just made him gun the accelerator even more, and they careened around one corner after another, tyres screeching, travelling at ridiculous speeds. It seemed the car was defying gravity at certain points of the hair-raising ride. Nobby was almost out of control, incensed yet focussed, maniacal in his driving. Steph needed him, and he had to get there. He could not let her down. What if it was too late? He put his foot down again, and the engine roared past oncoming cars, and he pressed his horn with the heel of his hand and just left it there.

'Have you got your peg with you?' Stark shouted to Nobby, above the roar of the engine and blaring horn. Stark realised that his truncheon and handcuffs were still at the station in his office.

'No, it's in my drawer. I've got cuffs on my belt. I don't need my peg. Trust me I will hammer that bastard.'

'Nobby, he is armed, we need to take him together, if he is there, don't just lunge at him.'

'Trust me; he will be eating that fucking knife when I get to him.'

'Watch out!' They swerved to miss a lorry that seemed to appear from nowhere. 'Jesus H. Christ, Nobby, seriously…' Stark's heart was pounding as he was thrown around with the recklessness of Nobby's driving.

'Boss, we have to get there. We have to.'

'Have you got a radio?'

'Nope.'

'Fuck me; we are on our own.'

'No, he is on his own. I'm going to ram that fucking knife up his twitchy little sphincter.'

Stark shrugged out a nervous laugh. 'Just get us there alive, will you? We can't do anything lying in a ditch, Nobby.'

The drunkard had stepped out into the road without even looking, and as Nobby swerved to avoid him, he oversteered, and then yanked the steering wheel the other way and overcompensated, but his nearside wheel hit the pavement, and he lost it. The car rolled over three times, and the gravitational forces rattled the pair of them around like ragdolls.

The vehicle struck a wall with the front end, and the metal closed in around the officer's feet and heads, dented by the incredible forces being applied to it. The detective's breath was knocked out of their lungs, and they were incapable of drawing in any more as the car rocked on its suspension. Finally stationary, it thankfully rested with its wheels on the tarmac rather than the roof. The Granada looked like it had been through the scrap yard crusher; it was a third less the size it had been, with all the metal crunched in and the front concertinaed. All the windows were broken, and smoke wafted from under the crumpled bonnet. There was a smell of petrol and oil. All went quiet; the silence momentarily penetrated only by the tinny rolling of a hub cap which then took its time in settling flat to the road. The two detectives sat there, stunned, their chins resting on their chests, neck muscles torn to ribbons. They each groaned, and Nobby raised an arm for a moment, but it flopped back down almost immediately. The two friends were covered in fragmented glass, and tiny cuts were in their skin along with glass shards. Stark was bleeding from the nose, and Nobby was unconscious. The engine had been hammered down onto both their feet and they were trapped. Both were unable to speak or move. The gravitational forces to their brains inside their skulls were the equivalent of putting a marble in a tin and shaking it. As always with such a severe accident, it wasn't always the visible, external injuries that were the most dangerous, but rather the internal ones. When a vehicle abruptly stops the seatbelt stops you, but nothing stops your internal organs, and they slam into your skeleton and muscle. Organs can be torn away from their connecting valves, tears of internal structures can cause unseen bleeding, and you can go into clinical shock.

A passer-by ran to a telephone kiosk to call for an ambulance. Another tried pulling at the men to get them out but to no avail. They just groaned. Both doors were crumpled and locked in place in any case.

Thankfully, for the detectives, the vehicle had rolled over several times before slamming into the wall which, despite being highly dangerous in itself, had at least lessened the impact and most importantly they had not struck their heads on the car frame. This would be their saving grace. There would be no saving grace for Steph; however, - she was on her own.

*

Welles had taken the belt from Steph's dressing gown which was hanging up on the inside of the door and wrapped it around her neck. Steph was unable to walk, and so she crawled back around to the bedroom like a dog, but with great difficulty because of the searing pain and loss of function of her right shoulder caused by Welle's first blow with the knife. Blood was running down her forearms and making her hands sticky. She could hardly put any weight on her right arm, and she kept collapsing face-first into the carpet as Welles continued to tug at her throat with the dressing gown belt.

'Get up, slut?' Welles pulled at the improvised ligature causing Steph to choke. She tried to loosen it with her left arm, which she managed to do, if only slightly.

'I can't.' She gurgled.

'Get up.'

'Give me time. Give me a chance.'

Steph managed to get on to her left arm and moved a couple of feet before collapsing again. Welles was impatient; he took hold of the ligature with both hands and pulled her along the floor to the side of the bed. The improvised noose tightened, and it felt like her head was being pulled from its neck. She tried to hold the belt with her left hand to ease the pressure. It helped slightly. Steph couldn't breathe and was in terrible pain. As she landed at the side of the bed, she managed to ease the ligature once more just a fraction, and she coughed and spluttered to draw in a breath. This was desperate. It was not going to end well, and time was running out for her, she knew that. Why had the neighbours not heard her and rung for help? She had a dull ache of fear in her stomach, and a sense of doom hung over her like darkening storm clouds. She began to cry a little. She did not want to die. All she could do was try to delay, somehow. Hope for an intervention. But who? It was down to her, it seemed hopeless, and she felt defeated.

On the floor at the side of the bed where Steph now lay, was the wrapping paper from Nobby's present. She suddenly had a glimmer of hope. Of course! Steph knew she had fallen asleep on top of the towel, but she had used kitchen scissors to open Nobby's present before that. Where did she put them? Where the hell were the scissors? She couldn't think; the pain was too much. The stress too great. The importance too high. She tried to focus, but it was hard. She had to; her life depended on it.

'On the bed, all fours.' Welles growled.

'I can't.' Steph whimpered.

'Just fucking do it bitch.'

Steph managed to claw herself up on to the mattress, it seemed to take an age, and she landed on the bed, but on her back. 'Do it on my back; I can't support my arms.' She gasped.

'Just do…'

Steph closed her eyes but opened her legs, displaying her privates to the beast.

'Oh fuck it.' Welles positioned himself, kneeling in between her legs.

Steph was carefully feeling under the towel for the scissors, slowly. She was sure she just left them on the bed. Didn't she? Where were they?

Welles had lost his erection with the exertion and distraction of pulling her along, but as he fiddled with himself, Steph could see that she only had a few seconds to find the scissors. Still, she could feel nothing. Were they on the bedside table? She moved her head to one side, and she could only see the mirror and the earrings there. No scissors. The killer was ready, and he had that look in his eye. Now was the time to try the one thing that a victim had told her, many years ago. What she did threw the offender off his stride. Might it work with Welles?

Steph relaxed her bladder and began to urinate.

It took Welles a second or two to register what was happening. 'What the fuck is that? You dirty fucking whore!'

'Sorry I couldn't help it.'

Welles began to punch her about the face. The force of the blows knocked her to the left-hand side, and her fingertips touched something under the sheets. The scissors! Before she could grab them, he took hold of her neck and began strangling her viciously. She couldn't breathe and thought that maybe this was it. She started to blackout when Welles threw her head down on the pillow. She coughed and gasped for air, making a wheezing noise and a rattle as she did.

'You are a filthy cunt!'

She knew where the scissors were, but she just couldn't reach them. A plan was emerging; she needed his defences down. 'Let me suck it, then.' She blurted out, in between gasps for air.

'Fuck you.'

After a couple of seconds, she managed to get her composure back a little. 'Please, let me suck it. Sorry for weeing, it just happened. I'm frightened.'

Welles was wary. 'I'm going to hold this knife over your head. One false move and you're dead. Understand?'

'Yes. I'm sorry.'

She opened her mouth. Again Welles was triggered, unaware that actually, he had lost control; Steph had suggested the bed, she had gone on her back, she had stopped him penetrating, and now she was dictating what was coming next. She was winning, but the end game was his. He owned it, and he would decide when it was time to take her head off her shoulders.

Welles put his knees each side of her body and walked himself up to her face, his semi-erect penis hardening as he did so. She could smell it now. It was filthy, and the end was blotchy and looked sore. It was almost in her mouth as Steph reached down and pulled the scissors out and with all her might rammed them up into his undercarriage, just behind his balls, severing his 'root' and his penis immediately flopped down.

He screamed and fell to his right, still on the mattress, blood spurting, clutching at his groin. It was his turn to scream like a little bitch. Steph, with clenched teeth, her pain numbed by adrenalin, was on top of him and rammed the scissors into his face aiming for the eyeball, but missing and the blade hit his cheek. She saw the momentary look of fear in his face. Within half a second she thrust the scissors down again, this time hitting the bullseye and they sunk through the soft tissue of the eyeball and into his brain, killing him outright. She was showered with his blood which spurted like a fountain through his eye, and he let out a prolonged gasp like a tyre deflating. She rolled off him and staggered to the open window and threw herself through the gap and landed hard on the grass, three feet below. As she lay there, she shouted for help. Quietly at first but then, hysterically at the top of her voice.

Lights flickered on, and faces appeared in windows. She heard footsteps approaching as she drifted into semi-consciousness.

The fire crew were working hard to cut the two men out of the wrecked car. One was conscious, and one was not.

'Get him out first; he's not breathing too well.' Stark said.

The young fireman was breathing erratically himself, as the hydraulic scissors clamped down near Stark's feet. 'There is someone else working on him too, don't worry.'

'Will he live?'

'Just worry about yourself, for now. Try to relax and not get too agitated. Try to regulate your breathing. Take longer breaths.'

'Anything hurting?' A paramedic appeared through the gap at the side of the fireman, and she shouted above the noise.

'My neck and…just everything, but I think I'm okay. It's my neck.' Stark repeated, his head flopped forward. He was aware of Nobby, who was groaning and snoring in his unconscious state. Nobby's head was also resting on his chest. Stark could just about see him using his peripheral vision.

Stark's heart was going at an alarming rate, and he was now trembling. He couldn't see if he was bleeding anywhere. His feet were numb, though. The woman in green reached through and put a neck collar around the Detective Inspector. He grunted in pain through gritted teeth as she raised his chin slowly.

Suddenly there was a loud crack. 'Gotcha!' The fireman exclaimed as the engine block fell away from Stark's feet.

'Thank Christ for that; I thought it was his bloody neck!' The paramedic said startled.

Stark felt agonising pain as blood started to return to his lower legs and feet, as whatever had been crushing them was released.

The two patients were slowly extracted in a well-rehearsed procedure, and placed in two separate ambulances on spine boards. Nobby had regained consciousness but was quiet, in between occasional groans of pain.

A crowd had gathered, and the police arrived. The officers quickly recognised the two patients, but they could only look on and inform control of the potential tragedy. A young PC peered in the ambulance to see if the DI was alive.

'Are you okay, sir?'

'Get to Steph's house. DC Dawson, she's in danger.' Stark said, shivering.

'A unit is already there, sir. We had a call a few minutes ago.'

'Is she alive?' His teeth were chattering.

'Hang on.'

The PC moved away and spoke into his radio before returning to the car.

'Injured but alive, sir. Not life-threatening. She will be okay.'

'Thank God.' He managed a fleeting smile of relief.

'Will he be okay?' Stark asked the paramedic. She was injecting something into the Inspector's arm, morphine or adrenalin. Stark wasn't sure what the hell it was, nor did he care.

'Your mate? I would think so. It's too early to say, love. We need to get you both to A & E. Sharpish.' She put a blanket around his shoulders.

The rear ambulance door slammed behind them, and they were off, with sirens blaring. Stark felt sick. This had not ended well. But at least Steph was alive. The paramedic lowered the gurney down a little, and she strapped the patient in, trying not to make the belt too tight. Stark closed his eyes, grimacing with the pain. Closing his eyes seemed to help; he just wanted to sleep.

18

'We'll never survive!'

'Nonsense. You're only saying that because no one ever has.'

William Goldman.

Stark had been discharged from hospital after five days, but Nobby and Steph needed more time. Thankfully none of them had suffered life-threatening injuries as it turned out. Nobby had concussion and breathing difficulties because of the muscle trauma to his chest, from the steering wheel, as well as neck injuries and three cracked bones in his foot. According to doctors, if the car had hit the wall any harder, Stark and Nobby would have needed amputations or the morgue.

Nobby's response was 'Oh, well, if my aunt had a pair of bollocks, she'd be my uncle.'

Steph's injuries were relatively superficial in the big scheme of things; no major arteries or organs were affected, but her healing was hampered by lack of sleep. She didn't feel safe and having only 3 hours sleep a night was damaging her overall health and recovery. Secondary complications like diarrhoea, nausea, lack of concentration, as well as general aches and pains and headaches plagued her. She hadn't reacted well to the sedation, and she was resistant to it. She didn't like the feeling of helplessness she was feeling. In the early days, she was twitchy and responding to every sound. A dropped tray, the wheels on a medicine trolley, everything put her back on alert. This had since eased, but she wasn't out of the woods yet. Steph's physical wounds were healing nicely, and she should have the stitches removed in a couple of days. There were signs of improvement, and in a moment of inspiration, doctors had moved her bed into a separate ward, alongside Nobby. Her sleeping hours increased, while his decreased, haunted by the tortuous dreams she was having and the screams and shouts accompanying them. Steph had been seeing a psychiatrist, and this too was helping. Generally, it boded well, but there was a heck of a journey ahead of them, particularly for Steph.

Stark was still walking strangely. To the uncultured eye, he looked okay, but to those that were used to his confident stride, he looked a bit disjointed, as he had to work harder to move his limbs, and everything seemed to be constantly trying to catch up with each other. As the day progressed, if you saw Stark from behind, you would think he was around seventy years old. His neck was the most painful of all, but he was sore from top to toe.

Stark was grinning as he walked awkwardly into the ward, a bit like Mr Bojangles. 'My God, isn't this just domestic bliss?'

'Really?' Steph looked to the heavens, in mock dismay. 'If I'd known I was going to have to spend every waking moment with the Sarge, I would have considered my options a bit more at the time.'

Stark laughed. He was clutching flowers and chocolates.

'It is a two-way street, you know.' Nobby grunted, grimacing as he pulled himself up the bed, still clearly in pain.

'You don't have to come every day, boss. Much as it is appreciated.' He said.

'Yes, I do.' He pulled a plastic chair up and sat somewhat exposed in between the two beds with the patients staring at him.

'How are you, sir?' Steph asked.

'Never mind that, how are *you* guys?'

'We're getting there.' Steph sighed. There were still some dim shadows in her eyes. He noticed that periodically she did a sort of double blink, like a nervous twitch. It would take time for her to get over such a traumatic event. She looked different; drawn and sallow.

'I'm alright boss, and I keep telling them I can go home, but they won't listen.' Nobby said.

'Leave it to the experts, Nobby.'

'It's alright for you; we have to struggle down to the smoking-room every hour. It's harder than the physio.'

Stark laughed.

'He's not wrong.' Steph laughed also. 'We look like a right pair, both leaning on each other, I am sharing his zimmer frame at the moment. It's like the blind leading the blind.'

'I'd love to be a fly on the wall.' Stark said as he handed Nobby a box of chocolate Brazil nuts and put yet another bouquet of flowers on Steph's bed.

'I'm going to have to ask for another vase. But thank you. Please don't keep bringing stuff, sir, there is no need.' She said. 'But thank you, anyway.'

'The two of you look a bit better in yourselves.' Stark lied.

'We feel a bit better. Don't we Nobby?'

'I've told you. I'm alright, and I don't know why they keep fussing over me.'

'At least you're together, joking aside.'

'We thought we might be able to get a week or two at the Police Convalescent Home at Harrogate? What do you think, boss?' Nobby said.

'Absolutely, that's why it's there. Do you want me to apply on your behalf?'

'Maybe, when we know when we are coming out. That would be great, nice one boss.'

'It shouldn't be too long, next week I shouldn't wonder.' Stark said. 'Have they not said anything?'

'No, nothing yet. Hopefully, it will be next week, as you say.'

'Old Wagstaff wants to visit.' Stark said. He wanted to get this out of the way while they were in good spirits.

'You're not back at work, are you?' Nobby asked.

'No, not yet, but he came to see me, all the lads have phoned or visited too, which is good of them. But he says he wants to come in the next couple of days.'

'Oh, that's sweet.' Steph smiled.

'Erm. Sort of.' Stark grimaced.

'Oh, what do you mean, "sort of?"'

'It's a bit awkward. Wagstaff has to investigate Welles' death. He has to interview you.'

'Ah. Yes, of course. Bloody hell!'

'Don't panic. There is not a problem with it. Wagstaff will do it properly, don't worry about that. You have nothing to be concerned about, and I am going to sit in with you anyway. Just in case Waggy starts getting it around his tits.'

'Can't he wait until she's off her bloody death bed, Christ!' Nobby was dischuffed.

'It's hardly my death bed, Nobby, don't be so dramatic.' Steph said.

'Well, what do you expect.' Nobby shook his head, a look of disdain on his face.

'It will be quite perfunctory.' Stark said.

'Oh, well, if it's going to be perfunctory, that's alright then.' Nobby said sarcastically.

'It is a bit worrying; these things can take a turn.' Steph bit at her lower lip.

Stark took hold of Steph's hand. She instinctively pulled it away but then let it return. Stark inwardly cursed himself for touching her without warning like that. He continued undeterred; he was just trying to put her mind at ease. 'Steph, the mad bastard, was a serial killer, look at your injuries. There is not a hope in hell of anything untoward happening, don't start getting wound up about it. Trust me. I've already had this conversation with Wagstaff, and there is no agenda. It is pure routine, I promise. It is just for the Coroner in the first instance.'

'There'd better not be any agenda.' Nobby grunted.

Cops were always paranoid when anything of importance was left in the hands of a senior officer; usually, they had little practical experience or indeed common sense.

'There isn't an agenda. Wagstaff wants to do it as soon as possible so he can get it knocked on the head and everyone can at least start to move on. He will wait if you want him to, but he is just trying to get it out of the way for you. I think the Coroner is getting a bit twitchy. That's what he's told me.' Stark said. 'And I tend to believe him.'

'I know, I get it.' Steph slowly nodded her head.

'I'm glad *you* do.' Nobby said, with a harrumph.

'Come on Nobby, we know how this works, we've all been involved in investigating fellow cops. It is a death, a homicide, and the Coroner will be itching to get it resolved. I'm not worried, I promise.' Stark said the word 'homicide' not as would be received by the media or the public, but the police understanding of the word - that it was the killing of a person by another person. Murder, of course, was a very different word.

Nobby sighed. 'I suppose you're right. It just grips my shit when,' Nobby stopped himself and wafted his hand at Stark as if throwing him an imaginary ball. 'anyway, you know what I mean.'

'The lads all send their regards.' Stark changed the subject, slowly releasing his hand from Steph's.

'Tell them they can come and see us now if they want.' Steph said.

'Are you sure?'

'Yes, I've stopped the crying. A lot of that was tiredness. It would be good to see them. Honestly.'

'You might have to go on a driving course, by the way, Nobby.' Stark thought he would drop it out while the going was good.

'Fuck that.'

'Nobby, it is the policy after such a serious accident.'

'Fucking driving course. If that pissed up prat hadn't stepped out into the road, there wouldn't have been a problem, would there?'

'Oh, you remember it now do you?' Stark asked.

'No, but I know that's what you told me.'

'Anyway, focus on getting better and concentrate on a nice relaxing week or two at Harrogate.' The DI smiled at the pair of them.

'It's hardly the Bahamas, but it'll do, I reckon.' Nobby grinned.

'It will have to. The budget won't stretch to the Bahamas, Nobby, you only pay a quid a month to be in the scheme.' Steph said.

'A quid's, a bloody quid.'

Stark smiled. 'It sure is. Is there anything you need doing, either of you?'

'What about our investigations, I've got a load of cases that need sorting out.'

'They're all being dealt with; I've split them out evenly. That's the last thing you need to worry about, Steph.'

'See, I told you.' Nobby said.

There was a lull in the conversation.

'I don't know how I feel. I think I just feel numb about it at the moment. What about you, folks?' Stark said.

'Funnily, enough, yet again, we were saying the same last night, weren't we Nobby?'

'Aye, we were.'

'I'm glad he's dead and gone, but it somehow feels like unfinished business, I don't know.' Stark offered.

Steph sighed. 'I know. I wouldn't want to go through that again in a hurry; I know that much. It was so terrifying. It was just beyond awful.' Steph became momentarily distant, and Stark cursed himself yet again for bringing it up. 'No, of course not.'

'She's thinking about putting her ticket in, aren't you Steph?' Nobby said.

'I've thought about it. I feel like I have lost all of my confidence. I can't see me going back into that world again. Not as things stand.'

Stark seemed taken aback. 'Resign?'

'Or a medical discharge.' Nobby said hurriedly, aware of the fiscal disparity between the two options.

'I understand but don't do anything rash. You won't always feel like this, Steph. Either way, everything can be worked out. Whatever you decide, you will have my blessing, and you know that. Selfishly I wouldn't want to lose you, but I know there are bigger things than that to consider.'

'I know.' Steph began to get a little teary. 'I was worried Nobby might finish with me, knowing what went off.'

Nobby reached over and held her hand across the beds. 'Eh, you, daft bugger. I've told you I wouldn't do that in a million years. Is that all you think of me? I am just amazed at what a wonderful, courageous human being you are. If anything, I love you even more. You just amaze me.' He squeezed her hand.

'Thanks, Nobby. I hope you cling on to those thoughts when the dust settles.'

'No need to thank me, and I will, nothing will change. I just wish I had got there in bloody time.' Nobby stared down at the bed.

'I've told you, Nobby, stop tearing yourself up about it. Tell him, boss.'

'Stop tearing yourself up about it. Honestly mate, it wasn't your fault. It was mine for letting you drive.'

'Sir, piss off.' Nobby said, laughing. 'You aren't having a chocolate Brazil for that.'

'That's good they are two weeks out of date, anyway.'

Nobby started searching for the 'sell-by-date' on the box.

'Bloody hell, Nobby, I'm joking, man. I think we are all in awe of you, Steph. There is talk of you getting the Queens Police Medal. I am looking into how to go about applying for it for you.'

She shrugged out a laugh. 'Hang on. A minute ago, you told me Wagstaff was going to have to interview me about being a potential murderer, and now I'm going to be honoured by the bloody Queen.'

'That just about sums the job up though, doesn't it?'

'I suppose it does. I wonder which it will be, life imprisonment or heroine status?'

'I wonder.' Stark smiled, adding a wink for good measure.

THE END

Keith Wright was brought up on a council estate and attended the local comprehensive school.

Keith went on to spend twenty-five years in the police service retiring in 2005 as Detective Sergeant in the CID, where he spent most of his service.

He then worked in the private sector, leading the Corporate Investigations Team for a global retailer, heading a team investigating blackmail, bribery, and other serious incidents.

His first novel, 'One Oblique One' was shortlisted for the Crime Writers Association John Creasey Award – for the best debut crime novel. He has received critical acclaim in prestigious newspapers such as The Times, Financial Times and Sunday Express.

'Murder Me Tomorrow' is Keith's fifth novel. All are set in the 1980s and involve the investigation of DI Stark and his team of diverse detectives. It is no coincidence that the author was a Detective in Nottinghamshire CID in the 1980s!

His short stories have previously appeared in various anthologies, such as The Crime Writers Association anthology 'Perfectly Criminal' as well as New York's Mystery Tribune magazine.

His earlier books are available on Audible as audiobooks.

He is engaged to Jackie and has four children. He lives in Nottingham.

Printed in Great Britain
by Amazon